PRAISE

M000189912

"You won't regret taking a risk on Elle Kennedy."
— *Hypable*

"With all the heart, witty banter, and toe-curling romance that you'd expect from an Elle Kennedy novel, *The Play* is a fantastic addition to one of my all-time favorite series!"
— #1 *New York Times* bestselling author Sarah J. Maas

"An opposites-attract romance with plenty of laugh-out-loud humor, steamy love scenes and swoony, heartfelt romance...a phenomenal reading experience."
— *USA Today*, about *The Chase*

"Kennedy fans and newcomers will relish the well-crafted plot, witty dialogue, and engaging characters."
— *Publishers Weekly*, about *Hotter Than Ever*.

"A steamy, glitzy, and tender tale of college intrigue."
— *Kirkus Reviews*, about *The Chase*

"Another addictive read from Elle Kennedy! *The Play* is a steamy, swoon-worthy romance you won't want to put down!"
— #1 *New York Times* bestselling author Vi Keeland

"When I pick up an Elle Kennedy book, I know I'm not putting it down until I'm done."
— International bestselling author K.A. Tucker

OTHER TITLES BY ELLE KENNEDY

AUTHOR'S NOTE

I am so excited to be re-releasing the *Out of Uniform* series! These new editions feature new titles and more discreet covers, but the characters and stories inside haven't changed.

For those of you who haven't read it before, this was one of my earlier series, and it also happens to be one of my favorites, probably because this is when I realized how much I love writing bromances. Seriously. The boy banter in these books still cracks me up to this day. You see more and more of it as the series progresses, and by the later books there are entire chapters of crazy conversations between my sexy, silly SEALs.

For new readers, you should know that a) you don't have to read the stories in order, though characters from previous books do show up in every installment. And b) four of the books are full-length novels (80,000+ words), while six are novellas (20-35,000 words).

I decided to release the novellas as two books featuring three stories each (*Hot & Bothered*, *Hot & Heavy*) making the total books in the series six rather than the original ten.

Sweet Talker (formerly titled *As Hot as it Gets*) is the fourth of the full-length novels.

**PLEASE NOTE: This book has NOT changed, except for minor editing, updating, and proofreading. There are grammatical differences and some deleted/added lines here and there, but for the most part, there is no new content. If you've previously purchased and read *As Hot as it Gets*, then you won't be getting more content, aside from a gorgeous new cover and title.

So, I hope you enjoy the cover, the better grammar, and the hot, dirty-talking SEALs who to this day hold such a big place in my heart!

— Elle Kennedy

SWEET
TALKER

OUT OF UNIFORM SERIES

ELLE KENNEDY

To all the fans of the Out of Uniform series—every book has been for you, and this last one is no different. Your enthusiasm and support for this series has made it a joy to write, and I appreciate all the lovely words and wonderful feedback I've received from you. Thank you for taking this journey with me.

CHAPTER
ONE

Mia Weldrick could think of a hundred better ways to spend a Saturday morning. Sleeping in. Eating breakfast at the diner across the street from her apartment. Jogging. Reading one of the gazillion unread books gathering dust on her shelf.

But she wasn't doing any of those things. Nope, because she was too busy trying to find the cell phone she'd accidentally buried in Tom and Sarah Smith's tulip bed yesterday.

"Oh, for the love of Jesus," she grumbled to herself. "Where are you, motherfucker?"

She desperately hoped her little brother Danny hadn't gone back to sleep after she'd roused him and ordered him to start calling her phone in precisely twenty minutes. She was going to flip the fuck out if she lost all her contacts. Unlike smarter and more practical people, she didn't have a backup list of passwords and phone numbers—everything was in her phone, which meant she couldn't afford to lose it.

Stifling a sigh, Mia scooted over a few inches and lowered her head to the yellow tulips. A sweet scent filled her nose, but no sound reached her ears.

Well, except for the loud throat clearing that suddenly echoed from behind her.

She swiveled her head and instantly spotted the source of the noise. He was obviously Tom and Sarah's neighbor, judging by the rolled-up newspaper in his hand and the serious case of bedhead he was sporting.

"Everything okay, sugar?" he called out.

Oh boy. He had a Southern drawl. That upped his hotness factor by a million, though even without the accent the guy was a perfect ten. Messy light-brown hair, whiskey-colored eyes, a chiseled jawline. And his body wasn't a pain to look at either. It was muscular but lean, his long legs encased in faded blue denim and defined biceps poking out of a wrinkled white tank.

"Not really," she called back. "Hey, you mind if I borrow your ears, *sugar?*"

He raised his eyebrows. "Beg your pardon?"

"Come over here and help me listen."

His dumbfounded look made her want to laugh. She knew she sounded like a total wacko, but she really could use his help. She had just a little over an hour to find her phone, go home to change, and hightail it over to the sandwich shop where she worked on the weekends.

"Can I ask what we're listening to?" her dark-haired stranger inquired when he reached her.

Mia tilted her head back in order to meet his gaze. "Holy crap," she blurted out. "You're ridiculously tall."

Her stranger grinned. "Maybe you're just ridiculously short."

"I'm five-three. That's average height." Her forehead was starting to sweat, so she pulled off her baseball cap and shoved a strand of damp hair off her face. "How tall are you?" she asked curiously.

"Six-five."

"Like I said, ridiculously tall. I'm talking to a giant. Do you play basketball?"

"Nope. Do you?"

"Sure, I shoot hoops every morning before work."

"For real?"

A laugh flew out. "No, not for real. You actually believed me?" Before he could answer, she gestured to the other side of the flowerbed. "Anyway, go over there. Tell me if you hear anything."

To his credit, he didn't question the command. He simply crossed the freshly mowed grass with long strides and knelt in front of the flowers. "What am I supposed to be hearing?"

"Well, if my brother is repeatedly dialing my phone like I ordered him to, then you should be hearing the faint strains of A-ha's 'Take On Me.' I'm really into '80s pop," she said in a self-deprecating tone.

Her stranger stared at her for a moment, before understanding dawned in his eyes.

"Wait a sec—you buried your phone in the dirt?"

Mia sighed. "Not on *purpose*. It must have slipped out of my pocket when I was planting yesterday. Hazard of the job." She flopped down onto her knees. "Now, hush. I'd like to find my phone sometime this century. I drove all the way back here this morning and I have stuff to do today."

From the corner of her eye, she saw his big body curling as he bent over the dirt. She had to give him credit—he was definitely being a good sport about this.

And gosh, he was *cute*. She couldn't stop taking peeks at him. So many peeks that she finally had to force herself to wrench her gaze away.

"Over here," he called a minute later.

As relief flooded her body, Mia bounded over to him with a spade in hand. She started digging in the spot he indicated, then stuck her hand in the moist soil and felt around for the phone. Her fingers connected with something hard and solid, the vibrations accompanied by her ringtone tickling her palm.

She triumphantly pulled out the iPhone, brushed dirt off the screen protector, and glanced at her savior with delight. "Hells yeah! We did it!"

He seemed to be fighting a laugh, but she didn't care how crazy or silly she sounded. He'd just saved her entire day.

The phone was still blaring out her favorite song with her brother's number flashing on the screen, so she quickly answered the call.

"Hey, Danny, it's me. I found it."

Irritation laced her brother's voice. "I'm so happy for you, dum-dum. Can I go back to sleep now?"

"Call me a dum-dum again and I won't bring home any breakfast."

"Don't care. I'm not hungry. I'm tired. You know, because someone *rudely* dragged me out of bed at *eight o'clock* on Saturday morning." He paused. "Are you coming back here before work?"

"Yeah."

"Fine. I guess you can bring me something to eat, then."

She choked back a laugh, not surprised by his complete one-eighty. Tired or not, teenage boys had voracious appetites, and at sixteen Danny ate like a damn horse. Her weekly grocery bill was proof of that.

"A food gesture will totes make me forget about being woken up today," he added. "But I swear, Mia, if you lose your phone one more time, I'm gonna kick your ass."

"Yeah, whatevs, dude. I'd like to see you try."

"I'll try and succeed," he declared.

"Uh-huh. 'Kay. See you soon."

She was smiling as she hung up. "Little brothers are such a pain in the ass," she told her waiting stranger.

"Trust me, I know. I have a younger sister and she used to be a real pest. How old is your brother?"

"Sixteen. He can be a total shit sometimes, but for the most part, he's a good kid."

The guy in front of her slid his hands into the pockets of his faded Levis. He filled out those jeans nicely, she noted. She was ridiculously tempted to ask him to do a little spin so she could check out his ass.

He's not a piece of meat, Mia.

A sigh lodged in her throat. No, he wasn't a piece of meat. And even if he was, she didn't have time to indulge. Her chaotic life didn't allow room for tall, handsome hotties who looked spectacular in a pair of jeans.

"So you're doing some work for Tom and Sarah?" he asked.

"Yep. But the job's all done, actually," she replied. "Sarah didn't want anything fancy, so it didn't take long to finish everything up."

The disappointment on his chiseled face was unmistakable, but his tone remained friendly as he stuck out his hand. "I'm Jackson Ramsey, by the way. I live next door."

"Mia Weldrick. And I'd shake your hand but mine is all covered with dirt."

"I don't mind getting dirty every now and then."

Her breath hitched as he moved closer, a grin tugging on his lips. When he took her hand, heat suffused her cheeks, burning hotter when she registered the naughty undertones of that remark.

"Was that a line?" she demanded.

"Was what a line?"

"You know, the whole 'I like it dirty' thing. Was that supposed to get me all tingly and weak-kneed?"

Because it worked.

Jackson laughed, a deep, sexy sound that rippled between them. "I didn't say I liked it dirty. I said I didn't mind it. And no, it wasn't a line." He was smirking as he met her eyes. "Why, did it get you tingly and weak-kneed?"

"Nope."

She took a step toward her truck, turning her head just in case her expression revealed the dishonesty of her response. She *was* feeling tingly. Her entire body pulsed with a strange rush of heat, all because of this man's proximity. She hadn't experienced a spark of attraction to anyone in months, maybe years, and she'd forgotten what it even felt like. But the symptoms were definitely hitting her hard at the moment.

"Would you like to have dinner with me sometime?"

The request was gruff and came out of nowhere, bringing a pang of agitation to Mia's stomach.

"Oh boy," she said with a sigh.

"'Oh boy'?" He smiled at her again. "Is that how you respond to all your dinner invitations?"

"No. But that's because I don't get a lot of them," she confessed. "I never go out, which means I don't meet a lot of guys. Honestly, I'm unprepared for this."

"Doesn't require much prep, sugar. A yes or no would do the trick."

She mumbled another "Oh boy," torn between lying and being brutally honest. In the end, honesty won out.

"Okay, I'm going to lay it all on the line," she told him. "You're hot, and I'm totally digging the height thing. It makes me feel dainty."

He chuckled. "All right..."

"But I don't want to have dinner with you."

"I see."

The visible disappointment in his eyes had her hurrying on.

"It's nothing personal. I bet you're a really awesome guy, and that Southern drawl is definitely a bonus, but I don't have time to go out on dates. I have a gazillion jobs and a teenage boy to raise."

"Your parents aren't in the picture?"

Mia swallowed the bitterness that rose in her throat. "Nope, it's just Danny and me. Which is why dating is the last thing on my mind right now and probably won't be until Danny graduates. So even though I'm flattered, I'm gonna have to pass."

Honest-to-God regret washed over her, which was weird because she'd truly meant every word she'd said. She *didn't* have time to date. Most days she wolfed down her meals in the company truck between jobs. And she was usually in bed by ten o'clock. When did she have time to get dolled up and share a nice dinner with someone other than her little brother?

The grim reality of her life only bummed her out, so she quickly pasted on a smile and took a step toward her pickup. "It was nice meeting you, but I've got to skedaddle now."

Jackson looked ready to protest, but she didn't give him the chance. She simply hopped in the truck and offered a little wave, then drove off before she changed her mind and accepted his invitation.

But she couldn't. She wasn't interested in dating, and as hot as Jackson was, she didn't want a fling with him either. Sex was way overrated. It was actually kind of boring, if she were being honest. So yeah, dinner with a cute guy who called her "sugar" wasn't in the cards.

Just another one in the long line of sacrifices she was forced to make in her life.

"Let me get this straight," Seth Masterson said in bewilderment. "You want to pay for a gardener to fix up our yard."

Jackson leaned back in the comfortable wicker chair and rested his bottle of Bud Light on his jean-clad knee. "Sure do."

"Because you have a thing for the gardener."

"Uh-huh."

"Even though you only talked to her for like five minutes."

"Yup."

"You're insane, Texas."

He didn't blame Seth for looking so confused. Jackson knew he was going to a helluva lot of trouble to see Mia again. And it sounded nuts when you said it out loud, but for the life of him, he couldn't let it end the way it had—with the first woman he'd connected to in ages driving away from him.

For the past couple months, he'd been striking out left and right when it came to the ladies. His friends' matchmaking attempts had resulted in some of the most disastrous dates he'd ever experienced, and last night had been the final straw. He'd come home to find one of his blind dates naked in his bed, mistook her for an intruder, and almost shot the poor girl with his nine mil. It had been the icing on the crappy cake he'd been eating for months now.

But just when he'd given up on women altogether, he'd met Mia.

Gorgeous, sarcastic, down-to-earth. And most of all, *normal.* So maybe he was veering toward borderline stalker territory, but could anyone really blame him for wanting to get to know the girl?

"I think it's sweet," Seth's wife said as she stepped into the small backyard.

Jackson glanced at Seth. "*See,*" he said smugly.

"She's only saying that because she wants someone to come

and clear out that jungle," Seth retorted, jabbing a finger at the overgrown yard.

"That's not true," Miranda protested. "I really do think it's wonderful that Texas finally met someone he likes."

"It is about time," Seth said grudgingly. "After all those horror-movie dates, I guess you deserve it, dude."

Miranda glanced at the two chairs occupied by the men, then sighed. "We need to buy more chairs," she informed her husband.

In response, Seth patted his thigh in invitation. Miranda wasted no time settling in his lap, her long dark hair cascading over one shoulder and onto Seth's bare arm.

As his buddy rested a hand on Miranda's hip and stroked absently, Jackson tried not to let his eyes linger on the couple's visible intimacy. But dang it, he wanted what they had.

He was sick and tired of being single. All his friends had found the women of their dreams, and what did *he* get? Naked nutcases who broke into his house, and a sore right hand from jackin' off every night.

Well, it was time to change that. He didn't know if Mia the gardener was the one, but he dang well knew he wanted to see her again. And he was confident that if she spent just a little more time with him, she'd change her mind about her no-dating thing and go out with him.

"I still insist on paying for half of the yard work," Miranda spoke up, interrupting his thoughts. "We don't want to take advantage of you."

Jackson waved a hand. "Don't even think about it, sugar. I never got to give you a wedding present because you two a-holes decided to elope, so this is my chance to right the wrong."

She looked ready to argue, but fortunately, two dark-haired tornadoes swirled onto the scene before she could get a word out.

Sophie and Jason, Miranda's seven-year-old twins, burst out of the sliding door with a degree of energy that made Jackson chuckle. He had no idea how Miranda had managed to raise those two on her own for so long. Even Seth, a Navy SEAL who'd had strenuous training in endurance, admitted that there were days he collapsed in bed thanks to the two energetic children he'd officially adopted last year.

"You wanna see my picture?" Sophie's brown pigtails swung around as she hurled herself into Jackson's lap.

He wrapped an arm around the little girl and peeked at the crumpled piece of blue construction paper in her hands.

"What exactly am I lookin' at, darlin'?" he asked with a laugh.

She pointed to the little stick figures. "Well, that's me 'n Jase —see, Jase is wearing his baseball hat. And that's Mommy in a pretty pink leotard. And that's Daddy over here. I gave him red eyes because he was really mad this morning because we woke him up by jumping on his head, but I don't know why he got mad because it was almost noon and nobody should sleep 'til noon—that's what Mommy always says."

"Mom always says that," Jason piped up, nodding vigorously.

Seth made an irritated noise. "I slept until noon because *somebody* kept me up all night. Maybe you guys should tell Mommy that binge-watching crappy TV shows isn't a productive pastime."

"I wouldn't have to binge-watch it if they didn't end every episode on a cliffhanger!" Miranda objected. She turned to Jackson and added, "I'm watching *Lost*. And yes, I know I'm several years too late but I never had time to watch it when it was on."

"She stayed up until five a.m.," Seth grumbled. "I'm lying

there trying to sleep and every five minutes she wakes me up to tell me how Sawyer is *soooooo* hot."

Miranda smirked. "I can't help it. I like bad boys."

Jackson had to laugh. There was no arguing that Miranda had landed herself the biggest bad boy of them all. With his scruffy face, tattoos, and smartass attitude, Seth was definitely rough around the edges. But he'd grown up a lot since marrying Miranda and becoming a father to her kids.

"Anyway, I should check on dinner," Miranda said, sliding off Seth's lap. She glanced at the twins. "Do you guys want to help?"

"Ya!" both kids declared, and then they were gone, scrambling after their mother into the house.

"Soph called you 'Daddy'," Jackson remarked when he and Seth were alone. "When did that start?"

"A few days ago. Jase introduced me as his dad at his last Little League game, and the rugrats have been calling me that ever since."

To Jackson's surprise, Seth looked vaguely embarrassed.

"You totally like it," Jackson accused, grinning broadly.

His buddy shifted awkwardly, a faint blush on his cheeks. "Kinda."

If someone had told Jackson two years ago that Seth Masterson, the wiseass he'd met during Hell Week, would marry a single mom with a good head on her shoulders and take on the task of raising her kids, he would've laughed in their faces. But life was funny like that.

"So, you really hit it off with that gardener, huh?" As usual, Seth changed the subject the moment the conversation got too squirmy for his liking.

He sighed. "I did. But she shot me down."

"You think she's playing hard to get or just not interested?"

"Nah, she was interested. I know when a girl's into me."

Seth snickered. "Maybe you'll come home tonight and find her in your bed wearing nothing but a cowboy hat."

"And a gun holster," he said with a frustrated breath. "Don't forget the holster."

Now his friend was laughing in earnest. "Fuck, I would've paid to see that. I can't believe you drew your gun on her."

"I thought she was a fuckin' burglar."

"Jesus. That's pure gold, man." Seth grinned. "Well, fingers crossed this gardener you've got a hard-on for isn't bat-shit crazy too. Though I still think you're nuts for hiring her to do our yard just so you can talk to her again." There was a pause. "Does that make her a hooker, you think?"

"I'm not paying to sleep with her, asshole. I just want another shot at asking her out."

Seth arched a brow. "Potato, potahto."

Jackson rolled his eyes and raised his beer to his lips. Fine, so maybe hiring Mia was going a little too far, but he didn't know how else to get her alone. She'd sped off without giving him her number. All he had was the name of the landscaping company she worked for.

But come Monday, he was going to have something else.

A date.

CHAPTER
TWO

"**D**anny, time to wake up!" Mia pounded her fist on her brother's door a few times before hurrying down the narrow corridor while raking a hairbrush through her knotted hair.

They were running late, as per usual. Seemed like their mornings always involved a lot of running around like chickens with their heads cut off. It didn't help that Danny slept like a rock and was impossible to rouse once he was REM-deep. Luckily, after two years on their own she'd finally mastered the difficult feat of waking him up. Meaning he had five more minutes of snooze time before she dumped a glass of cold water on his face.

She burst into the apartment's tiny kitchen, dropped the hairbrush on the linoleum counter, and hopped onto a plastic stepladder so she could reach the top cupboards. God, being short sucked. At sixteen, her little brother already towered over her.

Kind of like Jackson.

Sighing, she pushed all thoughts of her clients' sexy

neighbor from her head and focused on grabbing a box of cereal from the cupboard.

"Danny!" she yelled again.

There was no response. Apparently her brother was determined to sleep until the last possible second.

Normally she wouldn't care, but her boss was sending her to a new client today, and she couldn't afford to be late. Gillian had called last night and told her the client had specifically requested Mia over the other three gardeners who worked for Color Your Yard. Which meant she needed to make a good first impression, especially now that she was in the running to take Gillian's place once the boss opened up the Anaheim branch next spring. If she took over for Gillian in San Diego, she could quit her second job and live a stress-free life for a change.

"Danny!" she called out. "I'm standing in front of the sink about to pour some water into a glass!"

There was a beat, followed by a muffled groan that echoed through the apartment. "Coming!"

Grinning, she fixed herself a bowl of cereal and leaned against the counter to eat it. She was wearing her trademark landscaping "uniform"—denim shorts, a tank top, sneakers, and a baseball cap—and she had to admit, she loved having a job that allowed for such a casual get-up. She couldn't imagine working somewhere that required her to wear pantsuits and high heels. That sounded like pure torture.

She was just rinsing her bowl and spoon in the sink when Danny stumbled into the kitchen with a loud yawn. His green T-shirt was the same shade as his eyes and revealed his defined biceps.

Somehow, in the span of two years, Danny had transformed from a scrawny kid to a well-built young man. He was fourteen when he'd moved in with her, a lost, skinny boy who was dying to stay at one school long enough for him to play football. Now he was a sixteen-year-old heartbreaker, a junior at Madison High who'd just landed the coveted starting varsity quarterback position. He was over the moon about it, and Mia was thrilled for him. If anyone deserved to live his dreams, it was her baby brother.

"Eat your breakfast and make it snappy," she told him. "We're late."

"We're always late," he answered as he dumped a monstrous amount of cereal into his bowl.

"Yeah, and whose fault is that?"

"Yours." He smirked. "If you were a more responsible guardian, you wouldn't set your alarm for twenty minutes before we have to leave."

He had a point, but she refused to give him the satisfaction of admitting he was right. Instead, she stuck out her tongue and said, "If I'm such a bad guardian, go ahead and emancipate yourself. You wouldn't survive a day without me, bud."

Danny swallowed before offering a rueful smile. "You're totes right about that. I don't even wanna think about doing my own laundry."

Five minutes later, the two of them hurried out the door and descended the three flights of stairs to the small lobby of their building. Tenant parking was in the back, and Mia's work truck awaited them when they emerged into the early-morning sunshine.

They were on the road a minute later, carrying out their usual morning battle over the radio dial. Eventually she gave up and let Danny listen to his shitty hip-hop station. She'd only have to endure it for ten minutes, anyway.

"The season opener is this Friday," Danny said.

"Yes, Daniel, I'm well aware of that. You've only told me like a gazillion times." She clicked the right-turn signal and changed lanes, keeping her eyes on the road.

"You're coming, right?"

"Of course. I wouldn't miss it."

A sidelong look revealed the pleased expression on his face. No matter how much they bickered—or how many times he accused her of being annoying—she knew her brother loved her and desperately craved her approval.

Since he'd come to live with her, Mia had made an effort to be the parental role model he'd been lacking all his life. She helped him with homework, attended all his games, went to every parent-teacher conference. She was twenty-five years old, way too young to be the mother of a teenager, but she'd accepted her situation. You had to play the cards life dealt you, and she didn't regret taking on the mom role. If anyone deserved to live a normal life, it was her brother.

"So listen..."

Danny's hesitant voice instantly raised her hackles. When she glanced over and saw the cautious expression on his face, she grew even more uneasy.

"What's up?" she said.

"I just wanted to tell you this so you won't be blindsided if she actually shows up, but..."

Mia's shoulders stiffened. Shit. She knew exactly where this was going.

"Um..." Danny cleared his throat. "But yeah, I emailed Mom yesterday to tell her about the game. You know, just in case she's in town or something and wants to...um...you know... come see us."

A sigh the size of California lodged in Mia's throat. Along with visible discomfort, there was a flicker of hope in her brother's eyes. Fucking hope.

God. That woman deserved to rot in hell for everything she'd done to this kid.

"I see," Mia said in a guarded tone. "Well...look...I understand why you...I mean, I know you want to..." She finally released the sigh, at a loss for words. "I don't want you to get your hopes up, hon. She's..."

Not going to come, her internal voice finished.

Danny gave one of those teenage I-don't-care-about-anything shrugs. "I know she won't show. I just wanted her to know about the game, okay?"

Mia nodded. "Okay."

With that, her brother leaned forward and twisted the volume dial. A rap track blared out of the speakers, with a base-line so heavy it caused the entire truck to vibrate, but Mia didn't make a fuss about it. The mood had turned somber, a common occurrence whenever they spoke about their absentee mother.

Madison High came into view and Mia pulled up at the curb in front of the school. She stopped the truck, turning to Danny with a pained smile.

"Have a good day, kiddo. You've got work after practice, right?"

"Yup. Later, Mia."

He hopped out and slung the strap of his backpack over one shoulder, then dashed across the lawn toward the front steps of the brick building. As she watched him disappear through the doors, a wave of sorrow washed over her. He was such a good kid. Smart, sweet, talented.

Their mother was a damn fool for abandoning him.

Swallowing her resentment, she sped away from the school. She had exactly twenty minutes to get to the new jobsite, but traffic was surprisingly light as she headed across the bridge into Coronado.

The idyllic island was so small that it took no time at all to reach her destination. She was even five minutes early as she killed the engine in front of a pretty white house with an unkempt front lawn and a four-door sedan parked in the driveway.

All her gear was in the back, but she left it in the truck and headed for the front door instead of unloading. No point in lugging any equipment until she knew for sure what the clients wanted from her.

She was raising her hand to ring the bell when the door swung open to reveal a pretty brunette clad in black leggings and a bright pink T-shirt.

"Hi!" the woman said, sounding breathless. "Are you Mia?"

She nodded and stuck out her hand. "I am. And you must be Miranda?"

"Yep."

While they shook hands, two children appeared at Miranda's feet and peeked up at Mia.

She couldn't help but smile when she saw them. The kids were utterly adorable, carbon copies of their mother with dark hair and big brown eyes.

"Are you gonna make our garden pretty?" the little girl exclaimed.

"I'm going to try," Mia answered cheerfully.

"Can you put a baseball diamond in the backyard?" the boy chimed in, equally thrilled.

She fought a laugh. "I don't think so, kiddo. Not unless your yard is the size of Yankee Stadium."

The boy heaved out a big sigh. "It's not."

"Then I'm afraid we're outta luck."

The children's mother seemed to be fighting a laugh of her own. "Let me just take these guys to the car. I'll be right back."

The trio headed for the sedan, and after Miranda got the kids settled inside of it, she hurried back to the front stoop. There was a funny look on her face as she studied Mia.

For so long that Mia started to feel uncomfortable.

"You're a lot prettier than I expected," Miranda remarked.

Um.

Okay.

She tried to mask her confusion, but failed. "Thanks? So are you?"

The brunette laughed. "Sorry, I just realized how creepy that sounded. But you really are pretty. You've got great eyes."

O-kay.

Mia snuck a peek at Miranda's left hand and instantly spotted the wedding ring, which made the entire conversation even more baffling. She didn't get the sense that Miranda was hitting on her, but women didn't normally tell other women they were pretty and had "great eyes."

Did they?

Jeez, maybe she really was out of touch with the world.

"Anyway, let's go around back quick-fast so I can show you what I'd like to do in the yard," Miranda said, seemingly oblivious to Mia's train of thought. "Oh, and my husband should be home around noon, so don't be startled if a big, scruffy guy shows up. And you might also see—"

When Miranda stopped abruptly, Mia raised her eyebrows. "I might also see...?"

After a beat, the brunette shrugged, a strange expression in her eyes. "Nothing. Don't worry about it."

All right, there was something weird about this entire situation. Mia had no clue what it was, but she couldn't fight the feeling that she was being...being what? Duped? Hit on? Lured into a sexual encounter with a hot brunette while her husband watched?

Stop being paranoid. They hired you to garden for them.

The reminder was only about ninety percent reassuring.

The other ten percent maintained that a seduction in front

of Miranda's big, scruffy husband wasn't entirely out of the realm of possibility.

———————

After a long morning of underwater demolition training that started at four a.m., Jackson was dying to leave the base. He changed into his street clothes in record time, and was just about to march out of the locker room when his commanding officer stepped inside.

Lieutenant Commander Thomas Becker was as intimidating now as he'd been when Jackson first laid eyes on him three years ago. Built like an action star, the man had close-cropped brown hair and a pair of intense eyes that never failed to make a guy feel like he'd been caught with his hand in the cookie jar. Then again, when it came to Jackson and his teammates, Beck was probably right to remain eternally suspicious. He'd had to bail them out of more than one jam since they'd been assigned to his team.

"Hold up," Becker barked, jabbing a finger at Jackson.

Jackson experienced a flicker of unease, until he realized Beck wasn't singling him out. Seth, Dylan and Cash were also on the visual radar. The four guys exchanged a wary look as their CO crossed his arms over his bulky chest and scowled at each of them.

"I just wanted to give you the heads-up that we've got Team Eight coming in next week," Becker announced.

"What for?" Dylan asked.

Jackson shared his teammate's curiosity. It was rare for the West Coast SEAL teams to interact with the East Coast teams.

"Special Operations wants us to conduct some joint training missions," Becker replied. "I'll let you know the details when I've got 'em, but just be prepared to run a few ops with some new faces. They'll be staying in the barracks here, so none of you boneheads get any ideas about letting them crash at your places."

Seth hooted. "Are you ordering us to deny our fellow servicemen hospitality?"

Becker glowered. "They don't need your kind of hospitality, smartass. And from what I've heard, Team Eight is the East Coast equivalent of you troublemakers, so don't go inviting them to your swinging parties or whatnot."

"How dare you," Seth said in mock outrage. "I am a married man, sir."

"Swinging parties?" Cash echoed. "None of us are swingers."

"Trust me, I've got enough lovers to deal with at home," Dylan said wryly.

Their CO just scowled again. "I mean it. No partying with Team Eight. I'm not in the mood to bail anyone out of jail again. Understood?"

"Understood," they chorused.

After Becker stalked out of the room, Seth turned to the others and grinned. "Let's throw the Eighters a welcome orgy."

"Pass," Dylan answered. "Claire and Aidan would kill me if I touched anyone else."

"So would Jen," Cash said ruefully.

Seth sighed. "Yeah, you're right. Bad idea. Miranda would kick my ass."

Jackson stayed quiet, and experienced an odd pang of regret about it. He didn't have a lovely lady—or in Dylan's case, a lovely lady and a hot dude—getting all possessive over him. It bummed him out a little.

"I can't wait to get home and sleep," Dylan announced as the four men strode out of the locker room.

"Do you need a ride or did you take Aidan's car this morning?" Cash asked.

"Negative on the car. Claire took it to run a few last-minute errands before she leaves."

Jackson glanced over. "Where is she going?"

"Los Angeles, for business. She'll be gone three weeks."

"I guess that's the good thing about living a life of sin—your girl's away, but you'll still have your man at home," Seth cracked.

"Actually, Aidan's gone too," Dylan said glumly. "He's got some downtime so he's spending a few days in LA with the missus and then heading to Chicago to see his dad. Which means I'll be all by my lonesome for three whole weeks."

Seth rolled his eyes. "Poor baby."

"Poor baby is right," Dylan muttered. "That means no sex for *twenty-one* days."

"That's an eternity in manwhore years," Cash agreed solemnly.

Jackson snorted. There was nobody who loved sex more than Dylan Wade. Men, women, didn't matter the gender. Dylan was a serious horndog, which probably made it a good thing he was now in a relationship with not one, but two partners.

Truthfully, Jackson still had no clue how he felt about Dylan's unorthodox love life. Growing up in a tiny town in Texas, he hadn't encountered many polyamorous relationships. The residents of Abbott Creek were hard-workin', God-fearin' folks who loved their football and believed marriage was reserved for a man and a woman, thank you very much. If there were any liberal-minded folks in town, Jackson sure as heck hadn't encountered them. That was one of the reasons he'd skipped town and joined the navy. He hadn't been able to put up with those narrow-minded busybodies for one more second.

The fact that one of his best friends was involved in a permanent ménage a trois was a bit of a head-scratcher, but Jackson honestly couldn't say he disapproved. He adored Claire, Dylan's girlfriend. And Aidan, Dylan's boyfriend, was really fucking awesome. As long as Dylan was happy, who was Jackson to pass judgment?

The four of them continued chatting as they left the base, but Jackson's head was elsewhere now. He was going to see Mia again. In about, oh, ten minutes, according to the tactical watch strapped to his wrist.

He couldn't frickin' wait.

"See you boys later," Cash said when they reached the parking lot.

Dylan glanced at Jackson. "We still on for that COD sesh tonight?"

"He might have other plans," Seth spoke up with a barely restrained grin.

"Another date?" Cash said. "Oh man, if it's another date can you please, *please* record it on your phone for me?"

"Are you seeing the sex addict again?" Dylan demanded. "Because I want pictures of her cowboy outfit—oooh, and try to get a shot of the two of you where you're holding your gun."

"Fuck you both," Jackson said darkly.

Cash's blue eyes twinkled. "Aw, come on, turn that frown upside down. A sex addict broke into your house. Most dudes would consider that a high-fivable story."

"Seriously, though—you, me, Call of Duty tonight?" Dylan prompted.

"We'll see," he answered, shrugging. "I'll text you later."

"Cool beans."

Fortunately, neither Cash nor Dylan pressed him about why he might not be available. The duo waved goodbye and hopped into Cash's SUV.

Jackson had caught a ride with Seth that morning, so he slid into the passenger seat of Seth's Jeep and waited for his buddy to start the engine.

"You excited?" Seth grinned, then went on in a singsong voice. "Jackson and Gardener sitting in a tree—"

He slugged the other man in the arm. Hard. "And that's enough of that," he said, rolling his eyes. "You've been spending too much time with the twins."

Seth sighed. "I know, right?"

"And her name isn't *Gardener*. It's Mia."

"Gee, I'm so sorry. Jackson and *Mia* sitting in a—"

Another hard punch shut Seth right up.

"You're no fun today," the other SEAL mumbled. "I'm just showing some enthusiasm over your impending love connection, asshole. Not only that, but you should be thanking me. A strange chick is currently puttering around in my yard because of you. What if she decides to snoop inside and finds all the porn on my computer?"

Jackson had to laugh. "One, she's not gonna snoop around on the job. Two, why do you still have porn on your computer? I thought married men deleted all their porn once they tied the knot."

"No way." Seth steered the Jeep toward the security gate across the lot. "Miranda demanded I keep it all. We watch that shit together, bro."

Somehow that didn't surprise him.

As they drove off the base, Seth proceeded to tell him about the various pornographic movies he and his wife enjoyed, which, again, came as no surprise. Jackson had once thought it was fucked up and oddly incestuous how easily the other guys talked about—and shared—women. Folks in Abbott Creek didn't talk about sex—Jackson had found that out the hard way. But here in California he'd learned to go with the flow. Threesomes weren't really his thing, mostly because of the strict small-town mentality he'd endured growing up, but he appreciated that his teammates trusted him with their secrets, no matter how depraved.

One of these days he might even reciprocate, but he'd yet to find the balls to confide in his friends about the kinds of depravities *he* liked to indulge in.

His palms grew unusually damp the closer they got to Seth's place. Seth must have sensed his growing agitation because he glanced over with his trademark smirk.

"Relax, Texas. You've got this. Believe in your dreams, think outside the box, there's no 'I' in 'Team,' et cetera, et cetera."

"Are you just spitting out random inspirational sayings to pump me up?"

"Yep."

"I honestly don't know why I'm still friends with you."

Seth pulled into the driveway, where a familiar sky-blue pickup was already parked.

Jackson's pulse promptly sped up.

She was here.

"I'm going straight to bed," Seth told him as they got out of the Jeep. "Wake me up when you want me to drive you home."

"Thanks, man."

They walked into the house together. But while Seth made a beeline for his bedroom, Jackson continued down the hall toward the kitchen.

This was it. His second and last chance to persuade his sassy gardener to go on a date with him, which meant he couldn't screw it up.

He approached the glass sliding door and straightened his shoulders.

Time to unleash his God-given Southern charm and do some serious wooing.

CHAPTER
THREE

She was wearing those cute denim shorts again. That was Jackson's first observation when he stepped onto the stone patio. The fact that she was oblivious to his presence gave him ample opportunity to admire her petite body, and dang, he totally appreciated the view.

With a pair of earbuds popped in, Mia bobbed her head to the music as she raked the fresh layer of dirt in the empty flowerbeds lining the fence. When Jackson glanced around, he was impressed by how much she'd already accomplished today. The jungle-length grass was freshly mowed, all the monstrous weeds had been pulled out, and the beds around the perimeter were dug out and topped with new soil.

He took a step forward and cleared his throat, but Mia's back stayed turned. Her arms and shoulders were bare, her golden-brown tan shimmering in the sunlight. Lord, she was pretty. He couldn't take his eyes off her.

A few more steps and his scuffed-up combat boots met the grass, but Mia still didn't turn around.

So he raised his voice and called out, "Afternoon, sugar."

The rake clattered out of her hand, a loud shriek escaping

her lips as she spun around in surprise. The movement was so quick that her sneaker-clad feet got tangled together, her arms windmilled, and she went down like a stone.

Right on her ass.

Fuckin' hell.

"Oh my God! You scared the living crap out of me!" she yelled, her green eyes burning with annoyance. "Who sneaks up on people like that? *Who?*"

Despite himself, Jackson laughed, which only made those mesmerizing eyes burn brighter.

Mia yanked out her earbuds and shot to her feet, advancing on him like a predator. "Don't do stuff like that! What if I had a heart condition? And what if—wait, what are you *doing* here? Did you follow me here?" Her breaths came out in pants. "I'm flabbergasted right now. Jackson, was it? I'm flabbergasted, Jackson."

Another wave of laughter poured out of him. She looked so confused and upset and he knew he shouldn't laugh. He really, really shouldn't be laughing. But his attempt at reconnecting with this girl had failed so miserably it was impossible not to find it hilarious.

"And now you're laughing at me," she said in disbelief. "Wow."

"I'm sorry," he choked out. "I don't mean to laugh, darlin'. But the look on your face right now..." He tried to compose himself. "Shit. I really am sorry. Why don't we start over? Afternoon, Mia. It's good to see you again."

She gaped at him.

"I'm not following you," he added. "I'm friends with Seth and Miranda."

"You're friends with Seth and Miranda."

"Yup. I caught a ride with Seth from the base—"

"You caught a ride with Seth from the base."

"Yeah, we're both SEALs. Anyway—"

"You're both SEALs."

"—he's drivin' me home soon, but I wanted to say hi to you before we—"

"You wanted to say hi."

He stopped. "Are you just gonna keep repeating everything I say?"

"Are you going to prove to me I'm not being stalked right now?" she shot back. "Because I'm not sold on that yet, bud."

He swept his gaze over her indignation-flushed cheeks. "You're pretty when you're mad, sugar."

Her jaw fell open again. "Flirting? You're flirting with me? How about explaining yourself?"

Amusement tickled his throat. "All righty. Here's the thing, Mia. I'd really like to have dinner with you."

"Oh, for the love of..."

"Unfortunately, you were mighty difficult the last time we spoke, so I figured we needed to try this again."

Her mouth slammed shut. She looked around the backyard for a moment, and then understanding dawned in her eyes. "Wait a minute—you hired my company to work this yard so you could ask me out again? This job is a farce?"

His lips twitched. "The job is not a farce. It's my wedding present to Seth and Miranda. You saw the state of their yard. It definitely needed the work."

"But you specifically requested for *me* to do it."

"Yup."

She shook her head. "You do realize that's nuts, right?"

"Nah, it's not nuts. Just persistent."

"Persistent," she echoed.

"Persistent," he confirmed. When she didn't speak, he slanted his head and searched her gaze. "So, about that dinner..."

This time her jaw opened so wide it almost hit the grass. "Seriously? After everything I just heard, *sugar*, what makes you think I'd go out with you?"

"Because you want to."

MIA DIDN'T KNOW WHETHER TO KICK JACKSON IN THE SHIN or burst out laughing. Never in her wildest dreams had she expected to see this guy again, let alone *here*, at a new client's house. The lengths he'd gone to in order to ask her out triggered a wave of disbelief, but she'd be lying if she said she wasn't a tiny bit flattered. No man had ever pursued her so hard, especially one as spectacular-looking as Jackson.

But still. She couldn't go out with him. Her former shrink would tell her that enabling stalker behavior was a recipe for disaster.

"I told you, I don't have time to date," she finally responded, whipping off her cap so she could run a frazzled hand through her hair.

"One dinner, Mia." His tone softened, his whiskey-brown eyes taking on a vulnerable glimmer.

The vulnerability threw her for a loop. A guy as big and sexy as this one wasn't supposed to be so...sweet.

Sweet? Oh boy, she was in trouble. She wondered if there was a Stockholm Syndrome-esque diagnosis for women who developed crushes on their stalkers.

"You can't deny you're enjoying this," he went on, shooting her the most adorable grin she'd ever seen. "You, me, this easy banter we've got goin' on."

She had to sigh. "It's definitely rom-com-level banter, I'll give you that."

"Look, darlin', I like you." He shrugged sheepishly. "And I

think you like me too. So what's the harm in having one teeny weeny dinner together?"

Teeny weeny? Shit. The lame words only made him more endearing.

Oh, throw the guy a bone. He's practically groveling at your feet.

Argh. Truth was, she *did* like him. He was tall and gorgeous and charming as all get-out. And maybe saying yes to a date wouldn't be a *terrible* idea. She hadn't gone out with anyone in ages, and she couldn't live like a nun forever.

"Come on," he cajoled. "One dinner."

After a long beat of hesitation, Mia capitulated.

"Fine." When his expression lit up, she added a quick caveat. "One dinner," she said sternly. "We'll eat some food, banter some more, and that's it. I'm not committing to a second date, got it?"

His surprisingly full lips quirked up in a smile. "Got it. Don't worry, I'll be a gentleman. I won't demand a second date until we've got the first one squared away."

"Who says you'll enjoy the first one enough to request a follow-up?"

"Oh, I'll enjoy it." He cocked a brow. "So will you, by the way."

"I will, huh? I guess we'll just have to see about that."

"Yup, we sure will." He reached into his back pocket. "Give me your number, sugar. I'll call you tonight to set up the details for our date."

His confidence was a little unnerving. So was the cocky glint in his eyes.

But since it was too late to back out, she dutifully recited her number so he could enter it into his phone.

All the while wondering exactly what she'd just gotten herself into.

"I'm sorry, I think I misheard you," Mia's brother said the next evening. "Did you just say you had a *date* tonight?"

She ignored his shocked tone and brushed past him, her bare feet slapping the hardwood floor on her way to the bathroom.

"Really? A date?" Danny trailed after her into the bathroom, disregarding all the manners she'd tried to instill in him.

Mia glared at him in the mirror over the vanity. "Go away, kiddo. I have about ten minutes to learn how to put on makeup."

With that, she opened the medicine cabinet and grabbed the plastic bin that housed all the unopened beauty supplies she never used.

"I'm not going anywhere until you tell me about this date," Danny said. "Who is he? Where did you meet? And why does he want to go out with *you*?"

She ripped open a package of mascara and tossed the wrapping in the pink wastebasket. "Ha ha. You're a comedian. Hey, do you know how to use this thing?"

As she held up the plastic tube, Danny stared at her as if she'd grown horns and sprouted a tail.

Then he opened his mouth and shouted, "Angie, get in here! Mia needs you to make her look attractive!"

Mia glowered at him. "Eff you," she grumbled.

Danny's girlfriend dove into the bathroom in record time. Her face was flushed and her eyes shone with curiosity. "What's going on? What do you guys need?"

"Mia doesn't know how to put on makeup," Danny announced before rolling his eyes. "Jeez. I'm a dude and even *I* know how to put on makeup."

Mia stifled a groan. "I'm fine. I really don't need help."

"She really needs help," Danny said.

Angie's expression brightened as she released a happy cry. "Oh my God! I've been waiting months for this moment! BRB— just gonna get my makeup kit from my backpack!"

As the teenage girl flew off in a whirl of excitement, Mia scowled at her brother. "Now look what you've done. I'll never leave this bathroom."

"Trust me, Ang is good with this kind of stuff. She wants to be a makeup artist." Danny edged out the door. "I'm grabbing some chips so I have something to snack on while I watch you turn into a real girl."

As he wandered off, she stared at her reflection and heaved a massive sigh. Damn it, why had she agreed to this date? She hated all this girly shit.

And why was she even trying to pretty herself up? She wasn't planning on seducing Jackson—or even seeing him again after tonight. What she really ought to do was show up at the restaurant in sweats and with her hair in a ponytail. At least then he wouldn't want a second date.

Footsteps sounded from the hall, signaling Angie's return. Argh. Danny just *had* to open his big mouth. Now thanks to him, she was officially at his girlfriend's mercy.

Not that she disliked Angie or anything. Mia adored her. The sixteen-year-old was sweet, smart, and unbelievably kind. And a virgin, to boot. A fact Mia had discovered when grilling the girl the first time Danny brought her home.

Just because Mia had lost her own virginity at sixteen didn't mean she wanted the same for her brother, but as far as she knew, Danny and his girlfriend still hadn't done the deed even after a year of dating.

"Okay, tell me everything," Angie said after she'd ordered Mia to sit on the closed toilet seat. "Who is he? Is he cute?"

"His name is Jackson and he's very cute," she admitted. "But don't bust out any parades, hon. I probably won't see him again after tonight."

"Why not? You never go out, Mia. You totally deserve to have some fun."

"I'm too busy for that." Her jaw dropped when the younger girl placed an enormous zipped case on the counter. "What on earth do you keep in there? Rocks?"

"Every girl needs a fully stocked makeup kit," Angie said firmly. "We'll go out this weekend and buy you one."

"Nah, I'll pass."

Danny's voice came from the doorway. "Stop being a grouch. Angie's right. It's about time you started caring about your appearance. I don't want a spinster for a sister."

"Um, excuse me, but us spinsters prefer the term *old maid*," she said stiffly.

Angie burst out laughing. "You're so funny. Jackson is going to love you."

"Jackson?" Danny echoed curiously. "Is that his name?"

"Yes," Angie answered for Mia. "And supposedly he's *very* cute."

"What does he do? Like, for a job?"

Mia laughed at her brother's narrowed eyes. "Why do you care? If he's unemployed, will you forbid me from seeing him?"

"Of course. I don't want some bum taking advantage of my old-maid sister."

"Don't worry, he's not a bum. He's a SEAL."

Both teenagers gawked at her.

"For real?" Angie blurted out.

"For real."

Danny's suspicion transformed into glee. "That's so frickin' cool. Do you think he'll bring a gun on your date?"

"Why on earth would he do that? He's a soldier, not a cop."

"Is he picking you up? I've never met a SEAL before."

Jeez. Her brother looked scarily excited about the prospect of her going out with a navy man. Maybe she ought to send *Danny* on the date.

"I'm meeting him at the restaurant," she replied.

The interrogation didn't let up. "Which restaurant?"

"Go away, babe," Angie announced. "I have a lot of work to do and you're distracting me."

"Fine." Just like that, Danny left the room without a protest.

Mia raised her eyebrows. "I'm impressed. It takes me a minimum of five attempts to get him to do what I say."

"That's 'cause he likes making you mad. He thinks it's funny." Angie stuck her hand in the case and emerged with a tube of foundation. "'Kay, now quit talking. This might take a while."

CHAPTER
FOUR

Mia was late.

Jackson waited in front of the small Italian bistro on Market Street and checked his phone for the third time in the past five minutes. No new messages.

He would've been worried that he was being stood up, if not for the text Mia sent ten minutes ago informing him she was on her way. The gentleman in him still wished she'd allowed him to pick her up, but she'd been mighty insistent about meeting him here.

Clearly she was trying to keep her distance right off the bat, which didn't surprise him considering how difficult it'd been getting her to even agree to dinner. But her arm's-length approach didn't faze him. He was determined to win Mia over tonight, no matter what.

Truth was, he liked her. He really liked her, a rare and wonderful feeling he hadn't experienced in ages. He hadn't realized how frustrating dating could be. Sex? That was easy. San Diego was full of women eager to take off their clothes for a SEAL. But finding a girl who truly liked him and wanted to be with him? A whole other story.

"Hey, sorry I'm late!"

He lifted his head in time to see Mia round the side of the building, and the sight of her blew him away.

Her hair was loose, the dark shoulder-length tresses curling slightly at the ends. And her skin looked so soft and luminous his fingers tingled with the urge to stroke her face. She was wearing makeup, but not an obscene amount of it, just enough to accentuate her hunter-green eyes, high cheekbones and full lips. And she'd donned a dress tonight. A knee-length green sundress paired with brown platform heels that added a few inches to her tiny frame.

"You done checking me out or should I give you another minute?"

Her dry voice snapped him out of it. Clearing his throat, he shoved his fingers in the belt loops of his khaki pants. "You look amazing," he said.

Her lips stayed in smirk formation, but there was no mistaking the flicker of pleasure in her eyes. "Thanks. I'll have you know I endured forty-five minutes of torture at the hands of my brother's girlfriend in order to look like this. That's why I was late."

"Aw shucks, darlin'. You got a makeover just for me?"

"Don't you dare read anything into it. I'd have done it for anybody."

"I don't believe you." With that, he smiled broadly. "C'mon, let's go inside."

They walked through the bright red door of Tonio's, Jackson's favorite place to eat in San Diego. His teammates constantly teased him about it, maintaining that cowboys were supposed to eat steak and potatoes and nothin' else, but Jackson had always had a thing for Italian food. When he and Mia had messaged back and forth about tonight, he'd been pleased to hear it was her favorite food too.

"I love this place," she told him as they entered the waiting area. "Danny and I get takeout from here at least once a week."

Apparently she wasn't kidding, because a second later the dark-haired woman at the hostess stand greeted Mia like the two of them were old friends.

"Mamma Mia!" the older woman teased, her eyes crinkling. "You didn't call ahead to place an order, *cara*."

"No takeout for me tonight, Rosa. We're eating in."

The hostess shifted her gaze to Jackson, and a smile stretched across her face. "Ah, I see. A special occasion! Let's get you a table, then."

The woman led them into the cozy main room, which felt even more romantic than usual. The entire bistro seemed to glow from the soft light seeping out of the overhead fixtures. The faint strains of classical piano only enhanced the vibe.

They arrived at a table with a crimson tablecloth, lit candles, and gleaming silverware resting on pristine white napkins. After they were seated, the hostess hurried away and a waiter took her place, taking their drink orders before handing each of them a leather-bound menu. Yet for all the pomp and circumstance, the food wasn't overpriced and there was no air of pretension about the place.

"So," Mia announced, clasping her hands on the tablecloth. "You did it."

"Did what?"

"You lured me out of the house for the first date I've had in years." She raised her eyebrows in challenge. "Time to show me what you've got, *sugar*."

He flashed a grin. "Hmmm...I can take my shirt off if you want. That usually gets the ladies goin'."

She rolled her eyes. "I don't doubt it. But I was thinking more along the lines of you wowing me with your conversational prowess."

"All righty. Name a topic and I promise to rock the shit out of it."

Her answering laugh made his pulse race. He liked her laugh. It had a sweet lilt to it, like a pretty melody.

"Tell me where you grew up," she ordered. "'Cause I know that's not a California accent."

"I'm from Texas. Grew up in a little town called Abbott Creek, about fifty miles west of Dallas."

"Let me guess, you hail from a family of cowboys."

"Yup. My folks own a cattle ranch, so I spent my entire childhood waking up at the crack of dawn to do a shitload of chores."

"Did you like the ranch work?"

"I loved it," he confessed. "Growing up I wanted nothin' more than to stay on the ranch. Maybe buy a spread of my own someday."

Her eyes went thoughtful. "But you joined the navy instead. Why?"

He shrugged. "I needed a change."

"Well, *that's* vague." She laughed again. "Care to elaborate?"

Discomfort welled inside him, but he forced himself to offer a few more details. "Small-town life is...oppressive, for lack of a better word. Everybody's always stickin' their noses into everybody else's business. I got sick of it. I wanted to experience life beyond Abbott Creek, know what I mean?"

She nodded. "Yeah, I get that."

The server returned with their drinks, then waited patiently while they scanned the menus and ordered their entrees. Once he was gone, Jackson turned the tables on his date.

"Have you always lived in California?" he asked.

"Nah, we moved around a lot when I was a kid. I was born in Colorado, but my mom moved us to New Jersey when I was five. Then we moved to Philly, Chicago, Atlanta, Missouri, um —I think I'm forgetting a few places—and then after high school I came to San Diego for college and ended up loving it here. So I stayed."

He wrinkled his forehead. "Why'd you move so much?"

The edge that crept into her voice told him he'd struck a nerve. "My mom kept getting married."

Jackson blinked. "Huh?"

"She gets married a lot." Mia absently dragged her index finger over the trail of condensation clinging to her water glass. "I think she's on marriage number nine now."

"*Nine?*"

"Actually, I could be wrong. I haven't seen her in two years, so she could have tied the knot a couple more times, for all I know." Sarcasm dripped from her voice. "I think she's trying to double Liz Taylor's record."

"So each time she got married she packed y'all up and moved you to a new city?"

"Well, it was more like each time she got *divorced* we packed up and moved to a new city. Trust me, her divorces were as epic as her marriages—no city was big enough to accommodate both Mom and her latest ex-husband."

Jackson didn't need to be a genius to figure out there were definitely some unresolved issues when it came to Mia's relationship with her mother. He couldn't even imagine growing up with a parent like that. His folks were happily married, had been for nearly thirty years now, and they'd raised their family in the same little town where generations of their ancestors had put up roots.

"Moving so much must've been tough."

She gave a noncommittal shrug. "It was harder on Danny, I think."

"Your brother?"

"Yeah. He never really got to be a normal kid, and with the ten-year age difference between us, I was already out of the house when he was just eight."

"Sure, but you still had to deal with it for eighteen years of *your* life," he pointed out.

Another shrug. "I managed. I'm a lot tougher than Danny, truth be told. He's too softhearted for his own good. He always made excuses for our mom. Still does. He refuses to admit how selfish she is."

"Where is she now?"

"Who knows." Mia took a long sip of water, unmistakable sadness washing over her expression. "She showed up at my door two years ago with Danny in tow and asked if he could crash with me while she went on a one-month honeymoon with her latest husband. I said sure—I mean, I love that kid to death—but once the month was over, she never came back."

"Seriously?"

"Yep. She took off and never looked back. That's why Danny's living with me now. I filed for guardianship of him and the court approved my request on the grounds of abandonment."

"Shit, Mia, that's..."

"My life," she finished wryly. "But enough about that. No need for both of us to leave here bummed out and jonesing for antidepressants. Tell me about this SEAL thing."

He grinned. "SEAL thing?"

"Yeah, you know, your military career. How many times you've saved the world, that kind of stuff."

A chuckle slipped out. "Why? Does the idea of me saving the world get you goin'?"

"What is it with your need to 'get me goin'?"

"Can't help it. I want a second date, remember? That ain't gonna happen unless I make you fall in love with me."

Her laughter tickled his ears and made him want to jump across the table and kiss her.

"Ain't gonna happen," she mimicked.

"Fine. I'll settle for making you fall in lust with me."

"That probably won't happen either."

The remark piqued his interest. Cheeky as it was, he'd detected a note of resignation in her voice. "You don't experience lust often, darlin'?"

"Not really," she confessed. "I mean, I've been attracted to guys before, but never in a super *lusty* way. You know, like I can't wait to rip their clothes off and screw them silly."

"Are you a virgin?" he had to ask.

"Nope. Are you?"

"If I say yes, will you be my sexual tutor and make a man outta me?"

"Nope."

"Fine, then no, I'm not a virgin."

"Shocking."

He tipped his head, still intrigued by the entire conversation. "Do you enjoy sex?"

She laughed again. "This is *not* appropriate first-date subject matter."

"Well, seeing as there won't be a second date—" he shot her a pointed look, "—I figure any topic is up for grabs tonight."

"Fair enough." She sipped her water. "Fine, I'll answer the question. Do I enjoy sex? Not really. Honestly, I can take it or leave it."

His eyebrows soared to his forehead. "You don't like it at all?"

"It's okay, I guess, but I've never had a sexual encounter that's been any better than my solo sessions." An endearing blush appeared on her cheeks. "Actually, I have more fun alone than I ever have with a guy."

Damned if his dick didn't take that as a challenge.

Jackson shifted in his chair, trying to ignore the semi that had sprung in his pants. Mia's candid revelations had brought way too many visuals to mind. Like the image of her lying in bed, her fingers moving between her legs as she got herself off. Or the one of him in that bed with her, licking every inch of her body and proving to her just how much fun it could be having another person around.

"What, no response?" she said with a smirk. "Let me guess— my thoughts about sex have changed your mind about that second date."

"Not at all."

"Really? You don't think it's weird that I'd rather make myself come than—" She halted abruptly, her cheeks turning redder as their server strode up with their meals.

Jackson swallowed a laugh when he noticed the waiter's face. The man's expression was polite, but the flicker of amusement in his eyes said that he'd definitely overheard Mia's last remark.

Neither of them spoke while their food was served. After the waiter hurried off, Mia instantly stuck her fork in the tangle of linguine on her plate, then took a bite of the steaming noodles.

"Ugh, that's hot!" she burst out a second later, making a mad grab for her water.

Jackson chuckled. "That's what you get for trying to avoid the subject."

"I'm not avoiding. I thought we were done talking about it."

"A man is never done talkin' about sex."

That got him another laugh. "Okay. What else do we have to say about it?"

He picked up his knife and fork and cut into his massive serving of chicken Parmesan. After popping a small piece into his mouth, he chewed thoughtfully, then said, "Tell me one sexy secret nobody knows about you."

She wrapped her fingers around her glass. "Hmmm. Well. How's this? I keep a nine-inch dildo in a locked drawer beside my bed."

His semi-erection transformed into a full-blown boner.

Breathing through the wave of arousal, Jackson responded in a casual voice. "Interesting. Because my sexy secret was gonna be that I have a nine-inch cock."

"Wow. Congratulations, big boy." His date snorted, then raised her glass to her lips.

"Oh, and it's pierced."

A spray of water splashed the table as Mia did an honest-to-God spit take.

Smirking, Jackson took another bite of chicken.

"You're joking," she said.

He met her narrowed eyes. "Am I?"

Her tone grew even more suspicious. "There's no way a small-town Texas boy like yourself has his nether regions pierced."

"It's a dang shame you'll never get to find out," he said cheerfully. "I guess you should've thought twice before insisting this is a one-date thing."

She harrumphed, wiped her mouth with her napkin, and picked up her fork again.

"So..." he said pensively, "back to the topic at hand. You don't enjoy sex. Is it just the penetration part or all parts?"

"You're incorrigible."

Her chest heaved as she released another exasperated breath, drawing his gaze to her breasts. They were smaller than he usually liked, just a gentle swell of cleavage peeking out the bodice of her dress, but something about those perky little tits made his mouth water.

He wanted to fuck her. Getting to know her better had been the number one item on his agenda, but now that was joined by a hefty dose of desire. He wanted her naked. Naked and moaning while he thrust into her and drove her mindless with passion.

"And it's all parts of it."

Her voice brought him back to the present. To the table where they were both seated, fully clothed.

Mia went on. "The intercourse part, the oral, the kissing— it's all boring to me."

"Even the kissing?" he said in surprise.

"Yeah. I don't know if I'm the bad kisser in the equation, or if the guys I've made out with have just been abysmal at it, but make-out sessions have never really done it for me." She offered a knowing look. "You must think I'm a total prude, huh?"

"Nope. I think you're the most fascinating woman I've ever met."

"Clearly you don't get out much either." She rolled her eyes. "Now enough about sex. Let's talk about less stressful things. Tell me how you became a SEAL."

***

Two hours later, Mia had to face the indisputable truth: she liked Jackson Ramsey.

Not once during dinner had they run out of things to talk about. In fact, the conversation had flowed so smoothly that not only had they stayed for dessert, they were now lingering on their second cup of post-dessert coffee.

It was ridiculously hard not to like this guy. He was smart, charming, funny, down-to-earth. He listened when she spoke, laughed at her dumb jokes, was interested in her job. And she'd discovered in the course of their conversation that he wasn't just a soldier, he was also the medic on his SEAL team, which meant he was *extra* good at saving lives.

Oh, and his cock may or may not be pierced. Don't forget that part.

Right, who could forget that.

The strangest thing about the date was the way it made her feel. Or more specifically, the way Jackson turned her on. The pull of attraction was so strong her entire body had felt hot and achy from moment one. Every time he opened his sexy mouth, her heart began to race. Whenever her gaze strayed to his chest, hugged by a snug black T-shirt, her palms went damp. And each time she looked into his sultry brown eyes, she utterly melted.

It didn't help that he kept looking at her like he wanted her naked. The man had mastered seductive gazes to a T, and knowing he was undressing her with his eyes only caused her to mentally undress *him*—and that particular mental picture was so hot she was liable to burst into flames any second.

By the time Jackson paid the bill and helped her out of her chair, Mia was ready to flee. She couldn't get caught in the spell he was attempting to cast on her. As wonderful as he was, seeing him again wasn't an option.

But clearly he had other ideas.

"So when can I see you again?"

She stifled a groan and walked through the door he held open for her. When they stepped outside, the late-evening breeze snaked beneath her hair and cooled her warm cheeks.

"Jackson..." He was so tall she had to peer up at him to meet his eyes. "I had a good time. Seriously, I did. But this doesn't change anything. I'm still swamped with work and taking care of Danny. I don't have a lot of free time."

"I'll take whatever you can give me. One dinner a week, lunch every other week, I don't care, darlin'. I just want to keep seeing you."

For Pete's sake. The man truly was tenacious. She'd told him that she was pretty much a single mother, confessed her indifference to sex, and he still wanted to see her again?

"I'm not looking for a relationship," she said feebly. "Or a fling."

"I know that."

"Then what's the point? Why bother spending more time together if it won't go anywhere?"

"Because I want to. Because *you* want to."

She fiddled with the little brown pocketbook she was using as a purse, snapping it open to retrieve her keys. "It won't work. I've got too much on my plate to commit to anything more. Besides, I feel bad getting your hopes up about, you know, potentially having sex, because it probably won't happen."

"Why? 'Cause you think you won't like it?"

Because I know I won't.

She bit back the words before they could slip out. Truth was, she'd completely underplayed the whole sex thing during their discussion earlier. She found sex so boring and unsatisfying that she'd even raised the subject with her old therapist. For a long while she'd thought there might be something wrong with her, like maybe she was an asexual weirdo who'd never be able to function like a normal sexual being. But the fact that she could give herself wild, breathless orgasms without any trouble contradicted that.

She was so apprehensive about getting intimate with anyone again. She'd slept with four guys in her life, and each encounter had been more disappointing than the last.

"Y'know what, I've got an idea," Jackson said before she could respond.

She shot him a questioning look, but rather than elaborate he took her hand and started leading her toward the side of the building. The warmth of his fingers seeped into her palm and made her feel achy again. She didn't understand this effect he had on her. At all.

But although she was incredibly tempted to explore it further, she didn't want to set herself up for any more disappointment. Only one lover had even made her come before, and getting there had been a struggle, to say the least.

"What are you up to?" she asked warily.

He practically dragged her into the small parking lot behind the restaurant. Jackson scanned the lot and broke out in a grin. "Look at that," he drawled, "even our vehicles know we make the perfect couple."

Mia followed his gaze, groaning when she noticed the black pickup truck parked beside her blue one. "That's your pickup?"

"Sure is." Still grinning, he led her toward the trucks, then let go of her hand and crossed his arms over his broad chest. "Here's the deal, sugar."

"There's a deal?"

"Yup. I want to go out with you again. You're being difficult. So here's what I propose."

"I can't wait to hear this."

He ignored the sarcasm and swept his tongue over his bottom lip, an act so sexy she shivered.

"I'm goin' to kiss you."

Her breath hitched. "What?"

"I'm goin' to kiss you," he repeated. "And if you like it, then you have to agree to see me again."

Damned if her heart didn't start pounding. The heat in his eyes seared right through her clothing and sizzled her flesh, making her feel hot and dizzy.

"You're nuts," she stammered.

"Maybe, but that's the deal, sugar. You claim that nothin' gets you goin', not even a kiss. You also said you had a good time tonight, did you not?"

"I did, but—"

"The reason you don't want to pursue this is because you think I'll never be able to turn you on—"

She felt herself blush. "That's not what I—"

"—so it stands to reason that if I can prove to you I've got the moves, you'll have no choice but to give this a shot."

Her mouth closed. His reasoning was certifiably wacky, but she couldn't seem to argue with it.

"Do we have a deal?" he prompted, shooting her an adorably crooked smile.

It was sheer curiosity that had her nodding.

"Good. Then prepare to have your world rocked."

The laugh that flew out was cut short by the feel of Jackson's mouth on her neck.

Her neck?

Surprise jolted through her at the same time a flurry of shivers danced across her skin. His lips warmed the side of her neck, his dark hair tickling her chin as he bent his head to latch his mouth onto her bare flesh.

"Um...is this what you...consider a kiss?" she murmured between shivers.

"Quit distracting me. I'm busy," came his muffled voice.

Her neck was on fire as he trailed soft kisses along its column. The rasp of his stubble scraped her flesh, leaving tiny pricks of pleasure in its wake.

"You smell so dang sweet, Mia." His breath tickled her ear.

Jesus. What was he doing to her? She could barely stay upright, and he hadn't even kissed her mouth yet.

With a soft rumble of approval, he buried his face in the crook of her neck, then kissed his way up to her ear.

Mia shuddered. Her knees wobbled when he sucked gently on her earlobe. Her hands trembled so bad she had to rest them against his chest to steady herself. And oh boy, touching him was a bad idea. He was rock solid beneath her fingers, his muscles so defined they may as well have been carved out of stone.

Chuckling, Jackson slid his hands down to her waist, and the next thing she knew, she was being led backward to the shadowy strip of gravel between the two trucks. Still grasping her waist, he backed her up against the side of her pickup, then moved one hand to her face, his thumb sweeping over her cheek.

"Close your eyes," he said gruffly.

Her eyelids fluttered obediently. She stood there, eyes shut, heart pounding. Waiting.

The rustling of his clothing hinted that he was moving closer, and then his body heat surrounded her and the most intoxicating scent filled her nostrils. God, his aftershave was addictive. A hint of spice and lemon, with a woodsy fragrance thrown into the mix.

When his lips finally touched hers, she almost keeled over. His mouth was gentle, a featherlight brush against her trembling lips. His fingers traced the line of her jaw as he moved his mouth over hers again, firmer this time.

"C'mon, sugar, let me in." The tip of his tongue skimmed the seam of her lips, coaxing, teasing.

When she parted her lips, that wicked tongue slid inside without delay. Her core clenched the second their tongues met, a painful squeeze of lust that pulsed in her clit.

Oh my God.

She was insanely turned on.

"You taste like heaven," he rasped, pulling back slightly.

Her heart pounded even harder when she glimpsed the raw need burning in his whiskey eyes. His handsome features were taut with passion, and she could see his pulse hammering in the hollow of his throat. He wanted her. There was no denying it.

And there was no denying that she wanted him just as bad.

With a husky growl, he dipped his head and captured her mouth, driving the kiss deeper this time, taking it to a whole new level. His tongue teased her senseless, and when he nipped at her lower lip with his teeth, a soft moan slipped out and echoed in the night air.

"You okay?" he murmured.

She couldn't answer. Arousal had tightened her throat, making it impossible to speak.

He laughed quietly, and then his mouth found hers again. One warm hand tangled in her hair, angling her head so that she was at the mercy of his mind-blowing kisses, while his other hand glided down her body, snuck beneath her dress, and settled directly over her damp bikini panties.

Mia whimpered and tried to break away. "Someone might see us," she hissed out.

"No one can see us, sugar. We're completely hidden from view."

Another moan left her throat when he rubbed her with the heel of his hand.

"Ah, look at how wet you are," he muttered as his lips teased her neck again. "Your panties are soaked."

Embarrassment scorched her cheeks. He was right. She was drenched.

"You're blushing."

His teasing voice only made her blush harder.

"Don't be embarrassed. You're turned on. That's hot." His tongue circled her earlobe. "In fact, baby, that was exactly the response I wanted from you."

Sugar. Darlin'. Baby. The man certainly had a silver tongue.

Oh God, his *tongue*. It was in her mouth again.

And his hand... Rubbing, stroking, driving her crazy.

Mia's legs started shaking. She'd never felt this way before. Every square inch of her body throbbed relentlessly, and either she was imagining it, or those were the first ripples of orgasm tingling in her core.

"You like that, don't you?"

Jackson's thumb grazed her clit over her panties, his warm breath fanning over her lips.

When she moaned, he laughed seductively. "Ah, you *do* like it."

His thumb brushed her swollen bud again and she jerked.

"So is it safe to say that I've succeeded in—"

The orgasm came without warning, surging through her in a fiery rush.

Biting her lip to stop herself from crying out, she buried her face in Jackson's chest and rocked into his hand as waves of pleasure consumed her body. She fisted the front of his T-shirt, holding on tight, stunned by what was happening.

He seemed equally stunned when he finally withdrew his hand, which was no doubt covered in the moisture that had seeped through her panties. He gently tugged her by the hair and forced her to look at him.

"Sweet Jesus, did you just come?"

She managed a nod.

His eyes gleamed with pure male satisfaction before turning sheepish. "Shit, Mia. I'm sorry. I didn't mean for that to happen. I didn't think I was applying enough pressure on your lady bits —I was purposely trying not to."

She choked out a laugh. "My *lady bits*?"

He cast that little-boy grin that made her pulse race. "Yes, your lady bits. A gentleman can't say the word *pussy* on the first date."

Another strangled laugh popped out. "You just said it!"

"That didn't count." He swept his gaze over her. "Are you mad at me?"

"Are you seriously asking me if I'm mad that you gave me an orgasm?"

"It was only supposed to be a kiss. I crossed the line. I'm sorry."

Mia gaped at him. Who *was* this man? He'd just made her come apart in the parking lot of the restaurant. He'd barely touched her and she'd exploded like a Fourth of July firecracker, and now he was apologizing for it?

"It's okay. I forgive you."

Obviously he hadn't picked up on the sarcasm because he beamed at her. "You do?"

"Jesus. Yes. Oh my God, Jackson, you really are nuts."

"Good nuts or bad nuts?"

"There's no such thing as good nuts!"

Smirking, he lowered his hand and cupped his groin. "Sure there is."

Sheer exasperation had her fighting another wave of laughter. This guy was one of a kind. And damned if her pussy didn't clench again the second he touched himself like that.

"So..." His hand left his crotch, long fingers hooking in his belt loops. "When can I see you again?"

CHAPTER
FIVE

"You sure you're cool with going to a high school football game?" Mia asked Jackson on Friday night. She'd just slid into the passenger seat of his truck, which was parked in front of her building.

"I told you, as long as I get to spend time with you, I don't care what we do."

The smile he gave her made her heart do a silly little flip. She'd been thinking about that smile for three days now. And his husky voice. And his gorgeous face. His rock-hard body. His hands. Yep, definitely his hands—AKA what he'd used to make her come in the parking lot of Tonio's.

She'd gone to bed that night overwrought, confused, and stunned, analyzing every sexual encounter she'd ever had in so much detail she may as well have drawn diagrams and flow charts. What had her previous lovers done wrong? What did Jackson know that they didn't? Why had her body decided to respond to him when it had always been so *meh* about the other guys in her life?

She'd fallen asleep without reaching a single conclusion,

and seeing Jackson again now only raised a slew of new problems.

Because the moment she'd gotten into his truck, she'd wanted to fuck him.

"You look sexy as hell, by the way," he told her as he started the engine. "I'm lovin' the outfit."

Mia glanced down at her black Madison High Warriors T-shirt, skinny jeans with a hole in the left knee, and bright red flats, wondering how anyone could label the outfit "sexy as hell." But Jackson was eyeing her like he wanted to peel off her clothes and devour her whole.

"Um, thanks," she answered. "You look nice, too."

Nice? Ha. The man was a walking Adonis. She'd never met anyone who could pull off Levis, wifebeaters and plaid shirts better than Jackson Ramsey. He oozed raw masculinity in his casual get-up, and the fact that he hadn't shaved since she'd seen him last only aided his heartthrob cause. The dark stubble slashing his jaw was so hot her fingers itched to stroke all those sexy bristles.

"Thanks, sugar. That's sweet of you to say." He put the car in drive and turned to look at her. "So where am I goin'?"

She gave him directions to Danny's school and then they were off. When they reached the stop sign at the end of the street, he leaned forward and flicked on the radio. The upbeat tempo of a Temptations song wafted out of the speakers, prompting Jackson to sing along.

Mia started laughing. Never in a million years would she have pictured herself sitting in a pickup with a bona-fide cowboy, listening to him sing "My Girl."

"What, no country music?" she teased.

He shot her a sideways look. "Oldies are my guilty pleasure. I only listen to country when I'm feelin' down."

"I can't imagine you *ever* feeling down," she said frankly.

"You might just be the happiest, most well-adjusted guy I've ever met."

"Everyone gets sad sometimes, sugar. Even happy, well-adjusted folks like myself."

There was an odd chord in his voice, an emotion she couldn't quite put her finger on, but he flashed another smile before she could try to decipher it. "Anyway, tell me how your day was. Are you working a new job?"

She nodded. "Yeah, we just got contracted by the city to redo all those little parks near the waterfront. It's a lot of work, but it pays an obscene amount, so my boss promised everyone big bonuses once it's done."

"Nice. Oh, by the way, Miranda loved what you did at their place. She's telling all her clients about you. I'm not sure you know this, but she owns a dance school in the city."

"She mentioned that, yes." Mia paused. "I really liked her. We're going to try to have lunch next week."

He offered a mock pout. "So you'll make time for Miranda like that—" he snapped his fingers, "—but you make *me* beg for it? Evil woman."

"Hey, I made time for you, pal. Are we not having a second date at the moment?"

"Damn right we are."

He sounded so overjoyed about it that she had to grin. "Better make this one good too or you won't get a third."

"Oh, I'll get a third. Just you wait."

They reached Madison High five minutes later, then spent a full ten minutes cruising the jam-packed lot for a parking space. Apparently everyone and their grandmother had shown up for the season opener. Mia experienced a burst of pride that her brother was starting tonight. She'd taken him out for a steak dinner when he'd gotten the coveted position, an achievement made all the more impressive because the coach had chosen a junior for his varsity quarterback over the current senior starter.

A pang of nervousness tickled her belly. "I really hope he does well," she told Jackson.

"I'm sure he will. You don't become the starting QB unless you're good."

"And he better not get hurt," she added anxiously. "I'm always so worried he'll get sacked and break his neck out there."

"Injuries are a risk in every sport," he agreed in a serious voice. "But worrying doesn't achieve anything. There's nothing you can do to protect him when he's out there on the field, short of forbidding him to play."

She bit her lip. "I know."

They finally found an empty spot a million yards from the entrance, then trekked across the paved lot toward the gate. Jackson didn't take her hand or walk overly close to her, but she was completely aware of his presence.

And she wasn't the only one. Heads swiveled sharply as Jackson sauntered past, his long strides eating the pavement. Every single woman, young and old, gazed at him with blatant appreciation, gawking as if they simply couldn't believe their eyes.

Jackson, however, seemed oblivious to the admiring stares. "Football and injuries go hand in hand," he said, picking up where they'd left off. "My teammate Cash learned that the hard way."

"How so?"

"He was at Notre Dame, guaranteed to be the first overall pick in the NFL draft when he busted his shoulder. Took him a year to get back to playing shape, and by then the draft had passed and a whole new group of young QBs were angling for the pros. So he enlisted."

"I don't want that to happen to Danny. Not the enlisting

part—I wouldn't be mad if he did that. But he has his heart set on playing college ball and then making it to the pros. I want him to achieve his dreams."

"What about your dreams? What do *you* want out of life?"

"I'm doing what I want. Working outdoors, gardening, land-scaping. I love what I do."

"That's good to hear. Not many people are able to do what they love."

They reached the main gate, where three bored-looking teens sat behind a long table collecting entrance fees.

"Dang, shit's changed since I was in high school," Jackson remarked. "When did folks start paying to watch the games?"

"Nothing comes free anymore," she replied with a sigh.

Despite their murmured complaints, the tickets only cost five bucks apiece, and Jackson dutifully handed one of the kids a ten-dollar bill.

"Want somethin' to drink?" he asked.

"Sure."

A quick stop at the concessions stand got them two plastic cups of Pepsi, and then they wandered over to the row of bleachers that were closest to the home team's bench. The players weren't on the field yet, but the cheerleaders were, and Mia immediately spotted Angie among a large group of girls and guys clad in the black and silver Warriors colors.

She pointed the pretty teen out to Jackson. "That's Danny's girlfriend. She's a total sweetheart."

Angie spotted them as they climbed the first step. Her pony-tail bounced as she dashed over. "Mia!" she called. "Hey! I'm so glad you—oh. *Wow*. I mean...oh." The girl's cheeks turned the prettiest shade of red as she stared at Mia's date.

Smothering a laugh, Mia quickly made the introductions. "Ang, this is Jackson. Jackson, Angie. As you can see, Angie's on the cheerleading squad."

"Nice to meet you, darlin'," he said easily, extending one large hand.

Angie kept staring.

And staring.

Until Mia finally had to clear her throat to snap the girl out of whatever trance she'd fallen into.

"Oh. Right. Hi. It's nice to meet you, too," Angie stammered, leaning over the chain link fence to shake Jackson's hand.

A flurry of whispers sounded from the vicinity of the squad. Mia looked past Angie's shoulders and hid a smile when she noticed that all the cheerleaders were huddled together and sneaking not-so-discreet peeks in Jackson's direction.

"Um, well, I've gotta go warm up." Angie's eyes remained glued on the tall Texan. "I'll see you guys later."

"You're a hit with the teenage-girl demographic," Mia informed him once Angie was gone. "Don't you get tired of being so good-looking?"

He snickered. "Nope. Who am I to complain about my God-given gorgeousness?"

"Is gorgeousness even a word?" she asked as they sat down in a pair of empty seats.

"Sure. The dictionary people created it when they saw me."

Mia rolled her eyes. "I can't figure you out. Who are you exactly? The cocky ladies' man, or the super-polite gentleman?"

"Can't I be both?" he challenged.

"I guess. But that makes it damn difficult to peg you."

Jackson laughed so abruptly he spit out the drink he'd just taken a sip of.

She frowned. "What? What did I say?"

He let out another wheezy laugh and wiped his mouth with his sleeve. "Nothin'. It's just...you want to peg me, eh? You're into pegging?"

Her confusion deepened, which only made him laugh harder.

"What am I missing here?" she demanded.

Grinning with mischief, he leaned in so that his lips brushed her ear. "In the sex world, pegging is when a woman fucks a man's ass with a strap-on."

Her jaw fell open. "Seriously?"

"Mmm-hmmm."

She felt her cheeks turning bright red, but at the same time, her pussy squeezed almost painfully as she envisioned the wicked scenario he'd just painted.

"Are you into that?" She lowered her voice and searched his amused expression.

He shrugged. "Never had it done to me before, but I'm a big believer in trying anything once. Who knows, maybe I'd love it."

Oh boy. She wasn't used to being around guys who were so sexually frank. The fact that he was open to being "pegged" told her that this man had no qualms about sex. Try anything once. Jeez. Obviously they were polar opposites when it came to sex, and yet she couldn't deny she found his open-mindedness incredibly attractive.

The PA system crackled. A moment later, the announcer's voice reverberated in the outdoor stadium as he introduced the Warriors to the crowd. Each player burst out of the small tunnel and ran through the enormous banner on the field, then waved to the crowd before jogging over to the bench. It was a lot of fanfare for a high school game, but Mia had been to last season's opener and it had been equally extravagant. Madison High took its football very seriously.

Danny was the fourth player to emerge on the field. As he sprinted toward his coach, his eyes diligently searched the bleachers. When he spotted Mia, he smiled and waved, but his gaze kept seeking even after he'd acknowledged his sister.

Her spirits plummeted when she realized who he was looking for. Their mother.

Who, as far as Mia could tell, hadn't shown up tonight.

Shocker.

She watched her brother's face as he continued to scan the crowd, her heart aching when she glimpsed the disappointment that befell his expression. His shoulders slumped briefly beneath his pads, but then he straightened up and turned to talk to Ken Jones, the head coach.

"You okay?"

Jackson's voice was gentle, his touch even more so as he rested a hand on her arm.

She pasted on a smile. "I'm good. Just worrying about Danny again."

"Ah, he'll be fine, sugar. Check out those offensive linemen," he said helpfully. "Those kids are monsters. They'll have your brother's back."

I have his back, she almost blurted out, but she swallowed the words at the last second.

It was the truth, though. She was the only one in this world who had Danny's back. Who loved him unconditionally. Not his coach, not his teammates, certainly not their sorry excuse for a mother. Just *her*.

And God, it took so much out of her. Knowing that she was solely responsible for Danny, for raising him right, was so daunting it often kept her awake at night. Because what if she screwed him up? What if she made a wrong decision and he ended up in jail? Or the subject of a TV show like *Dexter*?

She was only twenty-five, damn it. Way too young to be taking on this kind of responsibility.

"Game's about to start."

Jackson's voice pulled her out of her head. Now wasn't the time to be pondering such heavy thoughts, anyway. This was

Danny's big night, and she needed to concentrate on supporting him.

By the time the game clock counted down to zero, Jackson's date had cheered herself hoarse. She'd jumped to her feet whenever the offense took the field, yelled out encouragements, whooped each time Danny successfully completed a pass. And when he'd run the ball in himself to score the winning touchdown, Mia had bounced up and down like a kid in a toy store.

Her excitement made the entire game even more entertaining, and Jackson stood up at the end of the final quarter with a grin on his face and a light feeling in his chest. *This* was what dating ought to be. Fun, easy, just a nice evening with a girl who didn't cry the whole time, or tell him she loved him on the first date, or broke into his house after he explicitly stated he wasn't interested in seeing her again.

"The kid did good," Jackson remarked as they descended the bleacher steps. "He's a natural. Got a great arm."

"He does, doesn't he?" Mia's eyes shone with pride. "Do you think he's got what it takes to play college ball?"

"Definitely. Only issue I saw was that he takes a few seconds too long to read his offense, but those kind of instincts will come with practice and experience."

They moved through the crowd, falling in behind a middle-aged couple who walked slower than molasses, but Jackson didn't mind the leisurely place. It gave him the opportunity to reach for Mia's hand and interlace their fingers.

She stiffened for a beat before relaxing, then looked up at him with a tentative smile. "I had a lot of fun tonight."

"Me too," he said gruffly. "What should we do now?"

"I usually go out for pizza with Danny after his games."

She actually sounded regretful, so much so that Jackson wanted to give himself a solo high five. He was winning her over. Hot damn.

"Is it a bonding thing or can I tag along?" he hedged.

"Let me see what Danny says. I always wait for him outside the clubhouse."

Jackson tried not to raise his eyebrows, but dang, football really *had* changed since his high school days. When he'd been a defensive end on his school team, they'd practiced on a muddy field and played every game on a baseball diamond that doubled as a gridiron. Madison High, in contrast, not only had its own stadium, but the team locker rooms were housed in a structure separate from the school. A "clubhouse." The boys were clearly living the life of luxury here, lucky bastards.

He and Mia headed for the small building next to the field, where several other people were already waiting. Most of them were older folks, parents of the players, but scattered groups of teenagers also milled around, many of them female. Football groupies.

At least that hadn't changed, he thought with amusement.

It was ten minutes before Mia's brother appeared, dark hair damp from the shower and lean body wired with leftover adrenaline from the game.

Jackson instantly noted the resemblance between the siblings. Same hair color, same dark-green eyes. Except while Mia was a tiny little thing, her brother stood close to six feet and would probably get even taller, Jackson suspected.

"Did you see that final play?" Danny demanded when he reached his sister. "The Panthers had no clue what was happening!"

"It was awesome," Mia declared. "You played brilliantly, kiddo."

"That was an impressive game," Jackson chimed in, smiling at the younger boy.

Danny shifted his gaze, and suddenly Jackson had a pair of shrewd eyes focused on him.

"You're Jackson?" the kid said bluntly.

"Yup. Nice to meet you."

"Yeah." The teenager made an obvious show of appraising him. "Mia says you're in the navy."

"I am."

"Officer or enlisted?"

"Enlisted. Petty officer second class. And one of the team medics."

"Cool." Danny cocked his head. "You're ridiculously tall."

Jackson grinned. "So I've been told."

There was a beat of silence, during which Danny continued to study him until Mia finally rolled her eyes and spoke up. "Are you done checking out my date, Daniel?"

Her brother rolled his eyes right back. "Just trying to figure out what he's doing going out with *you*."

She slapped a hand on her heart as if she'd been shot. "Ouch. That hurt so bad. I need to go find somewhere private so I can cry." She laughed. "Anyway, if you're done insulting me, I wanted to know if we're doing the pizza thing tonight."

"Ah...no. I was gonna catch a ride with Angie's folks and hang out at her place for a bit. Is that cool?"

"Yeah, it's fine. Can they drive you home?" When her brother nodded, Mia stepped forward and gave him a quick hug. "Okay, have fun. And be home by curfew."

"Or what? You'll ground me?"

"No, I'll just do what I did last time."

The kid's face paled at her chipper response. "Fine, I'll be home by midnight."

"Good boy."

Danny glanced at Jackson. "Later, dude. Glad you made it to the game."

As Mia's little brother dashed off, Jackson looked over at her in curiosity. "What'd you do the last time he missed his curfew?"

"I threw all his video games in the trash."

He let out a hearty laugh. "Sheesh, woman. You can't do shit like that to a teenage boy."

"I can, and I did." She raised one eyebrow. "You questioning my parenting methods, *sugar*?"

"Did he ever miss curfew after that?"

"Never."

"Then no, I think you're doin' a good job."

That earned him a big smile. "Thanks. Now, do you want to grab a late dinner? I seem to be free."

"Sure. Except I don't feel like sitting anywhere. Do you mind if we get takeout and head back to my place?"

She narrowed her eyes. "If I agree to come over, are you going to try to seduce me?"

"Only if you ask me to."

The answer got him another pleased smile. "Let's go."

CHAPTER
SIX

Jackson laced his fingers through hers again. As they walked toward the parking lot, he couldn't help but reflect on the easy relationship between Mia and her younger brother. It was obvious they adored each other. Their good-natured bickering reminded him of his relationship with his own sister.

An arrow of pain pierced his heart. Lord, he hadn't seen Evie in almost three years. He'd bailed on the holidays two years in a row, the most recent one because he'd been deployed overseas, the one before because...well, that had been cowardice, plain and simple. He hadn't been able to stomach the thought of seeing his brother Shane and congratulating him on his nuptials to Tiff.

In his defense, at least he wasn't completely out of touch. He spoke to his parents once a week and Skyped with Evie often, but Jackson knew it wasn't the same as seeing them face-to-face. He missed his mom's warm smiles, his dad's gruff voice, his sister's contagious laughter. He even missed his brother, despite everything that had gone down between them.

What he missed most of all was the ranch. The endless acres and lush pastures. The little creek that bisected the Ramsey land. The horses he'd grown up with and the cattle he'd brought into the world every calving season.

But he loved his life here, too. Loved knowing that he was serving his country and helping to keep it safe, loved the bonds he'd formed with his teammates, the crisp ocean air and the feel of warm sand between his toes. California would never truly be home, but it was dang close to it.

"Somebody's deep in thought," came Mia's teasing voice.

He smiled sheepishly. "Sorry."

"What were you looking so pensive about?"

"Nothin' really," he lied. "Just thinking about the game and how much fun I'm having."

"What are you in the mood for, food-wise?"

"Whatever you want, sugar."

He wasn't surprised when Mia ended up picking Italian. They called ahead to place an order at Tonio's, then swung by the bistro to pick up their dinner before heading to Jackson's house in Imperial Beach.

Inside, Mia spent a good five minutes marveling over how tidy his house was while Jackson placed their takeout containers on the wooden coffee table. He ducked into the kitchen to grab plates, silverware, and drinks. When he strode back to the living room he saw that Mia had made herself comfortable by kicking off her shoes and settling on the overstuffed leather sofa.

He smiled at the sight of her. He liked having her in his house. Something about her seemed to brighten up the sparsely decorated room.

As always, the conversation between them flowed smoothly during dinner. Afterward, when he suggested they put on a movie, he was thrilled by her easy agreement.

At least until she started dissing his Blu-Ray collection, which he refused to part with no matter how many new streaming services got released.

"How many copies of *Die Hard* does one person need?" she demanded, turning away from the entertainment unit to gape at him.

"What am I supposed to do?" he said defensively. "*Not* buy a new copy when a special edition is released?"

She ignored him. "And what is your obsession with Tom Hanks? You have every movie he's ever made. Even the shitty ones, like *Road to Perdition*."

"He's a good actor."

"Oh my God. You own every season of *Battlestar Galactica*. Nerd!"

He scowled at her. "Would you just pick somethin' already?"

Eventually she chose one of the Hanks films: *Big*, which Jackson had seen a hundred times and would never get tired of.

Mia sat beside him but kept a good foot of space between them, a travesty that he quickly remedied.

"Uh-uh, get over here." He slung his arm around her shoulder and pulled her toward him so that she was snuggled at his side.

Her body was stiff at first, but as the opening credits flashed on the screen, she started to relax. The warmth of her body seeped into him and brought a goofy grin to his face. It felt nice holding her like this, and when she shifted closer and leaned her head on his shoulder, he experienced a rush of serenity that spread through him and loosened every muscle in his body.

They laughed a lot during the movie but didn't say much save for the occasional observation about the plot. Jackson didn't mind, though. He was enjoying Mia's company, her laughter, the sweet scent of her shampoo. He hadn't felt this relaxed in ages.

Sadly, his state of relaxation didn't last. Nope, because Mia had suddenly placed her hand on his thigh.

As if on cue, his groin stirred. There was nothing sexual about her touch, yet it set his body on fire and pretty much eliminated any chance of paying attention to the movie. All night he'd been trying valiantly not to think about the kiss they'd shared on their last date or the accidental orgasm he'd given her. But now the memories flooded his brain, making it hard to breathe.

He'd jacked off when he'd returned home that night, coming hard to the memory of Mia's molten hot pussy tingling beneath his palm and the sexy little whimpering sounds she'd made when she'd orgasmed. He'd gotten her off in a parking lot, up against her truck where anyone could have caught them. And the entire situation had left him feeling...intrigued. For a woman who claimed to not like sex, she'd been so uninhibited, coming apart so fast his ego had inflated like a balloon.

Obviously Mia possessed a wild side she didn't know existed, but he'd witnessed it firsthand on their date, and he desperately wanted to explore it further. He wanted to unleash all that passion she kept buried deep inside. He wanted to make her whimper again, to find out what made her moan, what made her scream.

Somehow he made it through to the end of the movie without acting on the intense arousal wreaking havoc on his lower body—or alerting Mia to the fact that he had a raging boner. Fortunately, her gaze had stayed on the screen, sparing him the embarrassment of explaining why his cock was attempting to tunnel its way out of his jeans.

The moment the end credits scrolled across the screen, though, any hope of hiding his desire disappeared. All Mia had to do was take one look at his face. Which she did, and promptly gave a sharp intake of breath.

"Jeez, don't look at me like that," she grumbled.

"Like what?" His voice came out hoarse.

"Like you want to...um..."

"Want to what? Kiss you? Because I do, sugar." He moistened his lips with his tongue. "Actually, you know what? I'm totally gonna do it."

Before she could reply, he lowered his head and captured her mouth in a long, drugging kiss that made his head spin.

Her lips were warm and pliant, her tongue hesitant as it darted out to taste his. Jackson groaned. He slid his tongue into her mouth, teasing and exploring until they were both panting. When they came up for air, he took advantage of her hazy expression and nudged her backward onto the sofa cushions.

Breathing hard, he lowered his body over hers, propped his arms on either side of her so that he wasn't crushing her, and then kissed her again.

She moaned, a throaty, desperate sound that quickened his pulse. She was so soft, tasted so sweet. And Lord, he could feel her nipples poking against his pecs, right through her clothing.

"Your nipples are hard," he rasped, tearing his mouth off hers.

She sighed. "That's because you're rubbing your sexy chest all over them."

"You think my chest is sexy?"

"Are you kidding? I haven't even seen it bare but I already know I want to have a calendar of it made up."

He laughed and brushed his lips over hers. "I love kissing you, darlin'."

They exchanged a tongue-tangling kiss and she moaned again, which only summoned another laugh from him.

"See," he teased, stroking her cheek with his fingertips.

"Foolin' around *can* be fun." He arched his eyebrows. "Or are you gonna tell me you're bored?"

"Shockingly enough, I am the furthest thing from bor—" She squeaked in delight when he moved his hand to her chest and squeezed one breast.

"You like that?"

"Mmmmm."

"I'll take that as a yes."

He brought his other hand into play and began toying with her breasts, kneading and stroking until she was squirming on the couch.

His dick was an iron spike, straining against his zipper and pleading for some attention, but Jackson ignored the big guy's pleas and channeled all his energy on Mia. On making her feel so good she'd never use the words *sex* and *boring* in the same sentence again.

"I want to see these perfect tits of yours," he muttered, reaching for the bottom of her shirt.

She shivered as he slowly slid the cotton fabric up and over her head, leaving her in a black bra. "They're small," she warned him.

He disagreed instantly. "Perfect," he repeated.

"Yeah, I'm sure my barely-a-B-cup is a major turn-on."

"You sayin' I'm not turned on?" He ground his erection on her pelvis. "How's that for turned on?"

Her lips widened in a little O, a glaze of lust darkening her eyes. "My boobs get you that hard?"

"Yup."

He traced the swell of each one with his finger, then undid the front clasp and exposed her to his gaze. Her tits were indeed small, but they were damn perky, with pearly-pink nipples that made his mouth water.

"Sweet Lord, I want to eat you up."

With a growl, he dipped his head, took one rigid nipple between his lips, and sucked hard. He knew he was being a little too rough, but he was so overcome with lust he couldn't rein himself in. Luckily, Mia wasn't complaining.

The sexiest sounds he'd ever heard escaped her throat as he feasted on her breasts. He licked every inch of exposed flesh, teasing her, drawing out her pleasure. When his teeth gently nibbled on a nipple, Mia's lower body almost shot off the couch.

"Oh *God*. Do that again."

His breathing grew shallow. "You like the biting?"

"*Yes.*"

He bit harder this time, then flicked his tongue over the tip of her nipple to soothe the ache. He did it over and over again, focusing on one nipple, then the other, all the while grinding his pelvis against hers in a futile attempt to give his throbbing cock some kind of relief.

When the ache became unbearable, he shifted positions so that his groin was nestled beside her, then reached for the button of her jeans. He popped it open deftly and dragged her zipper down.

"I'm gonna make you come again, Mia."

An anguished noise left her mouth. "God. Please."

He had her jeans and panties off in the blink of an eye. His gaze roamed her naked body, and when it reached her completely bare pussy, his breath caught in his throat.

"I don't have a lot of time for grooming," she said sheepishly. "So I just wax it all off every month."

Saliva pooled in his mouth. Goddammit, he wanted to taste her. Wanted to slide down her body and fuck her sweet pussy with his mouth until she was screaming in ecstasy. But he wouldn't. Not tonight, anyway. Nope, tonight he had a plan and he intended on sticking to it.

The plan, of course, was to tease the living daylights out of her on every single date so she'd always be left wanting more.

He skimmed his palm over her belly, smiling when her muscles quivered in anticipation. Ever so slowly, his hand made its way lower. With the tip of his index finger, he lightly grazed her clit.

Mia jerked with a rapid breath. "More," she begged.

"More..." He trailed off thoughtfully. "More what?"

"More everything," she sputtered. "Just...touch me, damn it."

"I am touching you." To punctuate that, he idly stroked her clit again.

"Damn it, Jackson. I. Want. More."

For a woman who insisted she wasn't into sex, she had no problem voicing her needs.

With a faint smile, he applied more pressure on her clit, rubbing in a steady, circular motion.

The second she purred in pleasure, he stopped.

"*Jackson.*" Desperation and displeasure clung to her voice.

"Patience, Mia," he chided. "I don't just hand out orgasms willy-nilly."

Her hips moved restlessly as she tried to make contact with his fingers again. "I hate you."

He planted a quick kiss on her lips before meeting her gaze. "I'm gonna make you beg for it."

"I *am* begging!"

"Nah, this ain't beggin'. Not yet, anyway."

Very methodically, he rubbed his palm over her. Heat and moisture suffused his hand, and his cock grew impossibly harder, painfully pressing into his zipper.

He watched Mia's face as he stroked her, loving the cloudy passion in her eyes, the rosy blush on her cheeks, the way she kept licking her lips before parting them sensually. When he traced her slit with one finger, she let out a soft sigh. When he dipped that finger in the wetness pooling at her opening, the sigh became a groan of agitation.

His gaze remained locked with hers. Soon his finger was coated with her juices, which made it dang easy to slide inside her. Her inner muscles instantly clamped around his finger, trapping it there.

"You're so tight." His voice was strangled, his lower body an inferno of blind lust.

She whimpered and rocked her hips, trying to quicken his pace, but that only got her a soft *tsk*ing sound and the retreat of his hand.

"*No*," she choked out. "Please don't stop. Please."

A laugh rumbled out. "Aw, I'm sorry. I figured you were bored."

The taunt earned him a sharp thwack on the arm. Shit, her little fist was a lot stronger than he'd thought.

Grinning, he resumed his tormenting, his thumb seeking out her clit as he pushed two fingers in deep and stroked her tight channel.

"Oh my God," she moaned. "That's so good."

Her sweet juices soaked his hand, and he could feel her clit pulsing beneath the pad of his thumb. As he worked her pussy, he continued to watch her, each moan and shiver telling him exactly what she liked.

"I'm gonna add another finger, sugar," he murmured. "And I'm gonna fuck you hard now."

She shuddered, her eyes shining with excitement. "Do it. Please."

She was so tight that the third finger succeeded in filling her completely. Her pussy squeezed his hand like a vise, a wickedly hot omen of what it would feel like when his cock was buried inside it. Christ, he couldn't wait. Fucking this woman had just become his sole purpose in life.

He nuzzled her neck as he fingered her. When he heard her breathing quicken and saw her eyes go unfocused, he stilled his movements.

"*Jackson.*" She was practically wailing now.

He shot her an innocent smile. "Jackson, what?"

"Make me come. Please, please, *please* make me come. Please, please, plea—"

He cut her off by lowering his head to one breast, capturing her nipple between his teeth, and thrusting his fingers so deep inside her that her whole body convulsed against him.

The force of Mia's orgasm detonated the room. The air sizzled, the couch cushions squeaked. And through it all, her hot, wet pussy pulsed and rippled against his hand and her breathless moans vibrated in his shoulder.

When she finally went limp, he propped up on one elbow and smiled down at her. "That was some real nice beggin' at the end, baby."

Her green eyes took a long time to focus. "What...the...hell... did you just do to me?" she mumbled. "I've never..."

"Never what?"

"Come that hard before." Her cheeks were pink again, this time from palpable embarrassment.

He stifled a sigh. "You've gotta stop gettin' all embarrassed whenever you let go."

"I don't do that. Do I?" She sounded troubled.

"'Fraid you do. But there's nothin' wrong with coming so hard that you drench my couch, or letting a man get you off in public. Sex doesn't have to be confined to a bedroom with the missionary position and the lights off."

"Sex?" She choked out a laugh. "We haven't even done that yet!"

A grin stretched across his face. "Yet?"

As expected, she backpedaled. "I mean...I didn't...argh. I'm not saying sex is inevitable. It might never happen, okay?"

"Uh-huh. If you say so." The grin widened. "You better get dressed now, sugar. It's past eleven, and if we don't get you home by midnight, you'll be eating crow after that riot act you read your brother."

She blinked. "Wait—you're taking me home?" Her gaze lowered to the enormous bulge in his pants. "But you didn't..."

"Trust me, I enjoyed this as much as you did." He shrugged. "I don't need to come to consider this a successful second date."

"And let me guess," she said as she fumbled around for her discarded clothing, "you're about to demand a third date."

He beamed at her. "You already know me well, darlin'."

"I'm not sure when I'm free next..."

"I told you, I'll take whatever I can get." Noticing her hesitation, he let out an unhappy breath. "C'mon, Mia, I know you want to keep hanging out, and I don't wanna have to twist your arm for another date each time I see you. So can't we just say we're dating and go from there?"

She distracted him for a second by wiggling into her panties. "How's this?" she said once her jeans were on. "I'll date you—"

"Deal."

"—but," she rolled her eyes, "—that doesn't mean we're in a relationship. No strings, no commitments, and if I get really busy, you have to back off. You're not allowed to get possessive or clingy on me."

"I won't," he promised.

She blushed. "And despite what just happened here tonight, sex isn't necessarily a given, okay?"

"We'll go at your pace. Your terms."

It was difficult to say those words—when it came to sex, he liked to be the one calling the shots—but he knew that pushing her right now wouldn't be a smart move. He couldn't force her to lower her inhibitions. She had to reach that point all by herself.

But he was confident she'd get there. Mia Weldrick didn't know it yet, but she was about to embark on the sexual journey of her life. And she was going to love every second of it.

CHAPTER
SEVEN

Four days later, Jackson left the base after a grueling day-long workout that had turned his legs to jelly. A class of SEAL recruits had just arrived in Coronado, and the powers that be always requested that a few active-duty pros show the new hopefuls what they could expect during their training. Jackson and several of his teammates had been chosen to showcase their skills, which involved target shooting, timed dives, a HALO jump, and running the infamous obstacle course not once but three times.

He hadn't felt this exhausted since his own basic training, and it was a miracle his legs managed to carry him outside to his truck.

"Wanna hang out tonight?" Dylan asked, falling into step beside him. The man's blond hair was still wet from the ocean, his camo gear still covered in sand and dust, yet his expression was downright chipper as he moved with energetic strides that none of the others possessed at the moment.

"Can't," Jackson answered. "I've got plans with Mia."

Dylan sighed loudly. "Why doesn't anyone want to hang out with me?"

Seth stalked up, his eyes rimmed with fatigue. "Because we've all got women to go home to. After a day like today, all I want to do is lie naked on my bed while my wife fucks me senseless."

"Ditto," Cash said, sounding dead-ass tired. "Jen's gonna have to do all the work tonight."

"That won't be a problem for my girl," Matt O'Connor, one of their senior members, piped up with a grin. "Savannah likes being in charge."

Ryan Evans hooted. "That's because Savannah is a sex maniac."

Matt hooted right back. "And Annabelle isn't?"

"Face it," Cash said. "We're all involved with sex maniacs."

"Well, aren't you guys *so* lucky," Dylan said glumly as he opened the passenger door of Cash's SUV. "You get to go home and have sex tonight while I'm all alone feeling sad. Would it kill one of you assholes to put your friend ahead of your cock?"

"Dude, your cock gets more action than the four of us combined," Matt drawled in his Southern accent.

"Yeah, you've got two people pawing at it every night," Ryan cracked.

Dylan stuck out his chin. "Not at the moment. And not for *two* more weeks."

Seth lifted a challenging brow. "I swear to God, man, if you keep complaining about not having anyone to fuck, I'll call your bluff and fuck you myself."

The other guy smirked. "Sorry, you're not my type."

"Bullshit. I'm everyone's type."

As amusing as Jackson found the exchange, he was eager to get going. He still had to go home and shower before he headed over to Mia's. They would only have two hours of alone time before Danny came home from football practice. Jackson wanted to make use of every second he had her to himself.

With a hurried goodbye to his teammates, he got into his truck and hightailed it out of the lot. He didn't usually speed, but today he found himself going twenty over the limit. The anticipation coursing through him confirmed what he'd already known—he had it bad. He was tired as heck, hungry enough to pass out, yet he was so eager to see Mia that his sore muscles and grumbling stomach barely made a blip on his radar.

After a quick stop home to shower and change, he was on his way to Mia's, reaching her six-story building in record time. He was thrilled that she'd invited him over instead of insisting they go out or chill at his place. That she was willing to allow him into her personal space told him she was warming up to this dating thing.

Since her building didn't have an elevator, his tired legs were forced to make the climb up to the third floor, but when the door swung open and he saw Mia's face, his aching limbs were all but forgotten.

"Hey! You got here fast." She gestured for him to come inside.

He stepped into the front hall, kicked off his shoes at her request, then followed her deeper into the apartment. His curious gaze ate up his surroundings, taking in the cozy space. The living room offered mismatched furniture, bright blue curtains that led out to a small balcony, and a shit-ton of green plants and colorful flowerpots sitting on various shelves and ledges in the room.

He smiled when he noticed the framed photo of Mia and Danny on the television unit. In the kitchen he discovered even more pictures tacked on the fridge, including a series of photo booth shots that showed brother and sister making goofy faces at the camera.

As he looked around, he noted that the apartment definitely showed signs that a teenager lived there—piles of video games, a pair of scuffed-up sneakers, a stack of textbooks on the coffee table.

"Sorry I didn't get a chance to tidy up," she said with a blush. "I literally got home ten minutes ago and decided a shower was more important. I was covered head-to-toe in dirt."

He turned to her with a grin. "I already told you, I like you dirty."

She rolled her eyes. "Uh-huh. Anyway, what do you want to do first? Order pizza or make out?"

He laughed. "Mia, just for future purposes, you should know that the answer to that question will *never* be 'order pizza'." He waggled his eyebrows. "Now get over here and give me a kiss. I haven't seen you in four agonizing days and I'm gonna die if I don't kiss you right frickin' now."

"You're so melodramatic." Even as she threw the mocking words at him, she was leaning on her tiptoes so she could brush her mouth over his.

The brief peck was nowhere near enough to sate him. Groaning softly, he cupped her face with his hands and stole another kiss, this one deep and thorough with a helluva lot of tongue.

Mia was breathing hard when they broke apart. "How do you always manage to turn my brain into mush?"

"It's a gift." He slanted his head "What time does your brother get home?"

"Usually around seven."

Jackson's gaze drifted to the clock hanging over the kitchen doorway. It read five twenty-three. Dang, they didn't have much time.

"Wanna fool around until then?" He flashed her the little-boy grin he'd perfected over the years.

And it worked, just as intended.

"Bedroom," she announced. "Now."

They practically sprinted to the corridor, laughing like a pair of teenagers. Jackson couldn't remember the last time he'd been so excited to spend time with a woman.

Apparently Mia shared his thoughts, because she tossed him a wry look over her shoulder. "I turn into a horny teenager whenever I'm around you."

When they entered her room, he took a second to glance around. Bed, dresser, rug—the bedroom was empty save for those items, which didn't surprise him because Mia was the least materialistic woman he'd ever met. She wouldn't care for frilly curtains or designer furniture. The room was as no-nonsense as she was, and he appreciated that.

His gaze lingered on the perfectly made bed before shifting back to Mia. As cute as she looked in her black yoga pants and thin yellow tank, the garments didn't mesh with what he had planned for her.

"Lose the clothes," he told her. "Now."

"Aren't we bossy."

"Yup. But we both know you like it, so don't give me that indignant look, sugar. I want you naked and you wanna be naked, so let's not waste time."

The fact that she whipped off her shirt without a single complaint told him he'd been right about her. She liked letting him call the shots. It excited her. He could see it in her eyes, which burned with anticipation. Her cheeks, which were flushed with arousal.

She was out of her clothes in a heartbeat, standing before him in nothing but a bright red bra and skimpy black panties.

"What part of naked don't you understand, Mia?"

"Are you going to take your clothes off too?"

"Maybe."

"At least take off your shirt."

He just smirked.

She crossed her arms in defiance. "I'm not taking anything else off until you lose the shirt."

He supposed he could've argued, but he decided to throw her a bone. Very methodically, he began unbuttoning his plaid shirt.

Her eyes followed the movement of his fingers, those gorgeous green depths flickering with appreciation when he finally peeled open the shirt to reveal his bare chest. Her visible approval brought a rush of pure satisfaction.

"Like what you see, darlin'?"

"Uh, *duh*. Dude, you're shredded like lettuce."

He threw his head back and laughed. Lord, he liked her.

She took a step closer, her fingers toying with the thin straps of her bra. Jackson's mouth went drier than a desert. His pulse sped up as he waited for her to make a move.

Keeping her gaze locked with his, she reached behind her, undid the bra, and let it fall to the floor.

He licked his dry lips. "Now the panties."

Her fingers hooked in her waistband and the flimsy underwear joined her discarded bra on the floor.

"Lie down on the bed," he said in a low voice.

Again, he got no argument. Mia climbed on the mattress and stretched out on her back, naked as the day she was born.

His gaze roamed her sleek skin, focusing on her puckered nipples before settling between her legs.

"Spread," he told her. "Let me see your pussy."

He could see her pulse throbbing in her throat as she slowly parted her thighs. Her glistening folds gave him an instant hard-on, drawing Mia's attention to his groin.

"I think you should take off your pants," she murmured.

He shook his head. "I think I should put my tongue on your pussy."

She sucked in a breath. "You're...not at all what I expected."

Shrugging, he approached the bed with purposeful strides. "I get that a lot, sugar."

He eased himself down on the edge of the mattress, searching her expression for any sign that she wasn't into this. But all he detected was raw lust and the glow of excitement.

He knew he was a demanding lover, always had been, always would be. A lot of women weren't on board with that, which was why he didn't jump headfirst into sexual relationships the way his teammates did. He took the time to gauge his potential lovers, to make sure they could handle what he was going to give them, but Mia had passed his test the moment she'd let him get her off in a parking lot.

This woman liked to be dominated. She might not know it, not consciously anyway, but her body's responses to his commanding nature told him everything he needed to know.

He placed his hand on her firm thigh, enjoying the way she shivered from his touch. He skimmed his fingers downward and dragged his thumb over her heated flesh.

She shivered again. "That feels good."

He drew a lazy figure eight on her clit, then crawled between her legs and pushed them apart.

Mia moaned the second his lips pressed against her pussy. Her breathing quickened, slender hips lifting and straining for contact.

He gave her slit a long lick. Her sweet taste drew a groan of approval from his throat.

"Fuckin' hell," he muttered. "I'm never leaving this bedroom, Mia. I'm gonna stay here between your thighs for the rest of my frickin' life."

Her soft laughter echoed in the room. "You won't hear any complaints from me, *sugar*."

Heart pounding like a jackhammer, he explored her pussy with his tongue. Licked the delicate lips, then pulled them open with his fingers so he could suckle her clit. Her moans egged him on. Her restless writhing made him chuckle with satisfaction. He hadn't been lying—he wanted to lick her up from now 'til eternity.

"You're scarily good at this," she said hoarsely.

When he flicked his tongue over her clit, she let out a moan that vibrated against his lips. He promptly increased the tempo, tonguing her hard as his hand drifted to her opening. He pushed two fingers inside her hot channel and was rewarded with a cry of delight.

Lord, he wanted her to come all over his face. Wanted to taste her passion and hear her scream his name. But he paced himself, alternating between soft licks and hard suckling, the slow glide of one finger and the deep thrust of two. On and on it went, a gentle tease followed by a sensual assault, until Mia's legs began to scissor on the mattress.

Her fingers tangled in his hair, attempting to push his face closer, which only made him raise his head.

"No! Don't stop!"

She sounded so devastated he couldn't help a laugh. "You wanna come, huh?"

"Yes, damn it!"

He licked his lips, which were coated with her juices, then sat up and moved to the head of the bed. Mia watched him in a haze of confusion as he got comfortable on his back.

"Are you kidding me?" she demanded.

"C'mere," he said roughly, reaching for her. "I want you to sit on my face and come all over it."

"Oh," she squeaked.

"C'mon, don't keep me waiting. I want your pussy."

"Do people know how dirty you are?" she asked in a breathy voice. "Do they know that the gentleman thing is a total act?"

"I *am* a gentleman." He peered up at her with an evil grin.

"But I'm also a dirty motherfucker who wants you to rub your cunt all over his face. Got a problem with that?"

Her eyes went so wide he found himself laughing again. But the sound died in his throat when she positioned her knees on either side of his face and gave him exactly what he wanted.

He wasted no time devouring her. Mia braced her hands on the headboard, moving her hips and taking everything he had to offer.

His cock throbbed painfully, but he ignored it. Instead, he focused on the woman who was currently riding his face like a carnival ride. He loved every fuckin' second of it. Mia's husky moans, her swollen clit beneath his tongue, her wetness coating his chin.

"Oh my God...oh fuck...oh...*ohhhh.*"

The orgasm rocked her body and soaked his lips, and he lapped her up like a cat, so turned on he could barely breathe. Each time she shuddered, his cock twitched and his balls tingled. By the time her moans ebbed and her body stilled, he was so dangerously close to shooting his load that he had to think about baseball and carpeting for a full minute in order to stave off the release.

Mia slid off and collapsed beside him, letting out a contented purr that revved his engine all over again.

"You're my hero," she mumbled. "My mother-effing hero, Jackson."

"Glad I could be of service." He sat up with a grin. "Now what do you say we go out to the living room and order that pizza?"

Mia stared at him for a moment.

And then she flipped out.

"Are you fucking *kidding* me?"

CHAPTER
EIGHT

As Jackson continued to grin at her, Mia wondered if she'd somehow wound up on another planet. A planet where men got you nice and primed with a mind-blowing orgasm and then refused to have sex with you.

She didn't miss the irony of it, either. She was the one who usually needed convincing, the one who reluctantly followed her lover into the bedroom and then ran her grocery list over in her head the entire time. But with Jackson, she was always begging for it.

Craving it.

And how could she not? The guy was a sex god. He summoned orgasms out of her like a snake charmer luring a cobra from a box. The mere *sight* of him turned her on. Especially now, in all his bare-chested glory.

His torso was carved out of stone. Sleek and defined, with hard pecs, a dusting of dark hair, and the tightest six-pack ever. Actually, make that a twelve-pack. She'd never seen abs with that many damn ripples.

"Seriously," she grumbled. "Why aren't you getting naked and having your way with me?"

His hesitation generated a spark of confusion.

"Why?" she pressed.

After a beat, he raked a hand through his hair. "I'm trying to take things slow. I don't want to..."

She narrowed her eyes. "To what?"

"Scare you off."

The confession only confused her further. "Why do you think you'd scare me off?"

"Because..." His tanned, muscular chest rose and fell as he took another breath. "I'm not into slow, sweet lovemaking, Mia. I like it rough and dirty and I'm not always gentle. I don't wanna freak you out right off the bat."

She searched his deep brown eyes, utterly fascinated by his words. They didn't come as a surprise—God knew he'd already revealed some of that wicked dirtiness—but they didn't scare her, either. She'd been having vanilla sex her whole life, and she was starting to wonder if maybe that had been part of the problem.

Maybe she wasn't cut out for slow, sweet lovemaking, either.

"What's goin' on in that pretty head of yours?" He watched her intently.

"I'm just wondering if the reason I always found sex boring is because I was having boring sex."

Jackson reached up to rub his chin, which was still shiny with moisture. *Her* moisture. Because she'd just fucked his face and orgasmed on it.

"I want more," she blurted out.

He cocked a brow. "Do you?"

She nodded.

"Are you sure about that? Because once we get on this ride, I won't let you get off." He flashed a roguish grin. "Well, you *will* get off. But what I'm saying is, we will see this through 'til the end."

Mia swallowed. "What exactly do you plan on doing to me?"

"Everything," he said simply. "And you're gonna let me. You're gonna give me full control. When we're naked and alone, I call the shots."

Another gulp. "And if I don't like something?"

"Then I stop." The sensual smile returned to his lips. "But I guarantee you'll like it all. You'll beg for more every time."

Somehow she didn't doubt that.

But at the same time, the idea of handing over control of her body was incredibly daunting.

He must have sensed her hesitation, because he slid closer and dragged one callused finger over her lips. "Now you see why I wanted to take things slow?"

She nodded again.

"Tell you what, why don't we do a little warm-up? Give you a taste of what you can expect, and then you can decide if you wanna pursue this."

"What do you consider a warm-up?"

His whiskey eyes burned seductively. "You're gonna blow me."

Her heartbeat accelerated, and damned if her mouth didn't water.

Ever so slowly, Jackson slid off the bed and unbuckled his belt. "What do you say, sugar?"

Arousal tightened her throat and grabbed hold of her pussy. "Y-yes," she stammered.

"Good girl." He eyed her sternly. "Now get on your knees and pull out my dick."

Oh sweet Jesus.

The look in his eyes stole the breath right out of her lungs. Dark and dangerous and utterly sinful. She couldn't believe she was letting him order her around like this.

She couldn't believe it was turning her on.

Her entire body trembled as she scampered off the bed and sank to her knees, angling her face directly in front of his crotch. It was hard to unzip him with shaky fingers, but she somehow managed to pop open his jeans and tug on his waistband.

He kicked the Levis away, then took pity on her Jell-O hands by yanking down his black boxer-briefs.

Her gaze instantly swept over his gloriously naked body, so big and muscular and radiating sheer masculine power. Her breath hitched when his erect cock sprang up inches from her eyes.

A moan tore out of her throat.

He *was* pierced.

The sight of the silver ball bearings at the head of his cock got her so wet she could feel the moisture running down her thighs.

"Oh my God," she mumbled.

He chuckled knowingly. "Think of how nice it'll feel inside you. It'll rub on your G-spot when I fuck you senseless."

Her core tingled in response, suddenly aching for that very thing. She shivered involuntarily as she stared at him. He was hung like a bull, long and thick, the wicked piercing gleaming from the light streaming in through her pale blue curtains.

"But that's later," he said huskily. "Right now, you're gonna open your mouth real wide."

She did as he asked, feeling a tad silly as she knelt there with her mouth open awaiting his next demand. But he didn't say another word. Instead, he grasped the root of his cock, took a step forward, and guided the tip into her mouth.

Her lips parted even wider to accommodate his thick girth. When his piercing touched her tongue, she couldn't help but give it a tiny lick, but that got her a sharp jerk on the hair.

"You don't get to lick until I tell you, sugar," he scolded.

Oh gosh. Who *was* this man? And why did his gruff commands make her heart pound this way? She'd never had a dominant lover before. And she'd never dreamed, not in a million years, that she would get off from being told what to do.

"Relax your jaw. I want to see how deep I can go."

He pushed in farther. When his tip prodded the back of her throat, her gag reflex kicked in. She breathed through it, trying to get used to the feeling of a massive erection lodged in her mouth.

"That's it, Mia. Breathe. Take it all in."

He waited patiently as she inhaled through her nose, her lips stretched tight around the base of his shaft.

"You okay?"

She peered up at him and nodded.

"Good, 'cause I'm gonna fuck your mouth now and you're gonna suck hard on every stroke."

He wasn't kidding. He withdrew swiftly before ramming right back in, the force of the stroke nearly knocking her backward. Jackson immediately steadied her by threading his fingers in her hair, but he didn't slow his pace. His hips thrust and retreated as he drove into her mouth, plunging deep each time, filling her completely.

Flames engulfed her body. She couldn't breathe, couldn't think, couldn't focus on anything but the thick erection tunneling in and out of her mouth. The salty, masculine taste of him infused her senses. His low groans fueled her hunger. She was wetter than she'd ever been, a realization that shocked her. Blowjobs didn't usually turn her on, and certainly not to this level.

"Ah, you love this, don't you, darlin'?" His voice was low and mocking.

She whimpered against his shaft.

"Is that a yes?" He chuckled, his cock sliding out of her

mouth. "Yeah, I think that's a yes. Now be a good girl and give me your hand."

She quickly held out her hand, and he brought it to his hard shaft. Her pulse careened as he curled her fingers around him, then covered her fist with his and gave a sharp squeeze.

"Pump me hard," he muttered. "And tease the head with your tongue."

She wasted no time doing what he asked, and her eagerness to please him absolutely floored her. Every sound that reverberated in the bedroom sent a dark thrill shooting up her spine. Every time her tongue danced over his tip and he moaned, a rush of satisfaction flooded her core. He might be dictating her actions, but Mia realized she had all the power. Right here, right now, Jackson Ramsey was at her sexual mercy and damned if that didn't stoke the fire sizzling inside her.

"That's it. Lick me up, nice and slow. Just like that."

She swiped her tongue over his slit, moaning when a pearl of moisture formed there. She lapped it up, then explored the two silver ball bearings, sucking gently on each one.

"Fuck yeah." Growling, he grabbed her hand and forcibly moved it down to his sac, which was drawn tight. "Play with my balls, sugar. I'm gonna fuck your mouth again."

That big, throbbing cock plunged through her parted lips before she had a chance to breathe. She gasped and loosened her jaw again, while her fingers stroked and squeezed his sac.

"Put your other hand between your legs," he instructed. "Make yourself come while you're sucking me off."

She brought her hand to her pussy and found it slick and swollen. As she desperately rubbed her clit, Jackson maintained his relentless rhythm, pumping hard and deep, fast and furious, reducing her entire world to...to *him*, damn it. He was all she tasted, all she saw, all she felt, and it wasn't long before release consumed her.

Her cries were muffled against his cock, the overwhelming pleasure amplified by his low, satisfied laughter.

She'd barely regained her senses when his fist tightened in her hair, pulling to the point of pain that only heightened her pleasure.

"You wanna swallow or should I blow my load on your tits?"

She just increased the suction, telling him with her lips exactly what she wanted. And God, she wanted it. Wanted to taste him, to swallow every last drop.

"You ready for it, Mia?" His strokes slowed down, grew lazy. She moaned.

"Good, 'cause I'm coming," he rasped.

He rested his cockhead flat on her tongue and a second later, strands of semen jetted out. She swallowed heartily, milking him dry, taking everything he had to give her, and through it all, he kept a firm grip on her hair and shuddered with release.

"Ah, that was real nice, darlin'," he drawled after he'd pulled out.

Before she could blink, he yanked her onto her feet and kissed her. His mouth was hot and firm, his strong hands on her waist the only thing keeping her from falling to the floor in a sated puddle.

"So what do you say?" he murmured once they'd broken apart. "Do you think you can handle a demanding SEAL in your bed?"

It took a while for her to find her voice, and even then it came out hoarse and wobbly. "Y-yes."

"You sure about that?"

She spoke more firmly. "Yes."

"Good answer." His expression darkened with promise. "You ain't gonna regret this, Mia. I guarantee it."

CHAPTER
NINE

Mia's cell phone rang on Thursday evening as she was walking through the door. Her heart skipped a beat because she figured it was Jackson calling about their date tonight, but when she saw the unfamiliar number flashing on the screen, her excitement died.

It was a Nevada area code. She didn't know anyone in Nevada.

But she did know someone who moved around so much they might *be* in Nevada.

Anger rose in her throat, but she forced herself not to get unnecessarily riled up. She might be wrong about the caller. Maybe it was an old college friend she hadn't heard from in years. Or a lawyer calling to tell her she'd just inherited a gazillion dollars from a relative she hadn't known existed.

Wariness crawled up her spine as she swiped her finger on the touch screen to answer the call. "Hello?"

"Mia! Oh, baby, it's so good to hear your voice!"

The rage returned in full-force, hardening her insides and stiffening her shoulders. It took a serious amount of effort to respond, though her words were cold and biting.

"What do you want?"

On the other end, Brenda Whatever-her-current-last-name sounded devastated. "Baby, it's me. It's your mom."

"I know who it is," she said through clenched teeth. "And I repeat, what do you want?"

A soft sob met her eardrums, but Mia wasn't put off by her mother's crocodile tears. The woman was a master manipulator who knew precisely which buttons to push. In Mia's case, Brenda knew to appeal to her daughter's innate tendency to take care of others in need. But after years of playing this game, Mia knew better than to fall for it.

"I just wanted to see how my daughter was doing." Brenda sniffled. "It's been so long since we've talked."

A cloud of disbelief swirled through her. "And why do you think that is, Mom? You dropped Danny off on my doorstep two years ago and haven't been heard from since!"

There was another sniffing noise. "I told you, I needed to focus on my marriage, baby. I needed time to nurture the new relationship."

Mia was so angry she was ready to burst. "No, what you told me was that you needed me to watch Danny while you went on your *honeymoon*. I didn't think you were giving me a teenage boy to raise."

"Our wires must have gotten crossed. I thought you understood what I was asking for."

"Oh, you mean a two-year hall pass from motherhood?" she snapped. "Is that what you were asking for?"

"Mia, calm down. You know I get anxious when people yell at me."

Every muscle on her face froze in a mask of shock and fury. She wanted to whip the phone across the room and watch it shatter into a million pieces. No, she wanted to reach *into* the goddamn phone and strangle her mother through the telephone line. The woman was unbelievable. A despicable piece of work.

"Well, *I* get anxious when someone rearranges my entire life without asking me!" she yelled. "You left Danny, Mom. You just *left* him and expected me to take care of him."

"It's not like he's ever been a handful," Brenda argued. "Your brother is a wonderful, well-behaved kid."

"How the *fuck* would you know? You were never around when he was growing up, and you haven't been around these last two years."

"Well, I'm going to be around soon."

Horror slammed into her chest. "What are you talking about?"

"Danny emailed me last week begging to see me. I was swamped with work so I couldn't make it then, but I've been shuffling my schedule around. I'm going to try to drive up to San Diego in the next week or two. I can't wait to see you guys."

"Since when? You fucking abandoned us!"

"Watch your language, young lady."

"Don't you *fucking* 'young lady' me!" Mia struggled to regain her composure. "And don't bother coming here. Neither one of us wants to see you."

"Your brother's email says otherwise. He wants to see me, Mia."

"Danny is a naive kid. He doesn't know what he wants."

"He needs his mother."

"He needed you two years ago."

"Mia—"

"I mean it, Mom, don't come to San Diego. There's nothing for you here."

With that, she ended the call and let out a roar that bounced off the apartment walls. The fucking *nerve* of that woman! She disappeared from their lives for *two years* and now she wanted to waltz back for a visit as if nothing happened?

Breathing hard, Mia stormed into the living room and threw her phone on the couch in a fit of anger. She was going to slam the door in her mother's face. Yep, that's exactly what she would do if the woman followed through on her visit threat.

Brenda Weldrick-Jordan-Davis-Schwartz-Parker-Hassan-Reilly-Diaz-Reynolds had no place in their lives. Not anymore.

And not ever.

An hour later, Mia had calmed down drastically, thanks to a long shower and nonstop self-reassurances that her mother was full of shit. There would be no visit. Nope, because Brenda's ADHD rivaled that of a preteen in math class. She'd get distracted by something shiny and forget all about her kids again, just like she always did.

Mia didn't know what had inspired the phone call in the first place, and she wasn't sure she wanted to. No doubt another divorce. Or maybe there'd been a family-centered episode on one of her mother's favorite talk shows and the woman had felt guilty or something.

It didn't matter. If there was one thing Brenda could be counted on, it was *not* being counted on. She hadn't kept a single promise in her miserable, self-absorbed life, so there was really no reason to believe she'd actually show up in San Diego.

When Mia stepped into the living room, freshly showered and feeling centered again, she found her brother huddled over the coffee table with an open textbook, scribbling in his notebook.

"Hey," she greeted him. "When did you get home?"

"While you were in the shower," he answered absently, his gaze glued to his homework. "Practice ended early."

"You hungry?" She drifted toward the kitchen. "I can heat up that leftover lasagna."

"Actually, is it cool if I go over to Angie's for dinner?"

"Sure, but only if you finish all your homework first."

"What does it look like I'm doing, dum-dum?" He promptly buried his nose in the textbook and proceeded to ignore her.

She smiled and inwardly praised herself for bringing up such a good kid. But along with the joy came a pang of bitterness. How dare their mother ring her up out of the blue and announce a visit? The woman had deserted her son. She didn't deserve to see Danny again.

Swallowing her resentment, she focused on nuking yesterday's dinner. A part of her was tempted to tell Danny about their mother's call, just so she'd have someone to vent to, but she fought the urge. For some fucked-up reason, Danny had a soft spot when it came to their mom, and Mia feared the news might actually make him *happy*.

She couldn't tell him. And not just because she didn't want to see a flicker of excitement in his eyes. She refused to get his hopes up only to watch them splinter to pieces when their mother didn't show up.

"Oh, Mia, I forgot," Danny called out. "Can we stop at the bank tomorrow before school so I can deposit my check?"

"No problem," she called back, pulling the warmed-up lasagna out of the microwave. "Leon finally paid you, huh?"

"Yep. *Finally*."

She was glad he couldn't see her face, because her displeasure was written all over it. She really wished Danny would find another part-time job, but he insisted on doing manual labor for a landscaping company owned by a jerk named Leon, who openly took advantage of his young workers and always "forgot" to pay them. She'd urged her brother to quit on numerous occasions, but he was too damn trusting for his own good. She did appreciate his work ethic, though; he'd been saving money since he was fifteen, putting aside every penny in order to pay for college, or, hopefully, to supplement the athletic scholarship he was bound to get.

After she'd served herself a big helping of lasagna, she drifted out to the living room and ate her dinner while Danny finished up his work. Fifteen minutes later, just as her brother had slid out the door with a hasty goodbye, her phone buzzed.

A smile filled her face when she read the incoming text.

On my way. Meet me outside?

She typed back, *No need. Little bro went out, so we can stay here. Come up and let yourself in.*

Jackson responded with six words that sent a blaze of heat to her core.

Be naked when I get there.

They were going to have sex tonight. The s-word hadn't come up in the texts they'd exchanged these past two days, but Mia knew it was inevitable.

And she didn't plan on objecting.

In fact, she couldn't wait for it. After the other night's "warm-up," she was more than ready to explore a sexual relationship with Jackson.

But just a sexual one, a little voice reminded her.

She nodded in resolve as she rose from the couch and went to the kitchen to rinse her plate. She might have caved and embarked on a fling with the guy, but she had every intention of keeping things between them light and complication-free.

Because the truth was, her issues about sex didn't even compare to her issues about *love*.

As in, love didn't fucking exist.

She'd decided a long time ago there was no such thing as forever. If her mother had taught her one thing, it was that all love ever got you was broken promises and a broken heart, and another set of divorce papers to sign.

Well, screw that. She was perfectly content with her life, and she had no interest in letting a man destroy it. Jackson might be sweet and sexy and incredibly easy to be with, but this was nothing more than a temporary arrangement. Some good company, even better sex.

And nothing more.

MIA'S APARTMENT WAS QUIET WHEN JACKSON STRODE through the unlocked front door. He entered the living room and found it empty.

"Where you hiding, sugar?" he called out, a smile tickling his lips.

Her faint voice drifted from the hallway. "I'm in the bedroom."

His cock thickened with each step he took, growing into a full-blown erection by the time he reached her door, which had been left ajar. No light seeped out of the room. She must have closed the curtains. He liked that. There was something really dirty about fucking in the dark.

He walked inside to find Mia lying naked on the bed. One hand rested idly on her thigh, the other was flat on the mattress, toying with the soft blue bedspread.

She was so pretty she took his breath away. Shapely limbs,

perfect tits, a flat belly, and narrow hips. Her dark hair was loose and curling over one shoulder, looking silky to the touch.

"Beautiful," he said simply.

"What?" she murmured.

"You. I could stand here staring at you for hours."

"Is that what you're planning to do? Stand and stare?"

"No way, darlin'. I have more interesting plans for tonight."

Without delay, he began to strip. His shirt came off first, followed by his shirt. Socks and boots were next, and then his jeans and boxers joined the rest of his clothing on the floor.

Her breath hitched and his ego got a nice boost out of that. So did his dick, which hardened even more and rose to salute her.

He gripped his erection and gave it a firm pump, smiling when Mia's lips parted in delight.

"You like watching me jerk it?" he asked.

She nodded.

He continued to stroke himself, his gaze roaming her body as he did so. The signs of her arousal were hard to miss—bright eyes, a rosy blush on her breasts, the way her thighs clenched.

Jackson toyed with his piercing for a moment, enjoying the sharp tugs it gave to his cockhead.

"Let's talk protection," he said gruffly. "I brought condoms, but if you've got another method of birth control and you wanna forgo the condoms, I want you to know I'm clean as a whistle. I can show you my most recent results."

"I'm on the pill and STD-free," she admitted. Then she hesitated, those mesmerizing green eyes fixed on the tip of his dick. "Will I feel the piercing if you wear a condom?"

He shook his head. "Not really."

"Do you want to use one?"

He ran his tongue over his lips. "What I wanna do is come inside your pussy and watch my seed drip down your thighs.

And then I want to rub my come on my fingers and watch you lick it off."

"Oh Jesus." Her chest rose and fell rapidly. "Your dirty talk is..."

"Is what?" he prompted.

"The biggest turn-on *ever*."

"Damn right," he said smugly. "So what's your final answer, sugar? Do I need to reach into my pocket and get those rubbers?"

There was no more hesitation on her part. "No."

"All righty then."

He strode to the bed, knelt in front of her face, and guided his erection toward her.

"Suck," he ordered.

Her mouth immediately opened to let him in, and he shuddered with pleasure as wet heat surrounded his cock. The sight of her lips stretched around his shaft drove him mindless with need. Groaning, he stopped her from moving by resting his hand on the crown of her head, then brought his other hand south and traced her lips with one finger.

"You look so dang pretty right now." His finger followed the wide circle of her mouth. "Look at these sexy lips wrapped around my dick. Beautiful, baby. Fuckin' beautiful."

When she moaned, the husky sound tickled his shaft and had him pumping his hips. He buried his cock deep, gave her a moment to adjust, then withdrew and drove in again. When his tip poked the back of her throat, he went still and tightened his grip in her hair.

"Swallow," he told her.

She swallowed, and the feel of her throat muscles clenching around him summoned a low groan.

"Again."

Another swallow, another tight pull on his cockhead. His

dick was lodged in her mouth, but there was no suction, no thrusting. Just her throat clamping around him each time he instructed her to take a gulp.

He stroked her hair for a few lazy seconds, then slid out of her mouth.

"That's it?" she said in surprise.

He laughed. "I'll let you blow me again later, darlin'. Right now I'm more interested in fucking your brains out."

"Oh," she squeaked. "Okay."

Still laughing, he got on the bed and eased his body over hers, supporting himself by propping up on his elbows. His erection lay flat on her stomach. He made no move to push it inside her yet. What he did was dip his head and kiss her, a slow, thorough kiss that made her gasp against his lips.

He raised his head. "I'm gonna go easy on you today, seeing as it's our first time and all."

She peered up at him. "And what does 'going easy' on me actually mean?"

He planted fleeting kisses along her jaw. "It means—" he flicked his tongue over her earlobe, "—that I'm not gonna tie you up tonight—" his lips traveled to the hollow of her throat, "—or spank you until your ass is pink—" he kissed her throat before licking his way back to her mouth, "—or fuck your ass so hard you won't be able to sit down for days."

He bit hard on her lip, then sucked on it to soothe the sting, enjoying the way she moaned. Then he positioned his cock at her entrance and slid in. He didn't check to see if she was wet enough—he knew she was. He could see the glossy proof of it clinging to her pretty pink folds.

The first stroke was so fast and deep that she cursed loudly and twitched as if she'd touched a live wire. This time Jackson didn't give her time to recover or adjust. He pounded into her in a hard, relentless rhythm that had the headboard smacking against the wall.

"Oh *fuck*," she squealed, her arms coming around his shoulders to hold on tight.

Her fingernails dug into his spine, her legs hooking over his hips to deepen the contact. He was balls-deep in her pussy, the power of his thrusts rocking the bed and making the mattress squeak wildly.

"So tight and wet," he mumbled. "Your pussy belongs to me, Mia."

She groaned in abandon, desperately lifting her hips to meet each thrust.

He shoved his hand in her hair. "Say it."

Her voice shook like a leaf, tinged with the same lust glittering in her eyes. "My pussy belongs to you."

"Good girl. Now pry one of those sexy legs off my ass and bring it up here." He grabbed hold of her leg and raised it up so he could alter their position, so that he plunged in at an angle.

He knew the second his piercing hit her sweet spot, because she cried out, her inner muscles clasping his cock so tight he was surprised she didn't break the dang thing.

His heart pounded. He watched Mia's face while he fucked her, satisfied to find nothing but hazy passion there. He knew he was a rough lover, knew it freaked out some girls. But not this one. She moaned and whimpered, her pussy squeezing and rippling against his dick, coating it with her juices. No condom had been the right call. He couldn't imagine missing out on this wet paradise. It was sheer heaven.

"What are you *doing* to me?" she choked out. "You...your piercing...it's..." She quit talking altogether, her body telling him everything he needed to know.

His piercing intensified his own pleasure, too. The pressure on his tip was amazing, and each time the ball bearings scraped her hot channel, her muscles quivered and squeezed him harder.

As his pulse shrieked in his ears, Jackson knew he was getting close. His balls had drawn up, tingling incessantly. Strands of precome were already dripping from his head.

"I'm close," he warned her. "But I ain't gonna come until you do. So..."

He moved his hand to the place where they were joined and skillfully fingered her clit, knowing exactly how much pressure to exert on the sensitive nub. Then he quickened his strokes so that his cock was furiously hitting her G-spot on each inward thrust.

"*Jackson.*"

She shouted out his name as she convulsed, bringing a sizzling rush of satisfaction that unleashed the floodgates inside him. He almost blacked out as the orgasm tore through his body. Spots danced in front of his eyes, his heart damn near stopped, and the pleasure that seized his limbs made it impossible to breathe.

They shuddered together for what felt like hours. The air became stifling hot, the bedspread beneath them damp from their sweat, soaked with Mia's sweet juices and the come oozing out of her.

Not one for bluffing, Jackson pulled out and dipped his fingers inside. They emerged shiny and covered in his come, and when he brought them to her mouth, Mia raised her head to capture one with her lips. His nostrils flared, lust building once again, as she licked his fingers clean.

"Oh, sugar, that's so sexy," he muttered. "You want more?"

Her eyes were cloudy with passion as she nodded, prompting him to return to her pussy for a second dip. Watching her suck his seed off his hand succeeded in turning his semi-erect cock into a rock-hard spike. With a growl, he yanked his fingers out of her mouth and pushed his growing erection back inside her.

Her eyes widened. "Again?" she blurted out.

He started to move, his gaze never leaving hers as his hoarse voice ground out, "Again."

AFTERWARD, THEY LAY THERE IN A TANGLED, SATED HEAP, with Jackson's arm slung around her, and Mia's head resting against his bare chest.

"I'm sorry if I was too rough," he said repentantly.

Her muffled laughter shook her bare shoulders. "Rough? You nearly drilled me in half, Jackson. I've never been this sore in my life."

Concern washed over him. "Aw, shit. Why the heck didn't you say anything?"

"Because it felt so good I would have been an idiot if I stopped you." She craned her neck so she could look at him. "Relax. That was the best sex of my life, hands down. I'll just take a nice long bath in a bit, rub some soothing lotion on my lady bits, and I'll be fine."

His worry gave way to relief. "'Kay. But next time you start to feel sore, you'd better tell me about it."

"Deal."

As they both went quiet, a feeling of serenity floated through him and brought a smile to his lips. The best thing about being with Mia was that she didn't try to fill every silence. She was content to simply lie there with him, her hand absently stroking his abs, her warm breath heating his pecs.

"How was your day?" he asked a while later.

"Pretty good. I was out in the sun for eight hours, digging like crazy, but I'm looking forward to fixing up the park. All the plants there were terribly neglected." She paused. "My mother called when I got home today."

Surprise jolted through him. "She did?"

"Yep. She said she wants to come visit us." Resentment colored Mia's voice. "Can you believe it? Not a word from her in two years and suddenly she's calling out of the blue."

"What did you tell her?"

"I ordered her not to come. I don't want her anywhere near Danny."

He ran a hand over her back, which radiated tension. "Do you think she'll actually come to San Diego?"

"I doubt it. But if she does, she won't be receiving any welcome parades." Mia sighed. "I don't want to talk about her anymore. What's *your* family like? A lot less dysfunctional than mine, I bet."

"For the most part," he said gruffly. "My folks are still madly in love after thirty years of marriage. My dad works hard on the ranch, and my mom takes care of the house and makes sure there's dinner on the table when Dad comes back."

"Do you get along with them?"

"Yeah, I do. They're good people. Easy to talk to, always there when I need 'em. I wasn't a rebellious kid, so we never got into any screaming matches when I was growing up." He chuckled as a memory surfaced. "I did run away once, though."

"Really? Why?"

"Because my dad was gonna kill my pig."

She burst out laughing. "You had a pet pig?"

"Sorta. When I was seven, our sow gave birth to a dozen or so piglets, and I fell in love with the runt of the litter. But the little guy was damn sick. He couldn't move, wouldn't eat. The vet said he suffered oxygen-deprivation during the birth and that he wasn't gonna survive, but I was determined to nurse him back to health."

Mia sat up with a smile. "So even back then you wanted to save lives."

"Yup. But Frankie couldn't be saved. He was gonna die no matter what, but I refused to accept it. When I heard my folks talkin' about putting the little guy out of his misery, I shoved a few things in a backpack, snuck into the barn to get Frankie, and ran off."

"Where'd you go?"

He grinned. "This little cabin on the edge of our property. I was seven—I didn't know there was a world beyond our ranch. Didn't take long for my dad to find me."

"Did he kill Frankie?" she said softly.

"The minute we got home." Jackson swallowed a lump of sorrow. "I learned a hard lesson that night, which was that you can't save everyone. Sometimes you've gotta know when to let go."

"I'm sorry they killed your piglet, Jackson." Mia leaned down and brushed a kiss over his lips. "I bet he was really cute."

"He totally was."

"Are you an only child?" she asked, then answered her own question. "No, wait. I remember you mentioning you had a younger sister. What's she like?"

"Evie? She's precocious. And unlike lil' ol' me, she absolutely went through the rebel stage in her teens. Luckily I didn't witness most of it because she's eight years younger and I was already outta the house by then, so I was spared her purple hair phase and countless runaway attempts. Shane wasn't living in the main house at that point either, so he—"

"Who's Shane?"

He swallowed again. "My older brother. When he turned twenty-one, he told my folks he wasn't gonna keep working on the ranch unless he had some privacy, so my dad fixed up that cabin I was talkin' about before."

"So your brother and sister still live in Abbott Creek?"

"Yup. Shane works with our dad, and Evie lives at home and goes to the community college in the next town over. She's studying to be a massage therapist."

"Do you get to see them often?"

The lump in his throat grew bigger. He tried to gulp it down, but it stayed jammed in his throat like a piece of spoiled food, making it difficult to get any words out.

"Not as much as they'd like," he confessed. "I haven't been home in a few years."

"Because you're stationed here?" When he nodded, Mia wrinkled her forehead. "Don't you ever get shore leave, or whatever it's called?"

"I do, but I haven't had a chance to get back to Texas this last stretch."

Hadn't *wanted* to was more like it, but he was reluctant to share all the sordid details. Not yet, anyway. Not when this thing between them was still so new. His past wasn't something he liked talking about, and the last thing he wanted to do was ruin this moment of ease and connection with Mia.

"I have three days' leave for the holidays, though," he said roughly. "I'll probably head home then."

"You should," she advised. "It sounds like you've got a great family who loves you. You need to hold on to that."

Another silence drifted over them, until she finally let out a loud yawn. "Let's do something before I fall asleep," she suggested. "Do you want to watch a movie?"

"Sure. Except this time I get to pick something." Jackson heaved himself off the bed and embarked on a search for his clothing.

"Oh," Mia said, "I forgot to ask you—do you want to come to Danny's game with me tomorrow night?"

He answered with no hesitation. "I'd love to."

"Awesome. It'll be nice to have some company again. I get so bored watching the games by myself."

An idea crept into his brain. "Would you mind if I invited a few of my teammates? They're football nuts, so they'll have a blast. And I think you'll like 'em."

Her eyes narrowed. "Are they all bossy, sex-obsessed ladies' men like you?"

He blinked innocently. "Nah. They're the tamest, most polite guys you'll ever meet."

CHAPTER
TEN

The following evening, Mia was yet again the center of attention in the high school parking lot. Last week, her date had drawn all the admiring looks. Tonight, it was her date and the three spectacular-looking men he was chatting with.

She'd met Seth briefly when she'd worked in his yard, so she instantly recognized him as she approached the foursome. She didn't know the other two—a handsome blond with dancing green eyes, and a dark-haired one with amazing bone structure —but Jackson quickly remedied that.

"Hi, sugar," he said, leaning over to plant a soft peck on her lips. "Come meet the boys."

She tried to ignore the very noticeable stares of all the women in their vicinity, and focused on greeting Jackson's teammates.

"This is Cash," Jackson told her, gesturing to the SEAL with the dark hair. "Cash, my girl Mia."

She felt herself flush at the introduction, but didn't object to it. She supposed she *was* his girl. Tonight, anyway.

"Nice to meet you." Cash flashed a gorgeous smile, his vivid blue eyes twinkling with admiration as he extended his hand.

"Ditto," she said, shaking his big, callused hand.

"Blondie over here is Dylan," Jackson went on. "Be careful or he might just charm your pants off."

"Definitely a possibility," the guy agreed cheerfully, "considering I haven't had sex in—"

"Ten days," Cash and Seth finished, rolling their eyes.

Mia grinned as she and Dylan shook hands. "I take it you're not happy with your current situation?"

He sighed. "I most certainly am not, honey. But my partners are out of town, so I'm afraid I must remain celibate for a while longer."

Partners?

Before she could question the remark, Jackson finished the introductions by pointing to Seth. "And you've already met this smartass, right?"

"I have." She smiled at the scruffy-haired guy. "Nice to see you again. Why didn't Miranda come tonight?"

"Oh, she's here," Seth replied in his deep, gravelly voice. "She and Jen just took the rugrats to the bathroom. We're meeting them inside."

"Jen is Cash's girl," Jackson explained. "You'll like her. She's a real sweetheart."

Mia couldn't believe how many people gawked at them on their way to the stadium entrance. She supposed she shouldn't be surprised. The four SEALs made an imposing picture. They were equally tall and muscular, and walked with the same predatory swagger that made every pair of eyes gravitate in their direction.

As the guys paid the kid at the gate, she noticed all three of Jackson's teammates were wearing cargo pants that had a gazillion pockets. And yet strangely enough, she was able to get a clear sense of their personalities based on their outfits. Cash's cargo pants were olive-green and paired with a black long-sleeve shirt, giving him an intense, serious vibe. Seth wore black on the bottom and a gray pullover the exact shade as his silvery eyes, his dark stubble lending him a feral, badass air. In contrast, Dylan's pants were khaki-colored, and his blue polo shirt and white button-down told her he was the most easygoing of the bunch.

And then there was Jackson. Her sexy cowboy in his trademark denim and plaid, with a white undershirt and beat-up black combat boots. She wondered why he didn't just go all out and wear cowboy boots. And a Stetson. She suspected he looked spectacular in a Stetson. Like a military Marlboro man.

The five of them moved through the crowd and ascended the bleacher steps with Seth in the lead. His hawk-like gaze scanned the rows of seats. "There they are," he said, then moved purposefully toward his target.

Mia smiled when she spotted Miranda and the twins.

"Hello again," she greeted the woman, before turning to the two adorable children. "Hey, guys, remember me? I'm Mia."

Sophie dove out of her seat and threw her arms around Mia's legs.

"I remember!" Sophie declared, her dark head barely reaching Mia's stomach. "You made our garden pretty!"

She bent down to return the hug and was surprised when Sophie's brother Jason also jumped up to embrace her. She tweaked his hair before straightening up, then watched in amusement as the kids scrambled over to Seth and dragged him to the seat directly between them.

As Cash, Dylan, and Jackson flopped down and got comfortable, a blonde with a heartbreakingly beautiful face stood to introduce herself.

"I'm Jen," she said, her warm blue eyes sweeping over Mia. "Texas told us a lot about you."

"Texas?" Mia echoed.

Jen grinned. "Jackson didn't tell you about his nickname?"

"You guys call him *Texas*? You realize that's the least original nickname on the planet, right?"

"Hey, don't blame me." Jen tossed her long golden hair over her shoulder. "Smartass Seth is the one who came up with it. C'mon, sit over here with Miranda and me. We're way more fun."

Laughing, she followed Jen down the aisle. A moment later she was sandwiched between the two women while the guys and the Masterson twins congregated at the end of the row.

Since Mia didn't have many female friends—or friends, period, for that matter—she felt slightly ill at ease surrounded by so many new faces. But she quickly discovered that Miranda and Jen were the coolest people on the planet. They were both so friendly and laidback, their easy laughter and hilarious remarks making Mia feel like a real part of their group and not just some random interloper.

When the Warriors took the field, she pointed Danny out to everyone, which led to a conversation with Miranda about single parenthood. It turned out the other woman knew all about raising kids alone. She'd been a single mom to her twins before marrying Seth, and she confessed that having a partner to help out had made her life a million times easier.

"And surprisingly, Seth is a great dad," she told Mia in a low voice. "It took him a while to warm up to the twins, but now he absolutely adores them."

"It still boggles my mind," Jen admitted wryly. "I never imagined Seth could be daddy material."

The conversation shifted to their jobs next. When Mia

learned Jen was a freelance photographer, she couldn't hide her surprise.

"Are you sure it's not the other way around? Shouldn't you be in front of the camera?" she asked the breathtaking girl.

Jen rolled her eyes. "No thank you. I don't like being the center of attention."

Mia had to laugh, because at the moment, Jen was most certainly the center of attention. Every guy in their vicinity was checking her out, same way every girl in their midst was ogling the SEALs.

Miranda noticed all the stares and gave a dry laugh. "Jeez, you'd think they've never seen four smoking-hot military men before."

"What are you three whispering about over there?" Dylan demanded from down the row.

The women exchanged grins.

"Nothing," Jen called back. "Just watch the game and pretend we're not here."

"Impossible," Cash told her. "I always know exactly where you are."

"Yeah?" his girlfriend challenged.

"Oh yeah." He winked. "Your presence is like a shining beacon of light, sweetheart."

A faint blush stained Jen's cheeks. "Gotta love those sweet-talking men, huh?"

Mia smiled and moved her gaze back to the field, where Danny and his teammates were on their own twenty-yard line, getting into position after the kickoff. The whistle blew, the play clock started, and then they were off. The first snap resulted in Danny handing the ball off to the running back, who charged into a wall of defensive linemen and managed to eke out three yards, seven short of a first down. The next play was another running one, with the same kid finding a hole in the defense, cutting hard to the left, and rushing twenty-two yards before he was finally brought down.

"That kid can run!" Dylan whooped in delight.

"That's my son!" came a loud baritone voice.

Mia twisted her head and grinned at the bulky man in the row behind them.

"You should be proud," Dylan informed the happy father. "He's damn fast."

The man beamed. "And he's only a sophomore! What do you think of that?"

As Dylan launched into an animated exchange with the older man, Jen sighed and turned to Mia. "I swear, he makes friends wherever he goes. I think he might actually be the most charming person on the planet."

Mia dropped her voice to a whisper. "What's his deal, by the way? Earlier he said something about his 'partners' being out of town. As in, more than one?"

That got her simultaneous laughs from Jen and Miranda.

"He has a girlfriend named Claire," Miranda said.

"Oh, okay, so I must have misheard him when he—"

"And a boyfriend named Aidan," Jen finished.

She blinked. "What?"

"The three of them live together," Miranda explained. "They're poly. Like, a permanent threesome."

"Oh. I see." She shook her head a couple of times. "No, wait, I don't see. So he lives with two people and they're okay with sharing him?"

Jen hooted. "They *all* share."

"They're in love. All three of them," Miranda added.

"Oh."

Clearly Mia was not as worldly as she'd thought, because she was having a tough time wrapping her head around it. She'd never known anyone who was involved in an actual polyamorous relationship. She wasn't sure how that would even work.

"Don't worry, you'll meet Claire and Aidan when they get back from LA, and then you'll understand what we're talking about," Jen said with another grin.

A round of cheers from the crowd jerked Mia's attention back to the field, just in time to see Danny complete a fifty-five yard pass to a receiver in the end zone, officially putting six points on the home team's scoreboard.

"Did you see that pass?" Cash exclaimed.

Pride flooded her chest as Cash fixed his gaze on her. "Your brother has a ridiculous arm. Jesus. That kid is going places."

"I hope so," she said.

"Trust me, he is. You can see it in his eyes. He's got that glint of determination, and the arm to back it up."

"Listen to him," Jen advised. "Cash knows his football."

Mia's gaze focused on Danny, who looked calm and poised as he wandered over to the bench to receive a hearty pat on the back from his coach. The special teams unit hurried onto the field to kick the extra point, which sailed smoothly between the goal posts, and the score went from 6-0 to 7-0.

The opening touchdown served as a favorable omen for the rest of the game. By the time the final whistle blew, the Warriors had crushed the visiting team, 31-3. Danny and his teammates gathered in a celebratory circle, while Mia jumped to her feet and cheered herself hoarse.

As she hollered her support, she suddenly felt a pair of eyes burning into the side of her face. A slight turn of the head, and her gaze collided with Jackson's, her breath catching in her throat when she saw his expression. He was staring at her like he wanted to eat her up, whiskey eyes glittering with greedy promise. They hadn't spoken at all during the game, but she realized now that he'd been completely aware of her the entire time.

Without breaking eye contact, Jackson reached into his pocket and withdrew his phone. His long fingers moved over the screen even as his gaze stayed locked with hers.

A second later, her own phone buzzed.

The message on the screen was very succinct.

Give your brother the OK to chill with his GF so we can be alone. I want your pussy tonight.

As if on cue, a drop of desire dampened her panties. Which was clearly Jackson's intent, because when she lifted her head, he was smirking at her.

And then, the tease of a man had the gall to lick his lips, revealing the talented tongue that had already given her countless orgasms.

She couldn't wait to get home.

SINCE THEY'D TAKEN SEPARATE CARS AND JACKSON STILL had to drop Dylan off, Mia reached her apartment first. She sprinted up the stairs and hurried inside, where she promptly removed every last stitch of clothing. Jackson hadn't told her to, hadn't demanded a single thing of her when they kissed goodbye in the parking lot, but she knew he would appreciate her taking the initiative.

She was about to get comfy on the bed when another idea occurred to her. Grinning to herself, she went to the dresser, opened the top drawer, and rummaged around for the Victoria's Secret bag she'd stashed in there more than a year ago. She wasn't much of a lingerie girl, but Jackson made her feel so damn sexy she suddenly had the urge to look the part.

She finally found the bag and dumped its indecent contents on the bed. Putting on the black lace merry widow and matching thong was easy. So was rolling the sheer black stockings up her legs. But she spent an obscene amount of time trying to figure out how to hook the tops of the stockings to the straps hanging from the merry widow.

She'd just snapped everything into place when she heard the front door creak open.

No footsteps echoed in the hall. There was no sound at all, in fact, and yet a moment later, Jackson entered the bedroom.

Jeez, the man moved like a ghost. He'd appeared without warning, and his eyes grew heavy-lidded when he noticed her outfit.

But he didn't comment on it. Didn't utter a compliment. What he did was cross his arms over his red-and-black plaid shirt and make a *tsk*ing noise with his tongue.

"You were a bad girl tonight, sugar. Real bad."

She blinked in surprise. "I was? Why?"

His gaze rested on her cleavage before returning to her face. "Well, let's see," he drawled, ticking off each transgression with his fingers. "One, you didn't sit next to me at the game. Two, you didn't say a dang word to me all night. And three, you were checking out Dylan when you thought nobody was lookin'."

She frowned, slightly taken aback. "Are you actually mad about those things?"

"Nah, not at all." He shot her an evil grin. "I just needed to come up with something to punish you for, and those reasons seemed as good as any."

Her pulse kicked up a notch. Punish her?

With methodical strides, he crossed the room and sat at the foot of the bed. "You're gonna do two things for me."

"Which are?"

"First, you're gonna unlock that secret drawer of yours and get your nine-inch boyfriend." He arched a brow, waited, and when she didn't challenge him, he went on. "And then you're gonna drape your sweet body over my lap and not speak unless spoken to. Understand?"

Heat engulfed her body. Oh boy. What the hell did he have in store for her tonight?

And why wasn't she the least bit concerned by it?

Heart pounding, she walked over to the nightstand and grabbed the little silver key from the basket in the top drawer. She sank to her knees to unlock the bottom one, her fingers trembling as she pulled out the bright pink dildo. She'd never shown the sex toy to a man before, but she gave it to Jackson without a single complaint. Willingly. Shivering with anticipation as the toy exchanged hands.

When he patted his jean-clad thighs, she swallowed, tried to bring some moisture to her arid mouth, then climbed onto his lap. He positioned her so that her knees and elbows rested on the bed, while her breasts were crushed against his thighs and her ass jutted out in the air.

Mia was so turned on she could hardly breathe. The lacy fabric of the merry widow scraped her bare breasts and teased her puckered nipples, and her thong was already soaked from her excitement.

"W-what are you going to do?" she whispered.

His sharp voice reprimanded her. "I said no talking, sugar. That's two extra smacks right there."

"Smacks?" she couldn't help but echo.

"And lookey here, that's three more."

She craned her head to look at him. "Out of curiosity, how many 'smacks' did I start with?"

"Ten." He smiled pleasantly. "But that question just cost you five more, so we're at twenty now."

She gulped.

His hand was warm as he glided it over her bottom and toyed with the dental-floss strap of fabric nestled between her cheeks. His touch was so gentle she relaxed beneath it, but just as the tension left her body, his hand disappeared and then came down to slap her ass.

She jerked. Opened her mouth to protest, but then she remembered the no-talking rule.

His pleased chuckle hung in the air. "That's a good girl. You're gonna stay nice and quiet until I say otherwise."

The second smack connected with only one cheek, the third bringing a sting to the other. Fourth and fifth used more force, no doubt leaving marks on her bare ass.

"What a sweet little bottom you have," he muttered before smacking it a sixth time.

If someone had told her she would enjoy getting the hell spanked out of her, she would've told them they were insane. But here she was, completely at Jackson's mercy, growing more and more aroused each time his palm connected with her buttocks.

The seventh slap elicited a soft moan from her lips. The eighth had her wiggling her bottom in anticipation for the ninth. Number ten was the hardest yet, slicing the air with a loud thwacking noise and bringing a dull ache to her butt.

Jackson's mocking voice echoed in the room. "What number are we on? I seem to have forgotten."

She couldn't get a word out thanks to the arousal clamped around her throat.

"What number?" he repeated sternly, his free hand tugging on her hair.

"Eleven," she panted out. "Eleven!"

"Good girl." He spanked her again, then rubbed away the ache with the light graze of his fingertips. "Now count it out."

She was gasping for air now. "I...can't."

"And why's that?"

His palm struck her flesh and she shuddered uncontrollably. "Because I'm so turned on I can't concentrate."

"Don't care. You're counting it out. Starting now."

The number "twelve" flew out of her mouth on his next hard stroke.

"Thatta girl."

Another smack.

Her head started to spin. "Thirteen."

And another one.

"Fourteen."

Her ass was on fire. So was her pussy. Every inch of her sizzled with overpowering need that had her seeing stars.

In between fifteen and sixteen, Jackson hooked his finger beneath the thin strap of her thong and tugged hard, causing the lacy fabric to tighten over her clit.

Mia moaned as a shockwave surged through her.

On the seventeenth smack, he tore the thong right off her body, muttered something about "replacing it," and skimmed one finger along the crease of her ass.

"Eighteen," she wheezed, already anticipating—craving— the next one.

But he threw her for a loop—number nineteen was infinitely gentle, swiftly followed by him pushing his finger into her sopping-wet channel.

"Oh my God!" Pleasure blasted into her, nearly knocking her out of his lap.

His finger disappeared so quickly she almost broke down in tears.

"I said count, Mia. No other commentary allowed." He laughed. "That's five more."

Her brain turned to mush. She didn't know what he was doing to her and she didn't care. All she knew was that it felt so good. So fucking good.

The erotic game continued, fierce whacks intermingled with Jackson's fingers teasing her pussy, stroking her slit, flicking her clit. When they neared the end of the countdown, he shifted on the mattress, and suddenly she felt something cold and foreign probing her entrance.

The dildo. Oh sweet Lord.

He pushed the tip of the sex toy inside her just as his palm stung her ass again. On the second-to-last smack, he wedged the dildo in farther. On the final one, the toy was buried deep inside her.

Mia had no fricking clue why she hadn't come yet. God knew she was wet enough. Achy enough. She was ready to combust as she lay there draped over him, her ass sticking up in the air like a sacrificial offering.

"Oh, sugar, you should see your bottom right now. Bright red and so goddamn pretty. Do you want to come? I think you do, huh?"

She groaned in response.

Jackson slowly pulled out the dildo so only the tip filled her. He twisted it around a couple of times, his movements utterly indolent, thoughtful even.

A strangled moan ripped out of her throat when his finger slid down the crease of her ass, breached the puckered ring of muscle, and plunged right through it. He wasted no time driving the sex toy back into her core, fucking her hard with it while he fingered her asshole with the same merciless tempo.

Mia didn't remember climaxing, wasn't sure how she got on her back, didn't know how Jackson's cock had wound up inside her, but her limp muscles and the unbearable pleasure pricking her flesh told her she'd come, and come hard. And then it was happening again, a rush of bliss overtaking her as his muscular body moved over hers.

"Fuck, oh fuck yeah. I'm gonna come," he whispered as their mouths met in a blistering kiss.

His tongue devoured her mouth, his lips staying locked with hers through his entire orgasm. Mia's pulse drummed loudly in her ears as the heat of his release soaked her aching core. His piercing—that goddamn incredible piercing—hit her sweet spot as he shuddered on top of her.

She would never get used to it. The bone-melting pleasure, the intensity, the feeling of pure liberation that consumed her whenever this man had his way with her.

Temporary, her brain reminded her.

Even as she gasped for air and let Jackson roll her over so they were lying side-by-side in a sweaty mess, she was telling herself this wouldn't last forever. That she'd be a fool to think it even could.

They would say goodbye eventually. She knew that.

But until that happened...until then...she was going to cling to the way Jackson made her feel and enjoy every last second of this mind-blowing fling.

CHAPTER
ELEVEN

"So here's what we've got." Commander Roger Doyle swept his razor-sharp gaze over the group standing before him. "Enemy rebels captured two of our boys who were conducting a reconnaissance mission in North Korean waters. The men are being held in a sub off the west coast, just north of Namp'o in the South Pyongan Province. Sub is also believed to be harboring sensitive data pertaining to US Special Operations, stolen by the rebels during a siege on the American navy base in Yongsan. We've got two objectives: rescue the hostages and destroy the sub. Any questions?"

Thomas Becker, the commanding officer of Team Fifteen, spoke up briskly. "How many tangos in the sub?"

"Eight."

"How many on the surface?"

"Eight stationed on a fishing boat nearby. Armed with assault rifles and a few other nasty surprises."

"Any way to approach the red zone by vessel?" Lieutenant Carson Scott asked from his perch against the wall.

"Negative. They'll have eyes on the water. The op requires a HALO jump and scuba approach." Doyle moved away from the chalkboard and headed for the door. "I'll leave the op specs with Lieutenant Commanders Becker and Walsh. Team Eight, tangos. Team Fifteen, you're the good guys."

Dylan and Seth high-fived, while the members of the newly arrived Team Eight let out simultaneous groans.

"Why are we always the bad dudes?" the dark-haired ensign who'd introduced himself as Hunter complained.

"Seriously," a petty officer named Duke griped.

Miguel Delgado, the team's tall, balding commander, just grinned. "Have fun," he said before following Doyle out the door.

As Becker and Walsh, the teams' respective COs, huddled over the plans left by their superiors, Jackson found himself under the intense scrutiny of a guy with light-blue eyes. Max, if Jackson remembered correctly.

"Can I help you with anything?" he asked with a cock of his eyebrows.

"Just trying to figure out what all the hype is about," Max said thoughtfully.

"The hype?"

"You guys have this huge reputation, but I don't see what—"

"Wait, what reputation?" Dylan had overheard the comment and was drifting over to them.

Max shrugged. "You know, that you're all major players."

"He means whores," Duke said with a grin.

"And party dudes," their teammate Hunter added.

"And rumor has it, y'all got arrested for streaking last year." That came from the enlisted SEAL that Team Eight called "Lancelot," a tall man with dirty-blond hair.

"How dare you." Seth usurped the conversation with a smirk. "It was for brawling, thank you very much, and no charges were filed."

The members of Team Eight hooted. "Sorry, my mistake," Lancelot said in amusement.

Duke grinned. "Notice they haven't denied the *whore* part."

Seth grinned back. "I didn't realize the East Coast teams were a bunch of gossips."

"And FYI," Dylan said, "we were warned about your reputation too, so don't go all pot-kettle on us."

"Dude, we're not judging," Hunter replied, sounding sincere. "We were just fishing 'cause we want to party with you."

Jackson chuckled, though he honestly wasn't surprised by Hunter's response. From the moment the members of Team Eight had walked into the classroom, he'd known they were the East Coast clones of him and his buddies. Most of the Eighters were young, in their early to midtwenties, and they were rowdier and more outspoken than the majority of soldiers stationed on this base. Team Eight did have its Beckers, though —there were definitely a few stoic faces in the room, all business from moment one—but these four were clearly kindred spirits. Sporting cocky grins, quick to laugh, and giving off party-dude vibes.

"Seriously," Duke agreed. "We've gotta get some beers while we're here. Exchange war stories."

"Whore stories, you mean," Max cracked.

The next round of laughter was interrupted by a sharp whistle from Team Eight's CO. "I need my tangos over here," Walsh barked.

The SEALs snapped to attention and marched off without delay, while Jackson and his teammates were ushered to the door by Becker, who needed them in a separate room in order to go over the details of the mission.

"Enough chatting, ladies," Becker said briskly. "We've got a rescue to plan."

A LITTLE OVER SEVEN HOURS LATER, THE TRAINING mission was underway. It wasn't nearly enough time to plan and execute a foolproof extraction, but the hasty timeframe was part of the exercise. The powers that be wanted to evaluate how well the SEALs could carry out a rescue with very little planning.

Jackson and Seth had drawn the short straw and were playing the hostages today. They were currently in the bowels of the *USS Hoover*, a submarine stationed at the Point Loma Naval Base. Their hands were secured to a pair of pipes with the same painfully tight wires that were also coiled around their feet, while their "guards" watched them closely to hinder any funny business.

It was the kind of training demo Jackson hated. Being left out of the action was frustrating as heck, and he knew Seth shared his dissatisfaction as they sat there on the damp floor while their teammates got to have all the fun.

Shooting the shit wasn't encouraged during these exercises, but the four of them broke the rules, captors chatting with hostages as they waited for their respective teams to make a move.

"Connor's gonna smoke your guys," Duke said smugly, an MP5 submachine gun hanging loosely from the strap on his shoulder.

While Jackson and Seth were completely unarmed, Duke's and Lancelot's weapons were equipped with blanks, but all four men wore the same camo gear with high-tech sensors that would register if one of them was "hit." The sensor emitted a white light for a non-lethal injury, blue for a lethal one, and red meant dead. Both Jackson and Seth sported a couple of white ones already from the "beating" they'd endured during interrogation.

"Which one is Connor again?" Seth asked.

"Black hair, black eyes, didn't say a word during briefing." Duke chuckled. "He's the strong, silent type. Best sniper you'll ever meet."

"Not if Evans gets in position like he's supposed to," Seth retorted. "Dude can hit a quarter off a man's head from a thousand yards away."

Jackson tested his bindings for the hundredth time, but the thin wire didn't budge. If anything, it dug deeper into his wrists, and the moisture dripping down his forearms told him he'd fussed with the cord so much he'd drawn blood.

"Aw, poor baby," Lancelot drawled when he saw Jackson shifting around on the floor. "Did we tie those wires too tight?"

He grinned at the other man. "It's really too bad you can't see my hands. 'Cause I'm givin' you the finger right now."

"That's a Texan accent, huh? Whereabouts?"

"Little town west of Dallas," Jackson answered. "You?"

"Charleston." Lancelot gestured to Duke. "And my man here is from Raleigh."

"I'm from Vegas," Seth piped up. "Which means I'm way cooler than all you losers."

"Oh man, I love Vegas," Duke declared. "Me and Hunter went there last year on leave and we hooked up with the hottest showgirl on the planet. She was so flexible it should be illegal."

Seth smirked. "Beat you again. I'm married to a former showgirl."

"No shit."

"Yes shit. And before you ask, yes, she's also insanely flexible."

Lancelot glanced at his watch. "Been almost an hour. I think you boys are SOL."

No sooner had the words left his mouth than the sound of gunfire erupted from far above them, prompting both Seth and Jackson to grin widely.

"Gee, guess one of you should go and investigate," Seth taunted.

Duke and Lancelot had already snapped to action, the former sliding out the steel door while the latter stuck around, his gun trained on his hostages' foreheads.

Jackson chuckled. "We both know you ain't gonna kill us. Rebel leader would've ordered you to keep us alive for leverage."

"Fuck off."

Whatever was going on above them sounded like pure chaos. Shots rang out in quick succession, the ceiling above their heads vibrating as footsteps traveled over it.

Seth joined in Jackson's laughter, his gray eyes dancing. "Looks like your sniper didn't do such a good job keeping 'em off the sub."

Another round of gunfire erupted from beyond the door, followed by a familiar voice shouting, "Clear!"

"Uh-oh, I think Duke's out of the game," Jackson said cheerfully.

A second later, the metal door flew open and more shots exploded in the air.

Lancelot managed to get off two rounds before he was KIA, lowering his weapon in defeat as Dylan and Matt O'Connor stormed the cramped space in strategically sensored wetsuits and armed to the teeth.

"You boys all right?" Matt drawled, his shaved head gleaming beneath the fluorescent light fixture.

"Peachy," Seth said sarcastically.

Matt touched his earpiece and barked out a report. "The little birdies are back in the nest. I repeat, birdies back in the nest."

Their comrades wasted no time cutting them free. Jackson

rubbed his aching wrists, then cursed when he saw the flash of blue on Dylan's thigh.

"You've been hit. Femoral artery," he muttered. "You've got three minutes before you bleed out, man."

Dylan sighed. "Do your thing, then."

Jackson was already ripping off his belt. Same as he would have done if this were a real op, he went through the process of applying direct pressure on Dylan's "wound" and fashioned a tourniquet to stop the bleeding. No way of knowing if Dylan would lose the leg, but the sooner they got out of there, the better the man's chances.

"C'mon, let's jump ship," Matt said briskly, his eyes and weapon trained on the door. "The corridor is wired with C4 and one of the Eighters managed to detonate half that shit before McCoy took him down. The entire lower level is in flames."

The four of them raced to the doorway, Dylan playing his part to a T by limping on his "injured" leg. Jackson shouldered the other guy's weight, breathing hard as he lugged nearly two hundred pounds of muscle toward the exit point. Matt took the lead, MP5 locked and loaded, then swore and touched his earpiece.

"Shit. Fishing boat is officially rubble at the bottom of the ocean. That was our ride home."

"Orders?" Seth asked, holding the weapon he'd taken from Lancelot, whose "dead" body was still in the other room.

"Little Mermaid it to the secondary rendezvous point," Matt answered. "Looks like you're swimming with a bum leg, Wade."

"Wonderful," Dylan mumbled.

Jackson knew the physical activity was bound to exacerbate Dylan's injury. He wasn't wrong—five minutes after diving off the sub and hitting the water, Dylan's vest buzzed and the sensor over his heart turned red.

"Goddammit!" he yelled in aggravation.

Jackson, who'd been dragging his teammate through the cold water, released him with regret. The waves instantly bobbed around the blond man, whose expression conveyed sheer annoyance illuminated in the moonlight.

A speedboat carrying Team Eight's CO swiftly cut through the water and slowed beside them to haul Dylan on board.

Jackson kept going, his arms aching as he swam fast and hard, several yards behind Matt and Seth. It was a three-mile swim in the dark ocean, which sucked ass considering his arms had been tied behind his back for the last several hours. And the saltwater stung his scraped-up wrists, which just pissed him off.

By the time he and his teammates reached the rendezvous— a low-lying black Zodiac that'd been dropped from the chopper earlier—he was thoroughly exhausted. But at least he was alive. He and Seth exchanged grins while the raft sliced through the waves and the wind slapped their faces.

Seth glanced over at Matt with a nod. "Damn good job," he shouted over the wind.

"Not good enough," Matt shouted back. "We lost a man."

Seth waved a hand. "Ah, it was just Dylan. Nobody's gonna miss him."

But when they reached the base a short while later, the deep scowl on their CO's face told them he agreed with Matt on this one.

"How the fuck did we lose Wade?" Becker demanded as they hopped out of the Zodiac.

The rest of the team was gathered nearby, including Dylan, who seemed to be taking a lot of heckling about his grisly demise.

Matt shrugged. "Lancelot is damn quick on the trigger. We couldn't have done anything differently."

"We'll see about that," Becker muttered. "Unload your gear. Debrief in ten minutes."

As the CO stalked off, Jackson ran a hand over his wet hair and let out a weary breath. He was so dang tired he was ready to crash, but he had plans with Mia tonight and he refused to miss out on the chance of seeing her. He'd definitely have to chug a cup of coffee or two before he left the base.

"I can't believe I died." Dylan sidled up beside him on the way into the building. "You suck as a medic, Texas. You fucking suck."

He rolled his eyes. "I'm not God, man. Here's a tip for next time: don't get shot in your femoral artery."

"I'll keep that in mind."

Dylan's strides were scarily energetic as the two men strode down the hall. "Wanna go out for a beer?" he asked with a hopeful look. "I already asked everyone else but they all pled exhaustion, even the supposed party dudes on Team Eight."

Jackson stared at his teammate. "How the heck are *you* not exhausted? I'm frickin' beat."

"It's all the sex I'm not having," Dylan said gloomily. "Has me wired."

"Sorry, but I can't. Mia's coming over around eleven to hang out."

"Why so late?"

"She had to go to Chula Vista for her brother's game, so she won't be back 'til later."

"It's only nine," Dylan pointed out. "Plenty of time for us to chill and still get you home before Mia shows up."

He hesitated.

"C'mon, don't make me go back to my empty condo yet." Dylan gave a mock pout. "Have some pity, bro."

After a beat, he surrendered with a tired chuckle. "Fine. I'll go out for a beer with you."

Mia couldn't remember the last time she'd had such a wonderful, stress-free day. She'd spent her morning at the nursery picking up plants for the waterfront park project, her afternoon working in the sun, and her evening in Chula Vista for Danny's first away game of the season. She'd watched Danny lead his team to another victory, crushing their opponent and officially putting the Warriors on a three-game winning streak. To top it all off, her boss had phoned during halftime to say she wanted to meet on Monday regarding the possibility of Mia taking over the San Diego location of Color Your Yard.

And now she was on her way to Jackson's house, about to finish off her day with some incredible sex.

Go, me!

She was smiling like a goofball during the entire drive to Imperial Beach, unable to remember the last time she'd felt this content. The only downside was that she couldn't stay at Jackson's for too long because she was working at the sandwich shop tomorrow morning. But not even the thought of waking up early could put a damper on her high spirits.

She doubted *anything* could spoil her good mood—or at least that's what she thought before her phone buzzed.

When she read Jackson's text informing her that Dylan would be hanging out with them tonight, a burst of disappointment went off in her chest.

So much for incredible sex.

She stifled a sigh, forcing herself not to message him back. She was almost at his house, anyway, and she knew she'd look like a total brat if she cancelled their date just because sex was no longer on the table. Besides, she'd really enjoyed Dylan's company last week, so hanging out with the charming blond SEAL wouldn't exactly be a chore.

And maybe a sex break wasn't such a bad thing. It was beginning to trouble her how addicted she'd become to these bedroom games with Jackson. A fun, platonic night might do her some good, clear some of the overpowering lust that had been fogging her brain for weeks now.

She arrived at Jackson's place a few minutes later and discovered that his truck wasn't in the driveway. But the little house was lit up like a Christmas tree. She wrinkled her forehead. His message had stated that he was home. Where was his pickup?

When Jackson opened the front door to let her in, Mia had her answer. He was clearly drunk, or at the very least, tipsy. He wasn't slurring or stumbling, but his slightly flushed face and bright eyes told her he'd had a few drinks.

"Hey," she said. "Where's your truck?"

"I had to leave it at the bar. We cabbed it here because I was too loaded to drive. Guess that's what happens when you down three beers on an empty stomach."

She frowned. "When was the last time you ate?"

"We just had some leftover pizza now. Before that...I dunno...since nine a.m. maybe?"

"You didn't eat a thing all day and night?" she gasped.

"We were a little busy, darlin'."

She was about to ask what had kept him so busy he'd forgotten to eat, but a voice from the living room interrupted her.

"Is that Mia?" Dylan called in delight. "Get in here, honey! I haven't seen you in ages!"

She had to laugh as she followed Jackson into the living room. She didn't bother reminding Dylan that they'd only met a week ago. She just returned the big hug he gave her and then joined him on the couch while Jackson went to the kitchen to grab her a drink.

It wasn't long before her disappointment about not being alone with Jackson disappeared. Jen was right—Dylan was the most charming guy Mia had ever met, and for the next fifteen minutes he chatted away and regaled her with funny anecdotes that had her in fits of laughter. Jackson had returned by then, flopping down beside her, and Mia found herself sandwiched between two drunk SEALs.

The TV was on, but the three of them didn't pay much attention to it. Easy conversation flowed between them, eventually landing on the one subject Mia had been desperately curious about.

"Claire and Aidan come home on Sunday." Dylan's face shone with excitement.

"Nice. Does that mean you're finally gonna shut up about how you're not gettin' any?" Jackson cracked.

"Nah, I'll just start babbling about how *much* I'm getting."

Mia met Dylan's eyes, a tad hesitant. "So you're in a committed relationship with two people, huh?"

"Yep."

"A permanent threesome."

"Yep."

"How does that work?" she demanded. "I mean, do you have sex with one person one night, and the other the next night?"

Dylan snickered. "Why would I do something so boring? It's all three of us, every night." He paused. "Well, unless one of them isn't in the mood. Then it's one-on-one, with Claire or Aidan watching. Or if I'm not feeling it—which is rare—I'll just watch the two of them get it on."

The craziest rush of heat traveled through Mia's body and landed right between her legs. Before she could stop it, the thought of Dylan in bed with a woman and another man flew into her head, followed by the wicked image of him in a chair while his two lovers fucked each other in front of him.

That the idea turned her on beyond belief confirmed what she'd already started to suspect: she was a dirty, dirty girl. Which totally explained why she'd never enjoyed sex in the past. Her previous sexual encounters had taken place in a bedroom, one-on-one, missionary all the way with the occasional her-on-top thrown into the mix.

But Jackson had introduced her to a whole new world. Dominance, spanking, toys, unbelievable oral. And who could forget the very first time she'd gone out with him, when he'd brought her to climax in the middle of a parking lot? Afterward, she'd realized that the risk of getting caught had contributed greatly to the explosive orgasm she'd had that night, and ever since then she'd started to anticipate her encounters with Jackson. It thrilled her, never knowing what he had in store for her. And she couldn't deny that she loved the way he ordered her around, not to mention his complete lack of inhibition.

Clearly Dylan was equally uninhibited, because for the next ten minutes, he explained—in great detail—the mechanics of having sex with more than one person. By the time he hopped off the couch to use the bathroom, Mia was squirming on the cushions, so turned on she could barely breathe.

Jackson, of course, wasted no time commenting on her agitated state.

"Ah, sugar, you're as red as a tomato." He slid closer so he could put his arm around her shoulder. "You like hearing Dylan talk about his sex life, eh?"

She sighed. "If I say yes, will you punish me for it next time I see you?"

He nipped her ear with his teeth. "Damn right I will. You know how much I love punishing you."

When he sucked gently on her neck, she shivered and tried

to pull away. "Don't start anything you can't finish," she warned. "Dylan will be back any sec."

"Don't care. I'm drunk 'n horny and I wanna kiss you."

His mouth found hers, and despite the fact that they had company, Mia was helpless to stop the kiss. Her lips parted to grant his tongue access, and another shiver danced along her skin when she tasted the alcohol on his lips.

"I'm sorry I sprung Dylan on you tonight," he said when he pulled back. "I know you wanted us to be alone, but he was just so miserable. All the other guys bailed on drinks and he would've had to go back to an empty house..." Jackson shrugged. "I felt bad for the guy."

She smiled. "It's all right, I really don't mind. He's fun to be around."

"Thanks for being so understanding." He offered a smile of his own before leaning in to kiss her again.

His spicy, masculine scent surrounded her. She breathed him in, loving that intoxicating fragrance. Loving the way his tongue swirled over hers, the warmth of his hand on her hip, the scrape of his stubble against her cheek.

It took all of her willpower to end the kiss, but she did so with a groan. "Jackson, we can't—"

He cut her off with another liplock. This one hotter, deeper, and accompanied by his big hands sliding underneath her shirt to cup her breasts.

She squeaked in protest, but his touch felt so good she didn't put up much of a struggle. Instead, she let him fondle her aching breasts for several seconds and tried not to moan when he pinched her nipples through her bra.

They needed to stop. She knew that. Or at least, her brain knew it. Her body had other ideas. It melted into him, tingling and quaking as Jackson devoured her mouth.

"Ahem."

They broke apart at Dylan's loud interjection and found him standing in the living room doorway, his eyes twinkling.

"Ah, sorry," Jackson said sheepishly, then offered the same excuse he'd given her earlier. "Three beers on an empty stomach. Y'know how it is, bro."

Mia's cheeks were scorching, but the pang of embarrassment did nothing to diminish her arousal. She was still turned on.

And from the looks of it, so was Dylan.

There was no mistaking the bulge in his khakis, or the flare of heat that ignited his expression.

"I have two questions," Dylan finally said. "One—are the two of you really gonna fool around right there on the couch?"

Mia's face went hotter. She opened her mouth, armed with an apology, but Dylan didn't let her voice it.

"And two—can I watch?"

CHAPTER
TWELVE

Jackson had been friends with Dylan for a long time, which meant he possessed the ability to know exactly when his friend was joking around—and when he was dead serious.

Right now?

Dylan was dead serious.

Leaning against the doorframe with a boner in his pants and lust in his eyes, the guy sought out Jackson's gaze and lifted one eyebrow.

Jackson's first instinct was to say "heck no," but the look on Mia's face stopped him. She was blushing like crazy, yes. Squirming with discomfort, definitely.

But her eyes flickered with undeniable interest.

He couldn't even say he was surprised. Mia had proven to be the most open-minded woman he'd ever been with. She gave him free rein of her body, agreed to every wicked request, and he knew she loved exploring this new adventurous side she'd always denied having.

"Voyeurism turns you on," he said slowly.

The flush on her face deepened. "I don't know. Does it?"

His gaze landed on the rigid nipples poking through her shirt. "Yeah, I think it does. I think you want Dylan to watch us."

Her pulse jumped in the hollow of her throat. "I...don't know."

Her gaze moved to Dylan, who eyed her expectantly.

"You're in a relationship," she sputtered. "Claire and Aidan will probably be furious if you..."

"If I what? Watch porn?" Dylan shrugged. "'Cause this would be the equivalent of that, and trust me, they have no issues with me jerking it to outside entertainment."

Mia still looked hesitant, which prompted Dylan to grab his phone from his pocket. He dialed as he strode toward them, put it on speakerphone, then sank down on the armchair opposite the couch and held up the phone.

After three rings, a happy female voice answered. "Hey, babe, what's up?"

"Hi, honey," Dylan greeted his girlfriend. "Is Aidan around?"

"Yeah. He's sitting right beside me."

Claire McKinley's voice held a note of mischief, leading Jackson to suspect that Dylan's lovers were doing a lot more than "sitting."

"Do me a favor, Claire-Bear, and put me on speaker so I can talk to you both."

A second later, Aidan's deep voice rumbled over the line. "Everything okay, man?"

"Yeah, I'm fine. I just had a quick question for you guys." Dylan glanced over at the couch with a faint smile. "Hypothetically speaking, would it be cool if I watched Texas and his girlfriend fool around?"

There was a loud snort. "Hypothetically, or, *happening right now*?" Claire demanded.

"Definitely hypothetical at the moment, with a fifty percent chance of becoming reality," Dylan said cheerfully. "Thoughts?"

The utter absurdity of the request made Jackson grin, which then caused him to question why the heck he was even cool with this. He'd always made an effort to keep his sex life private. Hadn't accepted any threesome invites from the guys, didn't talk about what he did behind closed doors. And yet here he was, entertaining the idea of letting his buddy witness him getting intimate with Mia.

Maybe the alcohol he'd consumed was affecting his judgment.

Or maybe Mia's desire for exploration had rubbed off on him.

Either way, his dick was rock-hard beneath his jeans, and the heat rushing through his veins had nothing to do with alcohol. He wanted to fuck Mia. Right here, right now. He didn't give a damn if he had an audience. All he knew was that if he didn't get inside his woman soon, he was gonna go crazy.

"Well," Claire said, sounding pensive, "I know how miserable you've been since we left. I guess you deserve to have a little fun."

Jackson's grin widened when he heard Mia's breath hitch.

"You should jerk off if it's cool with them," Aidan said graciously. "It's no fun watching and not getting off."

"Oh, and memorize every inch of Texas's body," Claire chimed in. "And then describe it to me later. I'm dying to know what he looks like naked."

"Fuck, me too," Aidan said instantly. "I bet he's hung like a stallion."

Now Mia's entire body vibrated with laughter, prompting Jackson to glare at her. Claire and Aidan had no idea he and Mia were listening in, and their interest in his dick made him feel...weird. And...well, he'd be lying if he said it didn't inflate his ego. Just a bit.

"So yeah, we're cool with it," Claire told her boyfriend. "But no touching. You can put your hands to good use when we get home."

Dylan was practically glowing. "Deal. Love you guys. See you Sunday."

After he disconnected the call, he gave a smug look and said, "See? It's all good."

Mia resumed her fidgeting.

"What do you say, sugar?" Jackson asked in a rough voice. "Feel like putting on a show?"

"I..." She licked her visibly dry lips. "Um...I...damn it, just fuck me already!"

Her outburst made both men chuckle. Jackson searched her gaze once more, needing to know she was fully committed. He saw in her smoldering eyes that she was.

She wanted to do this.

So did he.

Fuck if he could figure that one out.

Awareness sizzled in the living room, so hot and thick that Jackson's throat turned to sawdust. His erection strained against his zipper, demanding attention. Craving release.

A glance at Dylan's lower body confirmed that the guy was suffering the same discomfort. But Dylan didn't move a muscle, didn't blink, not until the silence dragged on, at which point he finally flashed Jackson a deep smirk.

"Well, *dang*, Texas," he said mockingly. "What are you waiting for?"

Not one to back down from a challenge, Jackson smirked back.

And unbuckled his belt.

Mia's heart stopped. It literally stopped in her chest, coming to a grinding record-screeching halt as Jackson undid his jeans. She couldn't believe this was happening. Dylan was sitting five feet away, and Jackson was taking off his pants.

She blinked a few times to make sure she wasn't imagining it, but nope, he was actually shoving his jeans down his legs. Kicking them away.

Reaching for the waistband of his boxer-briefs.

Tugging on it.

When his dick was revealed, Mia wasn't the only one who moaned.

In the armchair, Dylan's eyes had grown heavy-lidded. "Jesus fucking Christ, Texas," he hissed out. "I really want to suck your cock right now."

Another anguished moan slipped out of Mia's mouth.

Dylan responded with a rueful laugh. "I'm sure the idea turns you right on, honey, but you heard the mister and missus. I'm not allowed to touch."

He groaned suddenly, alerting her attention to the fact that Jackson was now stroking his erection.

"Goddammit," Dylan swore. "Why didn't I know about that piercing, Texas?"

Jackson chuckled and rubbed the silver ball bearings with his thumb. "'Cause I never participated in any of your orgies." He gave his cock a firm pump. "And don't you worry about not being able to suck me off. Mia knows exactly what to do. Don't you, sugar?"

She'd barely managed a nod when she found herself being yanked off the couch and onto her knees.

Jackson released a hoarse groan the second her lips clamped around him.

So did Dylan.

She took him in deep, just the way he liked it, then shifted slightly so she could look at Dylan. Her pulse burst into a gallop when she noticed that he'd unzipped his pants and pulled out his dick.

Oh Jesus. He was sitting there stroking himself, his sultry gaze glued to the sight of his friend's erection buried inside her mouth.

The pressure between her legs became unbearable. Her entire body was so hot and tight she felt like she was going to explode. Sucking Jackson's dick never failed to evoke that same response, except tonight the sensations were amplified. Tonight she was being watched as she performed the erotic act, and damned if that didn't flood her with excitement.

She flicked her tongue over his piercing for a few languid moments, then sucked on his tip and whimpered when a salty drop infused her taste buds. His fingers tangled in her hair, stroking gently as his low murmur of encouragement filled the room.

"That's it, sugar, nice and slow tonight. If I fuck your mouth hard I'll come, and I don't wanna come anywhere but inside you."

Mia continued to tease him, alternating between slow, soft licks and long, deep pulls. As she skimmed her tongue along the underside of his shaft, her eyes met Dylan's, who was watching her attentively. Her gaze lowered to his cock, long and hard and oozing with precome. Her inner muscles clenched almost painfully.

Without looking away, Dylan stroked himself faster, a satisfied smile tugging on his lips.

"Baby, I think it's time you got naked," Jackson rasped. "Up you go."

She was suddenly hauled onto her feet, while his hands

whipped her thin blue shirt up and over her head. He moved behind her to flick the back clasp of her bra. When it popped open to reveal her breasts, she was standing directly in Dylan's field of vision, offering him a perfect view of her chest.

Dylan still didn't say a word, but his nostrils flared as he gazed at her. His hand slowed down, working his cock in a leisurely tempo.

"I love these tits," Jackson muttered, reaching around so he could cup them with his warm hands.

He pinched both nipples, unfazed that his friend's eyes were following his every movement. Then those talented hands drifted down her belly and hooked beneath the waistband of her leggings, pulling them off right along with her panties. He straightened up, one hand finding a breast again, the other gliding over her mound before he parted her folds with his fingers and rubbed her clit with his thumb.

"Spread your legs wider, darlin'." His hot breath tickled the side of her throat as he nuzzled her sensitized skin. "Let him see your pretty pussy."

Mia knew she was blushing like crazy. She also knew that the second she widened her stance, Dylan would notice the moisture dripping from her core and sticking to her thighs.

But she'd already discovered that she couldn't say no to Jackson Ramsey, and so her legs parted of their own volition, officially putting her on display to the SEAL in front of them.

Dylan sucked in a breath.

"She's dripping wet, ain't she?" Jackson chuckled. "Yeah, she gets very wet when she's excited, right, sugar?"

"Y-yes," she breathed.

The expression on Dylan's face grew tortured. He finally broke his silence. "Damn those assholes for laying down the law. I want to join in so fucking bad."

Jackson's thumb grazed her swollen clit. "Wouldn't let you

even if you could," he told his friend. "This pussy belongs to me."

"No prob. I would have just fucked your ass instead."

The mocking words summoned another moan from Mia's lips, and another laugh from Jackson. "Jesus, man, you really are a manwhore. Don't care where you stick your dick as long as it's warm and deep."

"And tight," Dylan added with a grin. "Don't forget tight."

Laughter wafted all around her, but the moment of light-hearted banter didn't last. Jackson was suddenly spinning her around, arranging her body so that her torso was draped over the arm of the couch, her elbows on the cushions and her ass at level with his groin.

A quiver of anticipation traveled through her as Jackson came up behind her and ground his dick against her ass cheeks. She heard a rustling sound, and twisted her head to see him peel his shirt off his broad shoulders, leaving him bare-chested.

God, that chest. Golden skin and sculpted muscles, a feast for her eyes. And his cock...he'd gripped it with one hand and was rubbing the tip over her asshole.

She held her breath, shaking. Was he going to take her anal virginity right here in front of his friend? She wasn't sure if the idea thrilled her or scared her, but he quickly squashed the notion by driving inside her pussy with one fluid stroke.

She gasped when he filled her to the hilt. Groaned when he rotated his hips and allowed his piercing to stroke her inner walls.

Her gaze found Dylan's again. The glazed passion in his eyes robbed her of breath.

"You like watching him fuck me?" The breathy question popped out before she could stop it.

Surprise washed over his face, rapidly replaced by a glint of fire and a seductive grin. "Damn right," he murmured, squeezing his erection with his fist.

Jackson ran his hand over her buttocks, a thoughtful note entering his voice. "You know, I think your ass looks so much prettier when it's bright pink and trembling after I've smacked it."

She swallowed a laugh when she saw Dylan's eyebrows shoot up. "Damn, Texas, you're into spanking?"

Jackson drew his hips back. "Damn right," he said, mimicking Dylan's earlier response. "And Mia loves getting spanked, isn't that right, darlin'?"

He thrust his hips again.

"Yes," she cried out.

"What other secrets have you been keeping from us?" Dylan's voice sounded hoarse, and he was pumping his cock furiously as he watched the scene before him.

Rather than answer, Jackson fucked Mia harder, his breaths growing more and more shallow with each stroke.

The angle caused him to hit a spot deep inside her, making every inch of her throb. She was perilously close to toppling over the edge, but she tried to hold off, to milk every ounce of pleasure out of this experience. Since she couldn't see Jackson's face, she indulged herself by looking at Dylan. His features were stretched taut, and the sound of his hand jacking his cock matched the slap of Jackson's flesh against hers as he moved inside her.

"Gonna come soon, Mia," Dylan mumbled. "But I wanna hear you scream first."

"Easy peasy," Jackson drawled, and then he reached around and rubbed her clit in a circular motion that had the desired cry ripping out of her throat.

The orgasm sent her soaring. Black dots flashed in front of her eyes, clearing up just in time to see Dylan lose control.

Strands of come splashed the front of his boxers as his gaze locked with hers.

When Jackson groaned and went still, her pussy spasmed, gripping him firmly as his hot release filled her.

Her cheeks grew warm with embarrassment once the after-effects of orgasm retreated. Feeling self-conscious, she wasted no time getting dressed, which was silly considering what just happened in the living room.

Was it wrong that she'd derived so much pleasure from the experience?

The doubts swirling in her mind were familiar. She'd questioned herself this very same way after previous sexual encounters, back when she'd wondered if she suffered from some kind of sexual dysfunction.

Had she traded one deficiency for another, though? Absolute disinterest for depraved perversions?

Her worries eased, however, when Dylan spoke up. "It's cool if I describe all this to Claire and Aidan, right? Because they're gonna make me recap it in great detail when I'm screwing them tomorrow."

A laugh lodged in her throat. Well, if she was a depraved perv, at least she wasn't the only one in the bunch. Dylan's reminder that he was routinely sleeping with both a man and a woman was enough to make her realize that in comparison, her sex life was probably still as boring as it used to be.

Jackson put on his pants before wandering over to her with a gentle smile on his face. "You good?"

"I'm good," she murmured.

"No regrets?" He had to bend over so he could whisper the question in her ear.

Shaking her head, she slowly met his eyes. "None."

CHAPTER THIRTEEN

"You're panicking. Don't intentionally ground the ball unless you're a hundred percent sure that some sneaky defenseman isn't gonna snatch it up." Jackson voiced the advice to Mia's younger brother, who'd screwed up another practice play and was now grumbling with irritation.

The two of them were tossing a football around in the grassy field behind Mia and Danny's building until Mia got home from her shift at the Sandwich Stop. Jackson had already been on his way when she'd called to say she was running late, but fortunately Danny had been home to let him in. They'd started watching a college game on TV, during which Danny had confessed he was having trouble making split-second calls under pressure, so Jackson suggested they head outside and go over some plays.

Truth was, he genuinely liked spending time with Mia's brother, something he'd done a lot of these past two weeks. He'd been in the stands when the Warriors had won another game, then consoled the kid when the team lost their next one. He'd had dinner with the Weldricks on two separate occasions. And he and Mia had even gone to see a movie with Danny and his girlfriend the other night, a romantic comedy that made the girls cry.

Earlier today Jackson was startled to realize he'd been seeing Mia for more than a month. It was already the first week of October, and he couldn't believe how fast the time had passed. Not that he was complaining. He loved spending time with Mia. It was all he looked forward to when he was running training missions on the base, and he knew she felt the same way.

The only problem? She continued to refer to their relationship as a "fling," a label that didn't sit right with him. This thing between them had moved way beyond a fling for him.

Mia was the one.

Call him foolish or naive, but after a mere five weeks, Jackson knew with bone-deep certainty that Mia was the woman he was meant to be with. She was so dang smart, so incredibly generous. She made him laugh, she challenged him, she rocked his world in bed. If he could wake up to her gorgeous face every morning for the rest of his life, he'd consider himself the luckiest man in the world.

He was in this for the long haul. Like, forever type of shit. And though he desperately wanted Mia to be on the same page, he suspected she wasn't. And that troubling notion was beginning to keep him awake at night.

Danny's voice interrupted Jackson's train of thought. "I didn't see the sweatshirt." The boy gestured to the bright red hoodie that sat on the grass twenty yards away, serving as one of their open receivers. "I didn't think there would be an eligible receiver there when I grounded the ball."

"Always be aware of your surroundings," Jackson said sternly. "You've gotta keep your eyes open, kid."

"I know."

"C'mon, let's practice ball protection. This time I'll sack you for real and we'll see if you can hold on to the pigskin."

Danny eyed him dubiously. "You planning on coming at me full-strength?"

He chuckled. "Of course not. I've got five inches and forty pounds on you. I'd frickin' kill you."

They got into position, squatting so Jackson could snap the ball into Danny's waiting hands. The second Danny straightened up and got ready to throw, Jackson assumed the role of defenseman and launched himself at the boy.

The two of them hit the ground with a loud thud. Jackson's body landed squarely on the kid, and he immediately redistributed his weight so he wasn't crushing him to death. Despite the heavy hit, Danny kept a protective grip on the ball. His eyes sparkled as he hopped to his feet.

"Nice job," Jackson said proudly.

"Thanks. Let's do it again. There's no way I'm fumbling the ball again like I did during that last game."

The intensity on the teenager's face sparked Jackson's admiration. Mia's brother had focus and determination, two qualities that Jackson greatly appreciated. He suspected that Danny Weldrick would land a scholarship to any school of his choice. The boy was serious about going pro, and worked his ass off for it.

After they ran the same drill a few more times, they called it a day and wandered through the field retrieving the various placeholders they'd laid on the grass. Jackson was just picking up the last marker—an empty Gatorade bottle—when Danny approached him with a hesitant look.

"Hey, can I ask you something?"

Jackson tucked the bottle under his arm along with the two sweatshirts he'd collected. "Sure."

"So next week the team is heading up to Irvine for the weekend," Danny started. "We play a game on Friday against the Devils, then this charity game on Saturday as a joint fundraiser type of thing."

"Okay..."

He waited for Mia's brother to continue, but the kid didn't say a word. He just stood there fidgeting with the sleeve of his white T-shirt.

"Whatcha waiting for?" Jackson said with a laugh. "Spit it out already."

Danny's cheeks flushed with embarrassment. "'Kay, well... here's the thing. I—"

He stopped talking when a familiar blue pickup sped into the parking lot.

"So?" Jackson pressed.

The teenager shrugged. "Forget it."

Clearly Danny didn't want to talk in front of his sister, who'd just parked the pickup and was hurrying toward them.

"Hey!" she said breathlessly. "I'm so sorry I'm late. Bill and Wendy asked me to stay late and clean out the freezer, and it took a ridiculous amount of time. Did you guys already have dinner?"

"Yup," Jackson answered. "But we left you a plate in the fridge."

Her eyes flickered with gratitude. "Thank you. I'm starved." She glanced at the football in his hands. "Are you two ready to go inside or are you still playing?"

"Nah, we're all done, sugar."

The three of them entered the building through the back doors. They'd just reached the third floor landing when Danny's phone chimed.

He quickly checked the screen before looking at his sister. "Braden and the guys are going to this all-ages club in the Gaslamp tonight and they want me to come. Is that cool?"

She narrowed her eyes. "How will you be getting there?"

"Sean's getting his mom's car. And you know he's a good driver—you forced him to take you around the block after he got his learner's permit," Danny said with a pointed stare.

"I had to make sure he wasn't going to kill you!" she protested.

"Anyway, they wanna pick me up in an hour. Can I go?"

It didn't take long for Mia to cave. "Fine, you can go. But you have to be home by curfew, and if you see one of the bartenders serving minors, I want you to leave the club immediately. Oh, and don't you dare try to con someone to buy you alcohol or I'll kill you."

Danny just laughed and darted toward the stairwell door.

"You know you can't stop him and his buddies from getting loaded," Jackson murmured as they trailed after Danny. "Teenage boys are gonna experiment with booze sooner or later."

"Not on my watch," she vowed.

He grinned. "Good luck with that."

Mia instantly disappeared into the kitchen to warm up her dinner while her brother sprinted down the hall to shower and change before his friends showed up. Jackson wandered into the living room and channel-surfed for a bit, then chatted with Mia as she flopped down beside him to eat. She didn't stay long, though—the second Danny came out of the bathroom, she left to take a shower of her own, leaving Jackson to his own devices.

He felt unbelievably content lying there on Mia's couch. The apartment had such a homey feel to it, reminding him of his family's ranch house. You could always feel the love when you walked into his childhood home. At least before the rift that had torn him and Shane apart.

But he refused to let himself dwell on that situation. It was over and done with, couldn't be changed. What he needed to focus on was the present, and when Mia returned a little while later and curled up beside him, that sense of joy only intensified. He stroked her hair, twining one silky strand around his finger, enjoying the steady beating of her heart against his chest.

Danny popped back into the room almost an hour later, took one look at them, and made a gagging noise. "Can't you two cuddle somewhere else?"

Mia snickered. "Says the guy who was making out with Angie on this very couch last night."

"We wouldn't have to make out on the couch if you hadn't enforced your crazy keep-the-bedroom-door-open rule," her brother retorted.

"Don't you have somewhere to be?" she grumbled.

"Yep." He grabbed his letterman jacket from the armchair. "Later, Jackson," he said as he headed for the door.

"Goodbye to you too, Daniel!" Mia called out after him.

Jackson couldn't help but laugh. "You two kill me. Are you ever not bickering?"

"Not really. It's kind of our thing." Grinning, she sat up and tucked her hair behind her ears. "Hey, listen, so I wanted to ask you for a favor."

"I'll do it," he said instantly.

A laugh flew out of her mouth. "You haven't even heard what it is yet!"

"Fine, I'll humor you. What's the favor?"

"Danny's going to Irvine next weekend with the team. The game is on Friday night."

"Yeah, he mentioned that."

"Well, you know I usually go to all his games, right? But I just found out I have to work at the sandwich shop on Friday right after I finish up at the park." She nibbled on her bottom lip in dismay. "I promised myself I wouldn't miss a single one of his games, but I could really use the money, so I told Wendy I'd work that night."

He raised himself into a sitting position and touched her cheek in a reassuring caress. He knew how hard Mia worked to support herself and her brother, and he wished she didn't have to struggle so much. At the same time, he admired her for it. The woman was so amazing. She'd sacrificed everything for that kid—her privacy, her freedom, her love life. She juggled two jobs in order to take care of him, and no matter how stressed out or tired she was, she was always sitting there in the bleachers every Friday night to cheer her brother on.

"I was wondering if maybe you could drive up and be there for the game," she finished. "You wouldn't have to stay the weekend—the charity game isn't important. I mean, it *is* important for whoever they're raising money for, but Friday's game is the one that counts for the team's standings. So...yeah...do you think you'd be able to go in my place?"

"Of course."

His swift reply brought a big smile to her face. "Really?"

"Absolutely." He stroked her chin with his thumb. "I consider it my boyfriend-ly duty."

Her smile instantly faded. "Oh. Um."

He narrowed his eyes. "What?"

"Boyfriend, huh? Is that what you are?"

"We've been seeing each other for over a month. What else do you wanna call me?"

"I don't know." She gave a helpless shrug, her features lined with discomfort. "I guess I didn't think about...I mean...nothing's changed, Jackson. You know that, right?"

"And what does that mean?"

She bit her lip again. "I told you from the start I didn't want a serious relationship."

He nodded. "Because you were too busy. But far as I've seen, we're not having any trouble making time for each other."

"I know. But...look, it's not only my schedule. I just don't see a relationship in my future."

He frowned. "A relationship with me?"

"With anyone."

Her answer threw him for a loop. He didn't know what to say to that, and his silence had Mia hurrying on.

"I love having sex with you. I really, really love it," she said, her green eyes shining earnestly. "And I want to keep seeing you."

"But?"

"But I don't believe in forever." Her voice grew pained. "Relationships don't last. They always end eventually, and I promised myself a long time ago that I wouldn't put myself through all that sadness and heartbreak. I love being with you, but I'm always going to keep you at a bit of a distance. I know that's a shitty thing to say, but I'm honest to a fault, you know that."

He did know that, and her candid nature was one of his favorite things about her.

What he *hadn't* known was just how deeply her mother's actions had affected Mia. Because clearly this was all about Mia's mother and her countless divorces. He didn't need to be a shrink to figure it out, but he was surprised it had taken him this long to connect the dots. It made sense, though. If one of his parents had been married *nine* times, he'd probably have a skewed view of relationships too.

He wished he could make Mia see that just because her mom hadn't been in a lasting relationship didn't mean Mia wouldn't either, but he wasn't about to push her. Not now, anyway. She was one of the most strong-willed women he'd ever met, and she spooked faster than the skittish pony he'd ridden as a kid. If he put too much pressure on her, she'd bolt and he'd never see her again. Which meant he had to tread lightly from this point on.

"Hey, don't look so upset," he said roughly. "I'm not trying to force you into anything. All I'm sayin' is, we've been together for almost six weeks. There's really no harm in calling each other boyfriend and girlfriend, is there?"

She seemed flustered. "I guess not. But...the future..."

"Let's not worry about the future, sugar. All that matters is the present. As for the rest, we'll see where it goes. No pressure, no demands."

"And you're okay with that?"

"Yeah, I am."

"You're not harboring any grand illusions about falling madly in love with me?"

He supposed now was probably not the best time to tell her he was already halfway there.

So he just shrugged. "Like I said, we'll see where it goes."

"Okay." She paused. "Can we stop talking about all this serious stuff? Let's do something fun."

He raised a brow. "What do you have in mind?"

"I don't know. It's Saturday night—should we go out?"

"And not take advantage of this empty apartment? I don't think so."

Without delay, he scooted closer and covered her mouth with his.

She let out a delighted squeak before kissing him back eagerly. Her arms looped around his shoulders, warm fingers stroking the nape of his neck as her tongue met his.

Jackson never wanted the kiss to end. She tasted so sweet, and her hair, damp from the shower, smelled like roses and lavender and something uniquely Mia.

He was breathing heavily when he pulled his lips back an

inch and echoed her earlier words. "So you really, really love having sex with me, huh?"

"Like you didn't already know that."

"What do you love the most?" He planted his mouth on the side of her neck and sucked.

"Everything. I love everything you do to me."

"You like the way I boss you around?"

"Mmm-hmmm."

"And the way I make you come?"

"Definitely that."

He pushed her back against the couch and reached for her waistband. "What about the way I eat your pussy? Do you like that?"

She shivered in anticipation. "Duh."

He eased her yoga pants off her legs.

And discovered that she was completely nude underneath.

"No panties," he muttered in approval. "Aren't you a dirty girl."

She laughed ruefully. "I can't afford to wear underwear anymore. You keep ripping every pair I own."

"Can't help it." He smacked a kiss right on her belly button. "I love your pussy so much I can't bear to see it covered up all the time."

He was slow and thorough, teasing her with featherlight licks to her clit and fleeting openmouthed kisses to her inner thighs. Her skin was so soft and silky that he couldn't help but rub his stubble-covered cheek against it, leaving pink marks on her thighs before kissing his way back to his favorite place in the world.

When he captured her clit between his lips, she jerked on the couch and cupped his head to keep him in place. But he wasn't going anywhere. He welcomed the tight grip in his hair and started licking with gusto, his tongue exploring every inch of her wet paradise. The second it speared her entrance, she cried out and rocked into the gentle thrusts with abandon.

"*So* good," she burst out. "Keep doing that."

He gave his woman what she wanted, fucking her with his tongue while his thumb feathered over her clit. But just as she reached the brink, he retreated, lifting his head so rapidly she groaned in disappointment.

He stood up and held out his hand. "C'mon, we need a bed."

"Why?" Her eyes burned with impatience. "We seemed to be doing just fine on the couch."

"You arguing with me, sugar?"

Her mouth snapped closed.

"That's what I thought."

Chuckling, he scooped her into his arms and marched toward the corridor. Mia started kissing his neck as he carried her to the bedroom, momentarily distracting him. He groaned when she sucked hard enough to leave a mark, then gave her bottom a sharp smack and deposited her on the bed.

"Enough teasing," he said sternly.

The mattress bounced as she landed on it. She wasted no time parting her legs.

"Make me come," she ordered.

A laugh rumbled out of his chest. "Someone's bossy tonight."

"And *someone* is a tease. You knew I was close and you purposely stopped."

"I did indeed." He licked his lips. "But that's 'cause you're not allowed to come yet."

He walked over to the nightstand and opened the bottom drawer, while Mia craned her neck to try to see what he was getting.

"When am I allowed to come, then?" she demanded.

His hand emerged with a condom and a tube of lubrication. "When I'm balls-deep in your ass."

Her swift intake of breath made him laugh again.

"Got a problem with that, baby?"

She shook her head, wide-eyed.

"Good. Now roll over."

She shifted onto her hands and knees in an impressive display of speed. Grinning at her eagerness, Jackson started to undress. One-by-one, items of clothing fell to the floor, until finally he stood there naked, his erection rising to slap his abdomen.

"You don't know how sexy you look right now." His gaze swept over her, lingering on her firm, round ass.

Saliva filled his mouth, while a different kind of moisture seeped out of his cockhead. He reached down and rubbed the precome over his piercing, anticipation building in his balls.

After he'd sheathed himself, he slathered the condom with lube and climbed onto the bed so he could prepare Mia. She shuddered when he drizzled the warm lubrication between her ass cheeks.

"I've never done this before." Her wobbly whisper echoed in the air.

"I know," he said gruffly. "If you don't like it, I'll stop, okay?"

She exhaled slowly. "Okay."

He teased her puckered hole with his fingers, getting them nice and wet before he slipped them through the tight ring of muscle.

"Oh *fuck*," they mumbled in unison, then laughed.

"You good, darlin'?" he asked in concern.

"Uh-huh. You?"

"Oh yeah. You're so tight. I can't wait to slide my cock inside."

He pushed his fingers in and out, stretching her, getting her ready for a much thicker, much bigger intrusion.

Her soft moans told him she enjoyed every second of this, and when his fingers traveled south to explore her pussy, he discovered she was wetter than ever.

"Gonna fuck you now," he rasped. "I need you to relax for me."

The moment his dick prodded her ass, he felt her tense up instinctively.

He stroked her lower back. "Relax and breathe, Mia."

She took a breath, and he saw the tension leave her body like air seeping out of a deflating balloon. This time he managed to get the tip in, just a small, erotic inch that brought a fierce groan to his lips. Lord, it felt like a hot vise around his dick. He pushed in deeper. Her muscles clamped around him even tighter. His cock started throbbing like a motherfucker, engorged to the point of bursting.

He was never gonna survive this. The pleasure was too unbearable.

Slow and steady, he worked himself inside. Caressing her hips, murmuring encouragement, stopping every few seconds to give her time to adjust. By the time he was buried to the root, his chest was soaked in sweat and his balls ached as if he'd been celibate for twenty years.

"Feels good," she whispered. "Go faster now."

He drew his hips back, plunged in again, and almost lost his load. "Fuck," he mumbled. "This is gonna be fast. I'm dying here."

The evil woman took that as permission to bear down on him, and the tip of his cock dang near blew right off. Screw it. There was no way to pace himself, no possibility for a nice, slow ride. As stars floated in front of his eyes, he began to fuck her tight heat with fast strokes that made the entire bed shake.

Her moans bounced off the walls, the sweetest sound he'd ever heard in his life. Somehow, despite the white haze drugging his senses, he managed to reach beneath her so he could strum her clit with his fingers.

The second he made contact, she reared like a filly in heat and came hard.

And just like that, he was a goner—her full-body orgasm sent him right over the edge.

His pulse roared in his ears as red-hot pleasure consumed his body, sizzling him from head to toe until he was nothing but a limp, sweaty mess unable to support his own weight.

He wasn't sure how long it took for the body-numbing sensations to ebb. Minutes. Hours, maybe. All he did know, as he rolled them over some time later and held her tight, was that this girl was his. They belonged together.

And sooner or later, he was going to make her see it.

CHAPTER
FOURTEEN

"Okay, here's the next one—Jennifer Lawrence, Jennifer Aniston and Jennifer Lopez," Cash said from the driver's seat of his black Ford Escape.

Dylan, who was sandwiched in the back between Seth and Mia's sleeping brother, piped up with a grin. "Easy. I'll field this one. I'd fuck J-Law, marry J-An and kill J-Lo."

In the passenger seat, Jackson cringed as yet another F-bomb was dropped. Though it wasn't much of a surprise considering they were playing a game called Fuck, Marry, Kill.

He really didn't like exposing Mia's little brother to his filthy-mouthed buddies, but fortunately Danny was sound asleep, eyes shut and head resting on the window.

Jackson still wasn't sure why Danny had decided not to ride up to Irvine on the bus with his teammates. When the kid asked if he could drive up with Jackson and the guys, who'd all demanded to come along, Jackson had readily agreed. He got the distinct feeling that Danny had something on his mind—the teenager had started half a dozen conversations this past week, only to clam up before revealing what he'd wanted to talk about in the first place.

Jackson wondered if it had something to do with Mia and Danny's mother, but so far, the kid wasn't sharing. He'd hoped that Danny might open up during the drive, but the boy had fallen asleep within minutes of sliding into the backseat.

"That's your answer? Really?"

Jackson glanced over to see Cash furrowing his dark eyebrows as he questioned Dylan's response.

"I'd do that completely differently," Cash said. "Marry J-Law, fuck J-Lo and kill J-An."

In the rearview mirror, Jackson saw Dylan's jaw fall open. "How dare you. Do you realize how much Jennifer Aniston has suffered? The woman is a saint and she deserves a big fat ring on her finger."

"If you say so." Cash rolled his eyes before focusing back on the road.

Rather than take the freeway straight up to Irvine, Cash had decided to treat them to the scenic route, though Jackson suspected it was just an excuse for the guy to use the new fancy-pants navigation system he'd installed in the SUV last month.

"This game sucks," Seth griped. He was sitting next to Dylan in the backseat. "It's more fun when you actually know the people involved."

"Fine." Jackson lifted one eyebrow in challenge. "Here's one for you, smartass. Jen, Claire and Holly."

"I swear to God, Masterson," Cash said in a warning tone, "if you choose to kill my girlfriend, I'll break your fucking neck."

"And I'll choke you out if you pick Claire," Dylan added ominously. "For any of them."

"You win, Texas," Seth said darkly. "I can't answer that."

Jackson had to laugh. "Coward."

"Oh come on, like *you'd* have the balls to make a choice?"

"I'd marry 'em all," he said solemnly. "Because they're all wonderful, upstanding women who deserve to be worshipped."

Dylan nodded in approval. "Good answer, bro."

"I thought so."

"How about this one?" Seth challenged. "Me, Dylan and Cash. Go."

Jackson twisted around to smirk at the dark-haired SEAL. "Easy. I'd fuck Cash, marry Dylan and kill you."

"Ha ha." Seth flipped up his middle finger. "And just so you know, you ungrateful bastard? I would've picked *you* to marry."

"Who would you have killed then?" Cash asked curiously.

"Sorry, man."

Cash looked outraged. "*Me?*"

"What can I say? I suspect Dylan gives really good head," Seth replied.

"I do," Dylan confirmed. "Aidan can vouch for that."

"Wait—*what?*"

The disruption came from Mia's brother, whose eyes had flown open to reveal a look of surprise.

Jackson turned to glower at the kid. "Ah, for chrissake, you've been awake this whole time?"

Danny offered an impish smile. "Kinda."

Great. Mia would murder him if she knew he'd allowed her brother to eavesdrop on a convo involving fucking and killing female celebrities.

Some role model *he* was.

"Not a word about this to your sister," he told Danny, shooting him an I-mean-business glare. "And pretend you never heard any swearing."

"You got it." The teenager glanced at Dylan, his expression lined with hesitation and undeniable curiosity. "Are you gay?"

Dylan donned a deadly scowl. "So what if I am, homophobe?"

Danny immediately backpedaled. "What? No! I'm not a homophobe! I don't care about that kind of stuff, seriously, I don't. I mean, if a guy wants to do another guy, then why shouldn't—"

"Relax, kid," Dylan interrupted with a laugh. "I'm just messing with you. And to answer your question, I'm not gay. I'm bi."

"Oh. Cool, I guess. So that means you—"

Pop!

A loud noise rocked the SUV, bringing a curse to everyone's lips.

Panic flooded Danny's eyes. "What happened?"

"Tire blew," Seth answered grimly.

Cash effortlessly steered onto the gravel shoulder of the road, his features glittering with annoyance. "Goddamn it. This is just what we need."

"Are we gonna miss the kickoff?" Danny sounded even more panicked now.

Jackson glanced at the clock on the dashboard. "Nah, we'll be fine. It's only six. Kickoff isn't 'til seven thirty. We'll make it."

"Yeah, don't worry about it," Dylan assured the young quarterback. "We're only twenty minutes away. We'll change the tire quick-fast and be driving again in no time."

"Come on, let's do this shit." Cash flicked on the emergency blinkers, then hopped out and slammed the door behind him.

Stifling a sigh, Jackson got out and rounded the vehicle, loitering near the trunk as Cash opened the compartment that housed the spare tire.

A very loud, very angry expletive roared out of Cash's mouth.

"What's up?" Frowning, Seth drifted closer and peered into the trunk. "Aw, shit. Are you fucking kidding me, McCoy?"

Jackson finally released that sigh. The spare tire was flat.

Fuckin' hell.

"Dude, you're a United States Navy SEAL," Seth taunted. "How could you leave the house without checking your spare?"

"I checked it a few days ago," Cash retorted. "And it was just fine."

"Clearly not, idiot."

Mia's brother raked his hands through his hair, looking upset. "Should we call roadside assistance?"

Every man wrinkled his brow.

"What for?" Cash asked in bewilderment.

"Um, to get a tow to a garage so we can fix the tire?"

Cash shrugged. "We passed a body shop a while back."

"But that was like six miles ago."

"Kid, you're with four guys who can run a four-minute mile. We can get there and back in less than an hour, change the flat, and be at the Irvine field long before kickoff."

"We?" Seth echoed. "Dream on, bro. Your car, your fault. Later, McCoy."

Cash's hopeful eyes shifted to Dylan. "Wade, wanna come along?"

"Yeah, right. See ya, Cash."

"Texas?"

"Heck no."

Cash's broad shoulders sagged in defeat. Sighing, he shrugged out of his long-sleeve shirt and tossed it to Dylan. "Here, put this in the car. I don't want it to get all sweaty."

"Holy crap, you're *ripped*," Danny said in awe, his gaze fixed on Cash's chest.

"And stalling," Seth added. "Move your ass, McCoy."

"Fuck. Fine."

They watched as Cash took off in the direction they'd come from, his scuffed-up Timberlands kicking up dust and gravel as he sprinted away.

"Is he really going to run twelve miles?" Danny exclaimed.

Jackson laughed. "Nah, probably just the six. I'm sure he'll be able to catch a ride back with someone at the shop."

They wandered to the side of the vehicle that wasn't facing the road. As Jackson and Dylan leaned against the SUV, Seth reached into his pocket and pulled out a pack of Camels.

Danny eyed him in disapproval. "You smoke cigarettes?"

"No, I just hold them in my hand to look cool," Seth cracked as he lit up a smoke and blew a cloud into the early evening air.

The sun hadn't fully set yet, but it was dipping closer and closer to the horizon, giving the sky a pinkish-yellow glow and reflecting off the orange grove that dominated the landscape about a hundred yards from their car.

They waited around in silence for a few minutes—Seth smoking, Dylan checking his phone, Jackson worrying. Because if he didn't get Danny to the game on time, Mia would be furious at him. Heck, he'd be furious at himself. He genuinely liked the kid, and wanted nothing more than for Danny to have a long and successful football career.

But Danny didn't seem to have football on the brain as he approached the three SEALs, his body language conveying nervous reluctance.

"Hey, can I ask you something?"

Here we go again.

Jackson suppressed a groan. He'd been dancing this same dance with the boy for days, so he knew all the moves by now.

"Of course," he said aloud, all the while praying that Danny would finally spit out whatever was on his mind.

"It's kinda personal."

"Do you want us to leave?" Dylan offered, already starting to move away.

"Nah, it's cool if you guys stay." The teen shifted his feet. "Uh, anyway..."

They waited.

He didn't continue.

Jackson let out the groan he'd been holding back. "Seriously, kid, you've gotta stop doin' that. Just say it alrea—"

"Angie and I are going to have sex this weekend!"

The outburst was followed by crashing silence.

Tread very, very lightly, the voice in Jackson's head warned.

Shit. He should've known this had something to do with sex. Danny was a sixteen-year-old kid with no father figure, and as much as the boy loved his sister, Jackson knew Danny wouldn't feel comfortable discussing such an awkward topic with her.

"Okay. Well." He cleared his throat. "Have you ever slept together before?"

Danny shook his head.

"Have you ever done it at all?"

Another quick shake.

"Okay." Discomfort climbed up his spine. "Uh...shit, Danny. I can't give you advice about sex. Your sister would strangle me."

This time Dylan cleared his throat. Very loudly. "Texas?"

"Yeah?"

"Sidebar."

Jackson found himself being dragged away by Dylan and Seth, who didn't speak until they were well out of Danny's earshot.

"What the hell do you mean you can't give him advice?" Dylan hissed.

"Are you serious?" he hissed back. "Mia would freak out if she knew I was encouraging her little brother to fuck his girlfriend."

"He doesn't need encouragement," Seth said, rolling his eyes. "The kid's clearly got his mind made up. He's banging that girl no matter what you tell him."

"At least if we talk to him about it beforehand, we can prevent any disasters," Dylan said. "I mean, what if he doesn't use a condom? Someone needs to give him the safe-sex talk."

Seth nodded gravely. "Think about it, Texas. What'll make Mia angrier? You giving practical sex advice to her brother, or said brother coming home with an STD or a knocked-up girlfriend?"

Uneasiness continued to flow inside him, but he couldn't deny his buddies had a point. A teenage boy could be dumb as a bag of rocks when it came to sex. Without guidance, Danny might do something seriously stupid.

"Fine," he finally mumbled.

The trio strode back to the waiting teenager, who rolled his eyes at their approach. "Are you done freaking out?"

Jackson ignored the quip and crossed his arms over his chest. "So is this for real? You're actually gonna do this?"

Mia's brother nodded.

"What method of birth control are you planning to use?"

A blush stained the boy's cheeks. "Angie's on the pill."

Seth narrowed his eyes in suspicion. "Did you know that it takes a month before the pill is effective?"

"Yeah, I know. She's been on it for three months just in case." The flush deepened. "And I have condoms. We're going to use those too."

"Good boy," Dylan said in approval.

"What exactly are you concerned about then?" Jackson asked carefully. "It sounds like you've planned ahead and you're being smart about this."

Danny sighed. "It's not the safety part I need advice on. It's the...uh...mechanics."

Son of a bitch.

Jackson got uncomfortable all over again, and from the corner of his eye he saw his friends fighting back laughter.

"I mean, obviously I know what goes where," Danny hurried on. "I'm not an idiot, and I've watched porn before, so..." He released another breath. "I'm just worried about her, you know? I wanna make her feel...um...good. And I...I just wanted some tips on how to do that."

Jackson exchanged a look with Dylan and Seth, who were waiting for him to take the lead. But no way could he do that. Danny might have made up his mind about losing his virginity this weekend, but Jackson couldn't allow himself to high-five the kid for it.

Preaching safe sex was one thing, handing out sex tips was another altogether. Mia was insanely protective of her little brother. She'd never forgive him if he endorsed Danny's foray into the world of underage intercourse.

"All right, I guess I'll be fielding this one," Seth said when Jackson didn't speak up. "Uh..." His voice became gruff. "Okay. So. The vagina is a mysterious garden that—"

Seth didn't get to finish the thought because Dylan had keeled over in a fit of laughter.

"Oh fuck!" Dylan choked out, clutching his side. "Shit, I can't believe you said that." Another laughter-induced shudder overtook his body, tears forming in his eyes. "Oh sweet Jesus, I think I just pissed my pants."

Seth glared daggers at his teammate. "As I was saying," he said loudly, his gaze shifting back to Danny. "The vagina is a mysterious garden that requires a lot of tending. You work in landscaping, right?"

Danny nodded.

"So then you know that you can't just throw any old soil down and then wait for flowers to grow. You need to water them, give them enough sun, play with them for a bit. Oh, and you definitely have to go down on them."

"Are we still talking about flowers?" Danny said in confusion.

"We were never talking about flowers, dumbass." Seth let out an exaggerated sigh. "Texas, you take over. I'm all metaphored out."

Despite the misgivings coursing through him, Jackson joined the conversation. Heck, he was already in this deep. At this point, he couldn't imagine how his speaking up could make things any worse.

"What this moron is trying to say is that you can't make the sex entirely about you," he explained. "You've gotta think about the lady's pleasure first and foremost. Which means a helluva lot of foreplay."

Dylan, whose laughter had finally died, spoke up enthusiastically. "Lots of foreplay."

Danny bit his lower lip. "Like oral and stuff?"

Seth gave a decisive nod. "Oral, petting, dry-humping, finger-blasting—"

Jackson silenced him with a glare.

"We've done some of that already," Danny confessed, averting his eyes. "I mean, we haven't gone down on each other, but the rest—"

Jackson swiftly held up his hand. "Oh Lord, please don't give me any details," he pleaded. "Look, just remember that you can't snap your fingers and expect a woman to have an orgasm. You've gotta warm her up, get her nice and primed for it."

"And you can't expect her to come every time," Dylan piped up. "And especially not the first time."

Danny tilted his head thoughtfully. "My health teacher said if a woman has an orgasm every single time you have sex, she's probably faking a lot of them."

"Probably true," Seth said with a shrug. "Chicks are

different from men, dude. According to my wife, it takes a lot of 'mental energy' to come."

"So she doesn't, um, come every time?" Danny said shyly.

"There are times when she doesn't come at all, and other times when it happens more than once. But she's always into it, no matter the final result."

Danny looked ready to ask another question, but Jackson quickly redirected the conversation before the teen could ask him—God forbid—about his and Mia's sex life.

Because that would just be wrong.

"Here's another tip," he said. "This applies to the first time, and whenever else you think it's necessary, but jerking off an hour or so before sex is recommended."

"Definitely," Dylan agreed.

A crease dug into Danny's brow. "Why?"

"Because you're a virgin," Seth answered with a laugh. "The moment you see your girl naked for the first time, you'll be a stroke away from exploding. Which means you'll last thirty seconds, forty at the most."

"If that," Jackson said wryly.

"Which pretty much guarantees she won't get much pleasure out of the experience. So yeah, yank it beforehand," Seth advised. "Release all the pent-up energy, and then when you're getting it on, you'll impress her with your crazy stamina."

"But...what if I don't come a second time?" Danny asked in concern.

The three of them stared at him.

"Dude. You're sixteen years old." Seth rolled his eyes. "Trust me, you'll come again."

CHAPTER
FIFTEEN

It was nice having some time to herself. Mia loved her brother to death, but she had to admit that she missed waking up to a quiet, empty apartment. She'd lived on her own before Danny had moved in, and sometimes she longed for those days. Back then she'd had the freedom to do whatever she wanted. Sleep in until noon, stroll around naked if she felt like it, eat cold pizza for breakfast if the urge struck.

Being a parent involved rules and schedules, not to mention a total lack of privacy, so she treasured this feeling of liberation as she rolled out of bed on Sunday morning and headed to the bathroom to wash up.

The only downside was that she and Jackson hadn't been able to take advantage of her first teenager-free weekend in ages. Jackson had been in Irvine on Friday watching the Warriors win yet another game, and the following night he'd gone to the rehearsal dinner for a teammate's upcoming wedding, Ryan something or other. He'd apologized profusely for not being able to invite her since it was a wedding-party-only event, but Mia was slightly relieved to be excluded.

Truth was, she was still troubled by the way their relationship was progressing. She hadn't dreamed she'd still be seeing Jackson after six weeks. And when he'd referred to himself as her boyfriend she'd experienced a sense of panic that had stuck with her.

As much as she loved being with him, she worried that she was starting to care for him a little too much. He was on her mind more often than not, and the level of anticipation she felt about seeing him was kind of terrifying.

Was she falling in love with him?

The idea scared her to death. She couldn't let herself fall for him. That would only make it a million times worse when the relationship eventually ran its course. Because it would. Something this good couldn't possibly last, and when it reached its inevitable end, she refused to be left brokenhearted and destroyed.

She forced the disturbing thoughts from her head as she wandered into the kitchen to fix herself some breakfast. She was grabbing a carton of eggs from the fridge when a knock sounded on the door.

Sighing, she set the carton on the counter and left the room, wondering if Danny was back early and had forgotten his key. But if that was the case, she knew he would have texted to give her a heads-up. Ditto for Jackson, who was too polite to stop by unannounced. Which meant that the person on the other side of that door was most likely some rude jerk who'd decided to bother her at nine o'clock on a Sunday morning.

Times like these, she really wished her front door had a peephole, but the people who'd put up this building had been too lazy to install one. Frowning, she left the chain on and opened the door a crack so she could peek out.

Her blood ran cold.

"Mia!" Her mother looked overjoyed. "Baby, hi! It's so good to see you!"

Her jaw clenched so hard her teeth rattled. "What are you doing here?" she demanded, her tone icy and unwelcoming.

Brenda's expression filled with hurt. "I told you I was coming to San Diego for a visit."

"Yeah, last month. And surprise, surprise, you never showed."

"I couldn't get time off from work. I tried, I really did, but it didn't work out. Luckily, I had this whole weekend free so I'm finally here!"

Mia made no move to slide open the chain. She just stared at her mother suspiciously. "If you had the whole weekend off, why are you here today, on Sunday, instead of coming earlier?"

"I was visiting a friend in LA."

Disbelief coated Mia's throat, making it impossible to speak. Her mother had made such a big stink about wanting to see her kids, yet when the opportunity finally arose, she chose to visit a *friend* first? The woman wasn't going to win any Mother of the Year awards, that was for sure.

"Are you going to let me in?" Brenda asked with a loud sigh.

Mia studied her mom's appearance, noting that in the two years since they'd seen each other, Brenda had changed—and aged—considerably. She'd gotten some blond highlights in her brown hair, which looked incredibly tacky paired with her dark eyebrows. She also had a whole lot of new wrinkles around her eyes and mouth, and her petite frame now packed at least twenty extra pounds.

Just seeing her again sparked a flash of fury in Mia's belly. Her hand actually tingled with the urge to slap her mom in the face, and the fact that she was tempted to commit violence only angered her more. Brenda was the only person on this planet who evoked this much rage inside her. The woman was toxic, and Mia didn't want anything to do with her.

"Sorry, but you wasted a trip," she said coolly. "Danny's not home, and I'm on my way out."

Disappointment flooded her mom's expression. "When will he be back?"

"Tomorrow morning," she lied. "He's on a school trip."

"And you?"

Her voice was curt. "Late."

"Oh. I see." Brenda's bottom lip trembled. "I won't be here tomorrow. I'm heading back to Reno this evening."

"Darn. What a shame."

The two-inch crack in the door offered a clear glimpse of the tears that welled up in Brenda's eyes.

"I know you're mad at me, baby, but I really wish you'd let me in so we could talk this out."

"There's nothing to talk about. You left, end of story. And just in case you've forgotten, this isn't the only time you deserted us so you could run off with some worthless piece of shit who meant more to you than your own kids."

Her mother's tears kept falling, but Mia refused to be conned.

"So if you want to talk to someone, go back to Reno and talk to your husband," she finished angrily.

Brenda sniffed. "I don't have a husband. I'm single again."

Despite her better judgment, Mia narrowed her eyes and said, "You and Stan got divorced?"

"Stan?"

Her mom's confusion caused a wave of hysterical laughter to bubble in her throat. "*Stan*," she repeated. "You know, the husband you abandoned Danny for two years ago?"

"Oh. Right." Brenda visibly swallowed. "We split up not long after the honeymoon."

"Shocking." Mia gritted her teeth. "Just for my own sick curiosity, how many times have you been married since?"

There was a beat. "Just once."

The laughter spilled out, a high-pitched sound laced with desperation. "For fuck's sake, Mom. That makes ten now. I think that's a new record."

"Mia—"

"I have to get dressed," she snapped, her fingers trembling over the doorknob. "Go back to Reno. We're doing perfectly fine without you, and we don't want to see you, so don't bother coming back here."

"Mia—"

She closed the door and flicked the deadbolt, then sagged against the wood and sucked in a few shallow breaths. She knew her mom was still standing in the hall. She could sense her.

God, she wanted her to go away. To disappear off the face of the Earth.

Mia's heart ached as if someone had stabbed it with a dull knife, throbbing even harder when she heard soft sobs coming from the corridor. It took some serious strength of will not to throw open the door and comfort her mother. But she was done taking care of Brenda. Done wiping away her tears and dragging her out of bed whenever her latest divorce sent her spiraling into a black hole of depression. Done paying all the bills after Brenda got fired from yet another job because she blew off her shifts to fuck around with her boyfriends.

There came a point in a person's life when he or she had to learn to take care of themselves. Mia was the child, damn it. Her mother should have been taking care of her, not the other way around.

She blinked away the hot sting of tears. Held her breath. Waited. When she finally heard the footsteps retreating from the door, she exhaled in a hasty whoosh and started to cry.

DANNY STRODE THROUGH THE DOOR SEVERAL HOURS LATER with a spring to his step and a broad smile on his face. He'd never looked happier, and he surprised the hell out of Mia by giving her an enormous bear hug when he saw her.

She pasted a smile on her face, trying hard to share in his joy, but their mother's visit continued to play over in her mind like a shitty pop song. It was hard to convey enthusiasm for the Warriors' latest win when she couldn't stop picturing Brenda's devastated expression as Mia slammed the door on her.

But she couldn't let herself feel guilty about what she'd done. Her mother was a poison that killed everything in its path. She'd never cared about her children, only herself, and they were better off without her.

Mia clung to that reminder as she listened to Danny describe every single play of Friday night's game. She was tempted to cut him off and tell him about Brenda's appearance on their doorstep, but she resisted the urge. The best course of action was to keep Danny in the dark and forget that Brenda had ever been here.

"Wow," she remarked when her brother finally stopped babbling. "You really are happy about this win."

He blinked. "Yeah. Right. The win. I'm psyched about it."

"Do you think the team will make the playoffs?"

"If we keep playing this way, then for sure we will." He beamed. "You know the Warriors haven't made the playoffs in *four* years? And now not only will we get there, but everyone's saying we can actually win state."

"That's because your quarterback rocks." This time her smile wasn't forced, but bright and genuine. "So what's your plan for today? You're not working, right?"

"Leon gave me the weekend off."

The shit-eating grin never left Danny's face, making Mia wonder if he might be on drugs. But no, his pupils looked fine, and he was speaking in coherent sentences. Must be the leftover high from his win.

"Ang and I wanted to do something outdoors today," Danny added. "'Cause it's such a nice day."

"Do you need me to drop you guys off somewhere?"

"Nah, Angie's sister is giving us a ride." He paused. "We might walk around the harbor, or maybe go to the beach."

"Sounds like fun. Jackson's coming over later, around six. We were going to grab dinner at Tonio's. Do you and Angie want to come with us?"

"Probably, but I'll check with her. Her parents might want her to have dinner at home tonight since she was away all weekend."

There was an odd flicker in his eyes, but Mia couldn't decipher it. So she just shrugged and said, "All right, well, call me later and let me know."

"Cool beans." Danny bounded toward the hallway. "Gonna shower and get ready. Ang will be here soon."

Mia watched him hurry off. She'd never seen him so euphoric about a game before, which made her wonder if there was more to his happiness than met the eye.

A rush of suspicion suddenly coursed through her veins.

Had their mom somehow made contact with Danny?

Was that why he was in such a good mood?

She prayed that wasn't the case, but she wouldn't put anything past her mother. For some reason Brenda was determined to reunite with her children, particularly her son, and she was manipulative enough to use Danny's teenage naiveté to wrangle her way back into their lives.

The notion was maddening. It stayed with Mia all afternoon, bothering her so much that it was the first thing she brought up when Jackson arrived at the apartment later that evening.

"Do you think Danny's seen our mother?"

Shrugging out of his black Windbreaker, Jackson wrinkled his forehead, his whiskey eyes reflecting bewilderment. "I don't think so. Why do you ask?"

She chewed on the inside of her cheek, barely returning the soft kiss he gave her as he joined her on the sofa. Not even his handsome face or the ripped arms poking out of his sleeveless shirt could distract her from her troubling thoughts.

"She was here this morning," Mia confessed.

"Seriously?"

"Yes," she said flatly. "She just showed up on my door and demanded to be let in. Apparently she went to LA to visit a friend, and, I guess as an afterthought, decided to come see her kids. Oh, and she's divorced again."

"From the man she ran off with two years ago?"

"Nope, a different guy. Marriage and divorce number ten."

"Whoa." Jackson dragged his hand over his jaw, which boasted a five-o'clock shadow that normally would've made Mia's heart pound. "So what does she want from y'all? Just to catch up?"

"I have no fucking idea what she wants. She claims she misses us, but that's total bull. She's been AWOL for two years, not a goddamn word from her. So why now? What could she possibly want?"

He reached out and took her hand. "Maybe she wants to reconnect with her children."

Mia snorted.

"Maybe she woke up one morning and realized how badly she screwed up, and now she wants to make amends."

"Well, if that's what it is, then she's a little too late." Her teeth sank into her bottom lip. "I'm scared she might have made contact with Danny. He was super happy when he got home today—I half expected him to burst into song or something. I've never seen him smile so hard."

Jackson's hand stilled for a second before resuming its stroking of her knuckles.

"He's always made excuses for her," Mia went on. "Even after she deserted him, he refused to admit what a horrible person she is. What if he met up with her behind my back? What if—"

"He didn't."

She glanced at him in surprise. "How can you be certain of that?"

"Because I'm pretty sure I know why your brother is smiling like a fool and walkin' around like the big man on campus."

Wariness circled her spine, especially when she noticed the sheepish look on Jackson's face. "What's going on?"

He hesitated.

"Tell me."

His chest rose as he inhaled deeply. "Okay, promise not to freak out—"

Her lips puckered in a frown. Any conversation that started with 'promise not to freak out' was bound to end poorly.

"—but I'm ninety-nine percent sure your brother lost his virginity this weekend."

She gasped. "What? Are you kidding me? How do you know?"

The guilty flicker in his eyes was all the answer she needed.

"He *told* you?"

"Not after the fact. But he asked for my advice beforehand," Jackson admitted.

Her jaw dropped, then slammed shut as her lips tightened in a thin line. It was a few seconds before she could speak again. And when she did, it came as an explosion of accusation.

"And you didn't talk him out of it? You just gave him the go-ahead to have sex?" Her chest clenched with resentment. "He's sixteen years old! He's too young to be having sex! Why didn't you try to stop him?"

Jackson answered in a calm, even tone, unfazed by the indictment. "There was no way to stop him, short of tying him up, sugar. Trust me, I was a teenage boy once. All those lectures about abstinence went in one ear and out the other."

"Did you at least *try* to talk him out of it?"

"No."

Mia stumbled to her feet. "I can't believe you encouraged my little brother to have sex!"

"I didn't encourage a thing. He'd already decided to do it before he spoke to me, and nothin' I could've said was gonna change his mind."

She spoke through gritted teeth. "But you didn't even *try*. You say you're my boyfriend, right? Well, my boyfriend would have tried to stop my brother from making the biggest mistake of his life."

Jackson had the nerve to smile. "Believe me, Mia, having sex for the first time won't be the biggest mistake of his life. And as I recall, didn't you lose your virginity at sixteen too?"

"Yes," she grumbled, "but I was very mature for my age."

"Bullshit. You were a horny kid, just like Danny." Jackson's features hardened. "And I find it mighty insulting that you're laying the blame for this at my door."

He was right. Rationally, she knew it wasn't his fault—Danny's hormones were to blame—but she couldn't seem to stop herself from lashing out at Jackson. She was still on edge from the encounter with her mother, but Brenda wasn't here, and neither was Danny, and Mia's anger and frustration needed a target.

Unfortunately, that target was Jackson.

"I think you should go."

His mouth fell open. "Are you kidding me?"

"I'm not in the mood to hang out tonight," she said tersely. "I need to be alone right now."

"Mia. For fuck's sake. Look, I'm sorry I didn't hogtie your brother and throw him in the back of my pickup to stop him from gettin' busy, okay? But you've gotta face the facts—Danny is growing up. He's not the fourteen-year-old kid who got dropped off at your door anymore. He's becoming a man, and sorry to break it to you, sugar, but sex is a part of that."

She was stunned to feel tears pricking her eyelids. God, she *never* cried, and now she was crying twice in one day.

"Please, just go, Jackson," she mumbled. "I really need to calm down and clear my head, and I can't do it while you're here."

The frustration burning in his eyes was unmistakable, but Jackson was a gentleman to the core, and so he didn't push her the way other men might've done.

Instead, he nodded curtly and stalked out of the apartment without another word.

CHAPTER
SIXTEEN

"Seriously? *This* is the wild bunch we've heard so much about?" Duke smirked and started pointing to each SEAL, starting with Seth and ending with Ryan Evans. "Mr. Married with twins over here, McCoy with the serious girlfriend, LT with the pregnant wife, and Mr. I'm-getting-married-next-weekend. Pansies."

It was Team Eight's last night in San Diego, and the four party dudes of the bunch had finally convinced their Team Fifteen counterparts to join them for a night out. Jackson had initially turned down the invite because he was supposed to have dinner with Mia, but a major hole had opened up in his schedule after she'd pretty much kicked him out.

The last thing he'd felt like doing was going home to an empty house, where he knew he'd end up drowning his sorrows in a bottle of whiskey and stewing over their ridiculous fight. So he'd come to the Hot Zone instead, a nightclub in downtown San Diego, in the hopes that if he was surrounded by his buddies, he wouldn't be tempted to drink himself stupid and show up at the base tomorrow with a massive hangover.

Except the second he'd joined the others by the second-floor railing that overlooked the dance floor, he'd discovered that most of his friends were already calling it a night.

Carson set his beer bottle on the wide iron railing and shrugged in the face of Duke's taunts. "Hey, just 'cuz my wife is pregnant doesn't mean we don't have wild and crazy sex every night. With that said..." He flashed a smug grin, his eyes gleaming in the shadows bathing the club's upper loft space. "It's time for me to go home and do some of that."

Cash, Seth and Ryan followed suit, polishing off their beers in a rush.

"Yeah, I'm outtie too," Seth announced. "My wife is a million times more interesting than you dumbasses."

The foursome bumped fists with everyone and said their goodbyes, then headed for the wrought-iron spiral staircase that led to the main floor.

Jackson and Dylan were the only Team Fifteen members left, though Dylan's presence was unexpected. The guy had barely left the house since Claire and Aidan's return. Jackson hadn't expected to see him tonight. Heck, he hadn't expected to be here himself. All he'd wanted to do tonight was spend time with Mia, but the infuriating woman had sent him away.

And he was real ticked off about it, too. He understood why she felt the need to shelter her kid brother, but she was being naive about the entire situation. Danny was a teenage boy with a serious girlfriend. The two of them would've slept together sooner or later. At least Jackson had managed to drill the importance of safe sex into the kid's head before he went out to do what he'd already been dead-set on doing.

No way was Jackson taking the blame for Danny's decision, and he refused to beg and plead for Mia's forgiveness. As far as he was concerned, she was the one who needed to apologize to him.

"So you're the last two remaining bachelors, huh? Must suck losing your posse."

Team Eight's Max had to raise his voice to be heard over the loud house track pounding out of the speaker system. The flashes of strobe light illuminated his face and revealed the wry look in his blue eyes.

Jackson leaned against one of the floor-to-ceiling beams in the large, open-concept space and brought his beer to his lips. "Actually, Dylan's taken," he said.

"Very taken," Dylan confirmed.

"So that leaves one," Hunter remarked, glancing at Jackson. "You're carrying the torch alone, huh?"

He shrugged. "Not really. I'm kinda seeing someone too."

Or at least he had been, up until an hour ago.

"And he was never much fun even when he was single," Dylan piped up. "No threesomes or fourgies for Texas. He's a total prude."

As the other guys cracked up, Jackson didn't miss the sly grin Dylan shot him. Thankfully, the other man chose not to bring up the voyeur role he'd played in Jackson's living room, proving that he was smarter than he looked.

"So where are your girls tonight?" Lancelot asked.

"Claire's around here somewhere," Dylan responded.

"She is?" Jackson said in surprise. "I didn't see her when I came in."

"She made a beeline for the dance floor the second we got here." Dylan grinned. "You know I don't dance unless I've had at least four beers in me, so she gave me permission to come up here and get loaded first. But I'm sure she'll track me down soon to drag me out there."

Lancelot glanced at Jackson. "What about your lady?"

He slugged back some more beer, hoping the alcohol might lift his spirits. It didn't.

"She's at home," he admitted. "Actually, we got into an argument right before I got here."

"Yeah? What'd you fight about?" Duke asked curiously.

With a deep exhale, Jackson quickly filled them in on everything that had gone down earlier. When he finished, he expected the Eighters to laugh and make light of the situation, but they surprised him by taking it very seriously.

"That's bullshit," Duke declared. "What the hell were you supposed to do, chain the kid up and forcibly keep him away from his girlfriend?"

"That's what I said," he blurted out. "But she thinks I should've tried harder to talk him outta it."

"Bullshit," Max echoed. "You're not the kid's father. Not your responsibility."

"Besides, you can't stop a sixteen-year-old horndog from not acting on all that horniness." Hunter's expression took on a rueful glimmer. "Dude, I've got a thirteen-year-old sister and I'm already dreading the day when some young punk tries to weasel his way into her panties. I'm prepared to shoot him down like a rabid dog."

The resounding laughter was broken by a high-pitched whistle from Duke, whose gaze had focused on the dance floor below them.

"Sweet Jesus, check out that redhead. Dibs," he said immediately.

Every pair of eyes followed Duke's gaze. When Jackson glimpsed the source of the SEAL's admiration, he choked on a laugh.

It was Claire McKinley. And he had to admit, she looked hot tonight. A skimpy cornflower-blue dress hugged her X-rated curves and barely covered her thighs, and the strappy black heels she wore added several inches to her petite frame. With her reddish-brown hair loose and cascading down her shoulders, and her face flushed from the heat of the bodies filling the dance floor, Claire was hands-down one of the hottest girls in the club.

"Sorry, bro, but she's mine." Dylan casually sipped his beer.

"Sure about that?" Duke countered. "Because Mr. Dimples seems to be staking a claim."

Sure enough, Aidan Rhodes had come up behind Claire and was grinding against her ass, his hands taking more than a few liberties as they moved up and down her curvy body. The strobe lights flashed, revealing Aidan's handsome face as he leaned in to whisper something in Claire's ear. She responded with a laugh, then spun around and kissed him.

The Eighters burst out laughing again, but Dylan remained unfazed.

"Oh, don't worry about him," he said with the wave of his hand. "He's mine, too."

Four sets of eyebrows shot up.

"Huh?" Max said blankly.

With a faint smile, Dylan polished off his beer and slammed the bottle on the railing. "Gotta go, boys. I've got two drunk lovers to grind up against."

As the blond soldier headed for the staircase, Jackson noticed the expressions on the other men's faces, and couldn't help but snort.

"He's joking, right?" Hunter said warily.

The question was answered when they all saw Dylan enter the throng of dancers and yank Claire in the middle of a Dylan-and-Aidan sandwich. Her delighted laughter rose over the pounding bass line and drifted up toward them. A moment later, Claire spun around and kissed Dylan with the same degree of passion she'd given Aidan.

"Son of a bitch," Duke muttered.

"So he's doing both of them?" Max demanded, looking impressed.

Jackson nodded. "The three of them are together."

"For fucking purposes?" Lancelot drawled.

"For relationship purposes," he corrected. "It's unconventional, but they seem to make it work."

There was a beat of silence.

Followed by Duke's deep sigh of resignation. "Fine. I take it back. You Fifteeners *are* the wilder bunch."

MIA'S HEART RACED NERVOUSLY WHEN A PAIR OF headlights appeared on the road. She rose from the bottom step of Jackson's porch and peered at the approaching vehicle. The hum of an engine cut through the darkness as his pickup slid into the driveway. Her pulse grew even more erratic

He was home. Finally. She'd worried she might have to wait out here all night.

The engine died abruptly, and then Jackson was striding toward her, his chiseled features creased with unease.

"What are you doing here, sugar?"

She swallowed a lump of guilt. "I came to apologize."

His eyes softened. "How long have you been sitting out on the porch?"

"Three hours." She shot him a sheepish look. "I was on my way over pretty much ten minutes after you left."

"For chrissake. Why didn't you call and lemme know you were here?"

"I did. You didn't answer your phone." She bit her lip. "I figured you were avoiding my calls."

He pulled his phone out of his pocket, checked the screen, and cursed. "It's dead. I didn't even notice." He sighed. "I'm sorry. I wouldn't have stayed out this late if I'd known you were waiting for me."

"Don't you dare apologize," she ordered. "And I'm demanding you retract your earlier apology, too."

His lips twitched. "Oh really?"

"I'm the one who should be saying sorry. I was a total dick to you before."

"Nah, you were just upset. I know you didn't mean to be a dick."

"I didn't, but that's no excuse."

She climbed onto the top step so she could look at him without having to tilt her entire head. When she met his gaze, she hoped he could see the genuine remorse in her eyes.

The wave of shame and guilt had hit her literally two minutes after he'd left her apartment earlier. She hadn't been kidding—she'd driven to his house almost immediately. And the frustration she'd experienced when she'd realized he wasn't there had been twisting up her insides for three very long hours.

"I overreacted," she said quietly. "I was pissed about my mom showing up, and I took it out on you. I'm so sorry for yelling and for accusing you of encouraging Danny. It was never your place or responsibility to talk him out of anything, and I'm sorry for saying what I did."

"Apology accepted, darlin'." His smile was infinitely gentle. "And I'm sorry if I overstepped when I told you how to handle the situation."

"No, you were right. I can't stop him from having sex. All I can do is make sure he's smart and safe about it."

"Which he is," Jackson assured her.

"Then I'm not interfering. And by the way, I'm not going to tell him that you broke his confidence. He doesn't know that I know about him and Angie, and I'm not going to tell him." She felt awkward as she added, "I really do appreciate your being there for him, Jackson. Aside from his coach, he doesn't have any male role models. I know he likes you, and I think you're a good influence on him, I really do."

"Thanks for saying that. It means a lot." Jackson stepped onto the porch, his keys dangling from his long fingers. "You comin' in?"

She searched his gorgeous face. "Do you want me to?"

"Always."

"Then yes, but I can only stay for a little bit. I have to be up early tomorrow."

They walked into the dark house, but rather than switch on any lights, Jackson led her down the shadowy corridor toward his bedroom.

"I keep meaning to ask you..." He paused, looking slightly embarrassed. "What's the deal with your father? You never talk about him."

Sadness jammed in her throat. "That's because I never knew him. He took off when I was four months old."

A groove cut into Jackson's forehead. "Wait, does that mean you and Danny have different fathers?"

"No, we were sired by the same asshole. I know, the ten-year age difference is confusing." She dropped her purse on the floor and plopped down on the edge of the bed. "My dad ran off with another woman after I was born. He was a truck driver, and I guess he was fucking around a lot whenever he was on the road. Mom, of course, was a wreck. Her husband had cheated on her, she was raising a baby by herself, but instead of learning to stand on her own two feet, she immediately went on the hunt for a new man. From the ages of one to ten, I had five different stepfathers."

Jackson joined her on the bed. "And then your father came back?" he guessed.

She nodded. "He waltzed into our lives completely out of the blue. Mom was overjoyed. She hopped right back into bed with him, cheating on her latest husband. But of course, her happiness didn't last." Bitterness burned Mia's throat. "My father didn't say a single word to me in the four days he stayed with us. He just slept with my mom, stole some cash, and ran off again."

"Ah, sugar, I'm sorry." Sympathy hung from his voice.

"Nothing to be sorry about. The man was a total loser—I'm lucky he's not part of my life." She shrugged. "But yeah, Mom got pregnant during their four-day fuckfest, and nine months later, Danny was born." Mia scooted closer and kissed his cheek. "Okay, we're done talking now. I still have some apologizing to do."

"You already apologized," he protested.

"Yeah, but only with words. Now it's time to apologize with actions."

His mouth curved impishly. "I like the way your mind works."

"Thought you would. Now get on your back, *sugar*."

He indulged her, stretching his long, glorious body on the mattress. When she reached for his shirt, he sat up so she could peel it off him, then sank down again and propped his muscular arms behind his head.

Her gaze ate up every square inch of his massive chest. Tight six-pack, sleek sinew, roped muscles. He radiated strength and masculinity, and yet when her fingertips grazed his warm flesh, he quivered beneath her touch. She bent over and kissed him right between the pecs, then skimmed her tongue over one flat nipple.

She took his husky moan as the green light to continue. She explored the small brown disc with her tongue, nibbling on it with her teeth. Then she moved to his other nipple and played with that too, before kissing a path down his hard stomach, her tongue following the line of hair that arrowed into his waistband.

She cupped the bulge in his jeans, and pure feminine power surged through her when he moaned again and thrust into her palm. Normally he had all the control during their encounters, but tonight he'd handed over the reins. And it was so thrilling to have this big, strong man at her mercy.

She squeezed his package, hard, the way she knew he liked it, then undid his Levis and pulled them down his muscular legs. The jeans snagged on his black boots, so she quickly scurried to the bottom of the bed to rid him of them.

Once he was naked, his cock rose up in a plea for attention, harder than granite and oozing with precome. The shards of moonlight entering the room through the cracks in the curtains caught on the silver ball bearings adorning his tip, and the piercing only served as a reminder of how dangerously wicked this man was. On the surface he was the consummate gentleman. Sweet, polite, generous. But in bed he was a threat to her sanity, a demanding, greedy lover who took what he wanted, when he wanted it.

She loved that dichotomy, the delicious knowledge that she knew something about Jackson Ramsey that most people didn't.

"You gonna stare at me all night, or am I gettin' some action?" he mocked.

"I don't know... Maybe I'll just make you lie here and watch you squirm for a bit."

"Nah. You're not that evil." His tongue swept over his lips. "Besides, you're dying to suck my dick."

"Oh, am I?"

"Heck yeah. That's why you can't quit staring at it."

She supposed she could've denied it, but what was the point? They both knew she wanted him in her mouth.

So she took him.

Jackson swore and gave an upward thrust that sent him all the way to the back of her throat. His potent masculine scent captured her senses, coated her tongue, and she desperately wanted to gulp him up. Suck him hard, make him come, and swallow every last drop.

But she didn't.

She was having way too much fun teasing him. It was rare for the tables to be turned, which meant she had to take advantage of his powerless state and drive him absolutely nuts.

She moved her mouth over him, slowly, drawing out each stroke until he was mumbling incoherently, his fists clawing at the bedspread. When her hand found his balls and cupped the heavy sac, he tried to increase the pace, but she simply clamped her lips around his tip and gave it a soft bite of warning.

"Son of a bitch," he ground out.

His groan of pleasure told her he'd enjoyed the sting of her teeth against his sensitive flesh. So she did it again, gently biting the crown of his dick, then soothing it with the rasp of her tongue.

"Jesus, Mia. You're killing me here."

She lifted her head and met his tortured brown eyes. "Payback," she murmured. "For all the times you've done the same thing to me."

Yet for all her brazen threats, she found she couldn't tease him for much longer. Pressure had built in her core, a dull ache that was impossible to ignore. After a few more languid licks, she sat up and ripped her clothes off so fast Jackson began to laugh.

"Somethin' wrong?" he asked innocently.

She wiggled out of her panties and climbed up to straddle him with her thighs. "Shut up," she grumbled. "This is your fault."

"Aw, shucks. What did I do?"

"You cast a spell on me. Your naked body turns me on so much I don't even have the patience to tease it."

His seductive chuckle made her shiver. "Then what are you waiting for? Fuck me already."

Still glaring at him, she rose up, then impaled herself on his rock-hard shaft.

"Fuck," he muttered, his hands immediately landing on her waist. "We fit so well, sugar."

She couldn't argue with that. As her inner muscles stretched to accommodate his size, she was overcome with a sense of completion. That was the only way to describe it. Jackson completed her the way no other lover ever had.

Taking a breath, she started to move.

"Faster," he ordered.

"You're lying on your back while I ride you, and you're still trying to boss me around?"

"Yes." His eyes gleamed. "Now go faster."

"No."

She maintained a leisurely pace and ran her palms over his rigid abdomen. Each stroke caused her clit to brush over his pubic bone, until the sensitive nub swelled to the point of pain. The mounting pleasure made it difficult to go slow—she rode him harder now, watching as his gaze darkened with approval.

"That's it, fuck me." His raspy commands thickened the air. "Squeeze your pussy and bear down on my dick, Mia. Shit, yeah. Just like that."

His hands slid up her body to cup her breasts, and when he pinched her nipples, Mia literally saw stars. It felt so good. *So* damn good.

As the pressure continued to build, she could barely stay upright. Her knees wobbled, her thighs spasmed involuntarily, and eventually she collapsed on top of him, her breasts crushing his chest. He wrapped his arms around her and held her tight as she grinded against his cock. He stroked her back, squeezed her ass, and then, before she could blink, he rolled them over and took control. Plowing into her again and again, hips pistoning, until finally he let out a hoarse cry and came inside her.

Mia didn't come, but she felt sated nevertheless, suddenly realizing that an orgasm wasn't what she'd needed tonight. No, she'd needed to drown in Jackson's endless well of strength, to bask in the soothing comfort and endless support he gave so freely.

He made her feel safe. Like as long as he was around, everything would be okay.

They lay there in a tangle of arms and legs for so long that her eyelids began to droop. Jackson's even breathing and the gentle way he stroked her hair were liable to lull her to sleep, so she planted a kiss on his shoulder and sat up reluctantly.

"I have to go."

He let out a drowsy groan. "Wish you could stay," he mumbled.

"Me too. But I have to drive Danny to school tomorrow morning and then go to work."

Without a shred of enthusiasm, she got dressed and located her purse, which had been kicked under the bed somehow. Jackson stayed completely nude as he followed her out of the bedroom. His hair was rumpled in the most adorable way, bringing a smile to her lips.

After a tender kiss goodbye in the front hall, she stepped into the late-night air, shivering when the cool breeze snaked its way beneath her hair. A moment later, she was on her way home, a rush of tranquility floating through her body and her heart feeling fuller and lighter than ever before.

CHAPTER
SEVENTEEN

Three weeks later

Mia pried her eyelids open as two male voices snapped her out of slumber with their very loud singing.

"What the...?" She sought out the alarm clock, registered that it was eight a.m. and grumbled in disbelief.

Unbelievable. This was the third time this week that Danny had woken up before her, thanks to Mr. Early-Bird Ramsey. Clearly she needed to revoke Jackson's sleepover privileges, pronto. She didn't care that the two guys were bonding. Didn't care that her brother, as it turned out, was amazing at background vocals. Her mornings were sacred, and their noisy renditions of Jackson's favorite oldies songs weren't welcome in her holy ritual of sleeping in until the last possible second.

When it became evident that they weren't about to shut up, she dragged herself out of bed and staggered to the bathroom, griping under her breath the entire time. Fifteen minutes later, she was showered, dressed, and annoyingly alert.

The yummy aroma of bacon and eggs greeted her when she

entered the kitchen. Danny stood by the stove, flipping the strips of bacon sizzling on the pan, while Jackson was at the fridge, his big body hunched over as he searched for something on the bottom shelf.

Mia cleared her throat, prompting both guys to glance over at her.

"Mornin', sugar." Jackson greeted her with a huge smile.

Argh. She wanted to stay mad at them, but the sight of the tall, bare-chested SEAL instantly distracted her. He was barefoot, and his jeans rode dangerously low on his hips. He was so damn gorgeous she had to blink a few times to make sure he wasn't a mirage. Men this sexy didn't exist, did they?

They do, and he's one of them. Just shut up and enjoy it.

She took her brain's advice and stood there admiring him for a moment. For some reason he hadn't shaved or gotten a haircut these past few weeks, so his hair was scruffier than usual and his face sported a full dark beard that gave him a feral vibe.

"C'mere and gimme a kiss," he urged when she hadn't budged from the doorway.

"Gross," Danny announced.

"Oh shut it," she told her brother.

She crossed the small space so Jackson could brush his mouth over hers in a sweet kiss that made her heart skip a beat.

She ran her fingers over his beard growth, smiling up at him. "You keep looking more and more like a mountain man."

Danny chimed in with his agreement. "Yeah, you totes do. Seriously, dude, what's with the beard?"

Jackson's expression became veiled. "Just prepping, is all."

She narrowed her eyes. "Prepping for what?"

Shrugging, he headed to the refrigerator. The sculpted muscles in his back flexed as he reached for something on the top shelf. "There've been some rumors around the base."

His tone was gruff and careless, causing Mia and her brother to exchange a wary look.

"What kind of rumors?" she demanded.

His hand emerged with a tub of margarine. He turned to face her, but his eyes still revealed nothing. "Just some murmurings that there might be somethin' brewing in the desert."

"The desert?" A spark of panic ignited her belly. "You mean, the Middle East?"

Another shrug.

"Oh," Danny said slowly. "So you guys all grow beards before you ship out? What, so you can blend in?"

"Somethin' like that," Jackson said vaguely.

As if on cue, the phone on the counter rang. It was Jackson's. Mia's worry doubled as she watched him check the display.

Something indefinable flickered in his eyes. "I've gotta take this," he muttered. "I'll be right back."

"Is it the base?" she blurted out.

He shook his head. "Nah."

She didn't detect any dishonesty, but her uneasiness refused to dissipate. She knew that as a SEAL, Jackson was forever on standby. Even when he wasn't deployed, he could still get called to action at any time. The thought of him being sent on some dangerous mission in the "desert" scared the living crap out of her.

She'd actually spoken about this very topic with Jen last week, when Jen and Cash accompanied her and Jackson to another one of Danny's games. Jen confessed that being in a relationship with a SEAL wasn't all sunshine and rainbows—the woman worried like crazy whenever Cash was gone, and she admitted that she'd initially resisted dating Cash for that reason. Jen hadn't wanted to deal with the long absences, the constant worry, the frustration that came with never knowing whether her man was safe.

The candid conversation had triggered in Mia the realization that soldiers weren't the only ones who needed to be strong. The partners who loved them had to possess that same strength in order to make a relationship between them work.

Sadly, her talk with Jen also served as a reminder that anything long-term wasn't in the cards for her and Jackson. Before, the only terrifying outcome she'd foreseen was a relationship that ended in her broken heart. But a relationship with a soldier could have an even deadlier end—Jackson could actually *die.*

The grim reality hadn't sunk in until now, and yet, even knowing that she could lose Jackson in more than just the figurative sense, she couldn't bring herself to break it off with him.

"I'm sorry, I really am. I know how much you were looking forward to it..."

Jackson's low voice wafted into the kitchen from the hall, and the chord of sadness and remorse in his tone made her uneasy all over again.

She glanced at Danny, whose head was bent in concentration as he checked on the omelet he was preparing. Satisfied that her brother was otherwise occupied, she crept toward the doorway. She knew eavesdropping was beyond rude, but Jackson had sounded so upset she couldn't help but listen in.

"I'll see what I can do, Mom, but there's no guarantee I'll be able to get leave." A pause. "I know it's Thanksgiving, but I have orders." Another pause. "I'll try to get leave, Mom. I'll call you next week to let you know for sure, okay? Yeah...'kay...I love you too."

Mia ducked away from the doorframe as Jackson's call wrapped up. She furrowed her brow, trying to make sense of what she'd heard. Why was Jackson telling his mother he couldn't come home? Mia knew for a fact that he was getting three days of leave for the Thanksgiving holiday—he'd told her so himself.

So why was he lying to his mother about it?

She bit her tongue when he returned to the kitchen. She didn't want to confront him in front of Danny, who'd plopped down on the stool by the eat-in counter and was happily munching on his omelet.

"Man, it's nice eating something other than cereal for breakfast." Danny swallowed, then shot Mia a pointed stare. "See how nice it is to wake up earlier and have a balanced meal before school?"

"Uh-huh, go ahead and blame me. But we both know you enjoy sleeping in as much as I do." She glanced at Jackson. "He's conning you. Pretending he's an early riser in order to impress you."

Jackson chuckled and drifted over to the stove. "How many pieces of bacon do you want, darlin'? Six or seven?"

She gaped at him. "*Six* or *seven*? I was going to ask for *two*. Who eats seven pieces of bacon?"

"I do." His expression turned smug. "I'm a growing boy, Mia. Jeez."

Danny's laughter filled the kitchen. And as Jackson prepared two plates for him and Mia, she watched the scene in front of her and a twinge of yearning tugged on her heart. She could get used to this. Jackson in her kitchen, the easy banter, the happy expression on her little brother's face.

She and Danny hadn't been lucky enough to grow up in a Norman Rockwell household. They'd been carted around from city to city, barely unpacking their belongings before their mother dragged them to a new place. They hadn't had one father—they'd had *nine*. And instead of a mom who loved them unconditionally and put them first, they'd gotten one who cared only about her own insecurities and dived into one marriage after the other in order to feel fulfilled.

"You okay?" came Jackson's husky voice.

She lifted her head with a bittersweet smile. "I'm good. Just thinking about how delicious that omelet looks."

The three of them ate at the counter, talking about nothing in particular until Danny hurried off to gather his school things, leaving Mia and Jackson alone.

"You really don't need to worry about the beard," Jackson said in a voice thick with reassurance. "I doubt the team will be goin' anywhere. We're just taking precautions."

She was relieved. "But if you do have to go, you'll say goodbye first, right? You won't just—"

A knock on the door cut her off.

Almost immediately, her shoulders went stiffer than a slab of marble. She and Danny didn't get a lot of unannounced visitors.

Except for one.

She flew off the stool, but she didn't make it in time. Danny must have been in the living room because he was already on his way to the front door.

She froze, her heart sinking to the pit of her stomach. *Shit.*

She was tempted to sprint to the door and stop Danny from opening it, but it was too late. The door creaked open and his dumbfounded exclamation reverberated in the apartment.

"*Mom?*"

JACKSON WAS WELL VERSED IN ALL SORTS OF EXPLOSIVES, which meant he knew precisely when a bomb would go off. And right now, Mia's apartment was about to explode. The fuse had been lit, the countdown had started, and detonation was imminent.

He slid out of the kitchen in time to see Danny leading a petite middle-aged woman into the living room.

The resemblance between Brenda and her two children was uncanny. Dark green eyes, the same generous mouth and sharp cheekbones. Only difference was that Brenda's features had a weathered look to them. This was a woman who'd lived through a shitload of heartache and disappointment, and the evidence of that was etched into her face.

"Mia, look! Mom's here," Danny said with excitement that his sister clearly didn't share.

"I can see that," she answered tersely.

Disapproval crept into her brother's tone. "You're not even going to say hello?"

Mia spared a pithy glance at their mother. "Hello."

"Hi, baby," Brenda said softly. "I'm sorry I took so long to visit again."

"Again?" Danny echoed.

His mother looked at him in surprise. "Your sister didn't tell you? I stopped by last month, but you weren't home."

A fire of betrayal burned in Danny's eyes as he swiveled his head. "Mom was here last month and you didn't tell me?"

Jackson watched the exchange with growing uneasiness. He felt like he should leave the room, but any move he made would alert them to his presence and make things even more uncomfortable. So he stood by the kitchen doorway, shirtless and on edge, wishing like heck he could escape undetected but knowing he was stuck.

"I must have forgotten," Mia muttered.

"Bullshit!"

"Language," his sister said in a warning pitch.

"Fuck that! Why didn't you tell me Mom was here? Why would you keep that from me?"

"Daniel, it's all right." His mother spoke in a soothing tone. "I'm sure Mia didn't mean to be sneaky. She was just trying to protect you."

"From who?" he snapped.

"From *her*," Mia snapped back, jerking a finger at Brenda.

A deafening silence crashed over the room.

Jackson tried to inch his way back to the kitchen, but Mia saw him and shot him a panicked glance.

Don't leave me, her eyes clearly communicated.

He stifled a sigh and stayed put.

"Look." Mia cleared her throat and turned to her brother. "I know you're pissed, but now isn't the time for this argument. We have to go, otherwise you'll be late for school."

"I'll take him," Brenda piped up.

The look in Mia's eyes could have frozen the Pacific Ocean. "No."

"*Yes*," Danny corrected, his cheeks red with anger. "Mom can drive me to school. I don't want to be anywhere near you right now."

Mia's glacial expression transformed into an eddy of hurt. "Danny—"

"Come on, Mom, let's go." Ignoring Mia completely, he marched to the door.

Brenda lingered for a moment, her interested gaze flicking in Jackson's direction. Then she addressed her daughter.

"Is it all right if I come back this evening so the three of us can talk?"

Mia's jaw was tighter than a drum. "Fine. Whatever."

It was her mother's turn to look hurt. Without another word, Brenda awkwardly adjusted the strap of her bulky leather purse and left the apartment.

The moment the door closed, Mia's face collapsed.

"C'mere, darlin'."

She dove into his open arms, her breathing labored as she buried her head in his chest.

He hugged her tight and stroked her hair, his heart splitting in two when he felt her tears soaking his bare skin. In the two months he'd known her, he'd never seen Mia break down like this. If he could've taken away her pain and transferred it all on himself, he would've done it in a nanosecond, but all he could do was hold her close and offer gruff words of comfort.

She lifted her head to reveal tearstained cheeks and red-rimmed eyes. "Why did she have to show up again? She's done so much damage already—why can't she just leave us alone?"

He led her over to the couch, where he pulled her into his lap and wrapped his arms around her.

"I'm gonna say somethin' you probably don't wanna hear," he started roughly, "but I want you to hear me out, all right?"

She nodded weakly.

He paused, knowing he had to tread very carefully. "Have you considered that maybe your mother's motives are sincere?"

Bitterness splashed across her face. "They're not. She has an agenda."

"How can you be certain of that?"

"Because she *always* has an agenda. I don't know what she's up to this time, but there's nothing sincere about that woman. The only person she's ever cared about is herself."

He tenderly tucked a strand of hair behind her ear. "What if you're wrong?"

"I'm not," she retorted, but her voice faltered slightly.

"All I'm saying is, maybe you should keep an open mind. People *do* change, Mia. Sometimes folks take a good long look at their lives and realize how much their mistakes have cost 'em."

He swallowed. "At the end of the day, family is the most important thing you've got. Family, and love."

"Oh really?"

He suddenly found a pair of shrewd eyes focused on him.

"Why are you lookin' at me like that?"

"I overheard you on the phone with your mother, Jackson. If family is so important, then why did you lie to her? You have the time off, but you told her you couldn't come home for Thanksgiving."

Guilt trickled through him. "You're right. I did lie," he admitted.

"Why?"

His throat tightened. "I...don't like going home."

"Why?" Mia pressed.

"Because..." Desperation and resentment formed a lethal cocktail that coursed in his blood. "Because I don't wanna see my brother, okay? We had a falling out several years back, and things haven't been the same since."

A deep crease marred her forehead. "What happened?"

He didn't answer. Every muscle in his body was tight, too many emotions constricting his chest. The memories were still so raw, like a wound that refused to heal. Whenever the thought of Shane entered his head, it was accompanied by crippling pain and bitter anger, not to mention paralyzing sorrow.

"Jackson...tell me what happened."

He swallowed a lump of sadness, then forced himself to answer. "My brother Shane recently married my high school sweetheart—"

"Seriously?" Mia said in shock.

Jackson wasn't finished. "But that wasn't what caused the falling out. All the bad shit went down years before that, after she—" he sucked in a breath, then exhaled in a rush, "—after she accused me of forcing myself on her."

CHAPTER EIGHTEEN

There. He'd said it. Confessed the one painful secret that had been tearing him apart for years now.

Just as he'd expected, Mia's expression conveyed pure and total horror.

What he hadn't expected, though, was her immediate and staunch words of response.

"That's fucking bullshit. You would *never* force yourself on someone."

"And I didn't," he said hoarsely. "I would never take a woman against her will."

"I know." Conviction rang in her voice, and her hands were firm as she cupped his chin. "Tell me everything."

The enormous bulge of pain obstructing his throat made it hard to speak, but he managed to power through it. "Well, first thing you should know is that Tiff told the truth not a day later, so there was no arrest or trial or any of that nasty shit."

"Tiff? That was your girlfriend's name?"

He nodded. "Tiffany Griffen. She lived a few miles down the road from us. Her daddy owned a horse-breeding farm, and he'd been raising Tiff alone ever since her mama died. She and I started dating in junior year and we were inseparable. We dated for three years, but we didn't have sex right away. Tiff was a virgin, I wasn't. We made love for the first time on our one-year anniversary."

He stopped, unwittingly remembering their first time. He'd gone all out that night: candles, rose petals, the whole shebang. He could still picture the ecstatic smile on Tiff's face when she'd walked into the cabin and seen all the trouble he'd gone to in order to make her first time special.

"Anyway—" he cleared his throat, "—we were madly in love, planned on getting married and having babies and living happily ever after."

"So what changed?" Mia's fingers stroked his chin, skimming over the thick beard he was dying to shave off.

"Sex," he said flatly. "You already know I like to experiment. Well, I liked it back then, too."

Mia hazarded a guess. "But Tiffany didn't?"

"Heck, no, Tiff loved it. She loved everything we did in bed. Only problem was, it embarrassed her. She didn't want to admit that she liked it dirty, and she made me promise that our bedroom activities would stay between us, and us alone. I was perfectly fine with that." He shrugged. "I mean, I don't like people knowing my business either. So yeah, things were good. We were a nice upstanding couple in public, and a pair of kinky sex maniacs in private. The night before my twentieth birthday, Tiff had somethin' special planned. We were both living at home at that point, so we used to sneak over to the cabin on my folks' property to fool around."

He didn't mention that Tiff was now living in that same cabin with his brother, but the irony didn't escape him.

"She told me to meet her at the cabin, and when I showed up, she was buck naked and holding a length of rope. She announced that my birthday present was that I'd get to tie her up and fuck her in the ass. We'd always wanted to play around with ropes, so everything that followed was one hundred percent consensual. She initiated it, and she loved every second of it."

He stopped abruptly, a burst of resentment going off in his chest.

"Hey, don't stop now," Mia said softly. "Tell me what happened afterwards."

"That night? Nothin'. But the next morning, Tiff was out in the paddock with her father. It was sweltering outside, so she rolled up her sleeves without thinking, and her daddy noticed the rope marks on her wrists." Jackson released a weary breath. "I guess we weren't too careful the night before."

Mia's breath hitched. "Shit."

"Shit is right. When her father demanded to know where she got those marks, Tiff panicked. She blurted out the first thing that came to her head." He spoke through clenched teeth now. "She told him that I tied her up and had my way with her —without her consent."

Horror erupted in Mia's eyes. "No."

"Yes." His insides twisted with bitterness. "As you can probably imagine, Casper Griffen freaked the fuck out. He grabbed his shotgun, hopped in his pickup, and hightailed it over to my house."

"Oh my God."

"Tiff had already called to warn me he was coming, so we were all out on the porch when he showed up. He started hurling threats and accusations, said the sheriff was on his way." Bile coated Jackson's throat. "My father, God bless him, had his own shotgun out, and he ordered Casper to get the heck off our property, told him we'd settle it in court if we had to."

Even though years had passed, the mortification he'd felt on that awful morning was fresher than ever. Jackson's chest ached as he remembered the unwavering confidence on his father's face. Kurt Ramsey hadn't believed Casper's claims for a second. He'd stood protectively at his son's side, prepared to shoot Tiff's father if it came down to it.

"Neither of my parents believed Casper's accusation," he said roughly. "My sister, well, she was too young to know what was going on, so they sent her to a friend's house while we waited for the sheriff. But Shane... Shane thought I was guilty."

That elicited a livid curse from Mia. "How could he possibly think that?"

"I didn't know it at the time, but he was in love with Tiff. Turns out he had a thing for her in high school, but she was three years younger so he was waiting for her to grow up a little before he asked her out. But by then she was already with me. Shane didn't say a word to me about it, but secretly he was jealous that I was dating the girl he wanted. And when Casper showed up, Shane wasn't thinking clearly. He was only thinking about Tiff, and the thought of anyone hurtin' her, especially his own brother, sent him into a blind rage."

Mia gasped. "What did he do?"

"After my dad shooed Casper off our land, I headed out to the barn. I needed to be alone, to make sense of it all. I couldn't believe Tiff had accused me of doing that. I desperately wanted to talk to her and find out why she'd done it, but my folks advised me not to contact her, at least not until we spoke to the sheriff." The frustration he'd felt back then returned now in full-force. "I was already having visions of going to jail for something I didn't even do, so I went out to see the horses. Being around them always calmed me down. But Shane followed me into the barn and..."

He stopped. Couldn't go on. That hot July morning had been the single worst day of his life. He'd never told anyone about it. Hadn't allowed himself to *think* about it.

Mia twisted around so that she was straddling him. Her gaze shone with encouragement as she planted both hands on his shoulders and said, "What did he do?"

His lips formed a thin, angry line.

"What did your brother do?"

"He beat the shit out of me."

"*What?*"

"He beat me," Jackson said dully. "And I'm not talkin' about a mean right hook or a kick to the nuts. He busted me up real good. Two black eyes, split lip, broken nose, sprained wrist, three fractured ribs."

Mia was agape. "Oh my God."

"My dad heard the commotion and rushed into the barn— he had to wrestle Shane off me. My folks wanted to call an ambulance but I refused, so Dad carried me inside and my mama cleaned me up best she could." He set his jaw. "Wasn't long before the sheriff showed up, but before he could step foot in the house, Casper's truck was speeding up the drive again. This time Tiff was behind the wheel."

Mia scowled. "About fucking time she showed up."

"Apparently Casper came back to the farm in a rage, told Tiff he was pressing charges, and she knew she couldn't let the lie go on. She came clean, right there in front of everyone. My folks, Shane, the sheriff. I realized later how difficult that must've been for her, admitting to a group of people that she'd asked me to tie her up and fuck her in the ass—and that she'd enjoyed it."

"Difficult for *her*? Did she even stop to consider how difficult it would be for you to be accused of *rape*? What a...a bitch!"

A weak smile lifted his lips. He found Mia's outrage on his behalf oddly sweet, but still he had to argue, "She wasn't acting out of malice. She panicked, pure and simple."

"Don't you dare defend her. Tiffany Griffen is a first-class *bitch* for doing what she did. She could've destroyed your entire life!"

"She did," he said ruefully. "No matter her motives, and even though she recanted her story, the damage had already been done. I was beaten to a bloody pulp. Things between Shane and me could never be the same after what he'd done. And then there was the people in town..."

Mia narrowed her eyes. "What about them?"

"Let's just say the folks in Abbott Creek aren't the forgetting type. They like to whisper and gossip and spread shit that ain't true. I couldn't go into town after that without folks staring and pointing at me. No matter how many times I denied any wrongdoing, or how many times Tiff admitted that she'd lied, some people still believed I'd done it. I think Shane secretly believed it too, because he never apologized for beating on me."

"Please don't tell me you stayed with Tiff," Mia said in a menacing tone.

"I ended it the moment the sheriff left the house."

"Good."

"But yeah, life fuckin' sucked after that." Guilt swirled in his stomach as he thought back to those days. "I felt so bad for my folks. People were whispering behind their backs, half of them calling me a rapist, the other half—the ones who believed me—taunting them about having a kinky sex fiend for a son. Eventually I couldn't take it anymore, so I drove to a recruiting office in Dallas and enlisted."

"And this was, what, eight years ago?"

He nodded.

"But you've been home since?"

"Only a handful of times, and every time I go back I have to deal with the same whispers. Not to mention seeing Tiff and my brother blissfully in love."

"I can't believe they ended up together," Mia grumbled. "They don't deserve to be happy together after what they did."

He sighed. "It was a complicated situation. I don't begrudge them their happiness, but...fuck, I don't want to see it flaunted in front of my face, y'know?"

"So Shane really didn't apologize to you?" Disbelief lingered in her expression.

"Nope. The two of us have barely exchanged ten words in eight years. He does his best to avoid me whenever I'm in town."

"I can't believe this has been going on for so long. Why didn't you ever confront him?"

"I didn't want to put my folks through another confrontation," he said gruffly. "They've already suffered enough."

"And you think an eight-year-long rift between their sons isn't making them suffer?"

She had a point. And she was also spot-on. Jackson's mother had been pleading with him for years to make things right with his brother, but he couldn't muster up the desire to do it.

Whenever he thought about Shane, he remembered meaty fists smashing into his ribs. He remembered the coppery taste of blood in his mouth, the sticky feel of it pouring out of his nose. And each time he saw his brother in person, he experienced the sickest urge to return the favor. To show Shane what it felt like to have your body ripped to shreds by your own brother.

"Jackson..." Mia bit her lip as she met his eyes. "I can't believe I'm saying this—it probably makes me the biggest hypocrite on the planet—but I think you should go home for Thanksgiving and air everything out with Shane."

An ironic smile tickled his lips. "Yup, totally hypocritical."

"I know, but my situation with my mother is different," she protested. "I've given her a million chances to prove me wrong. You and Shane never even *talked* about what happened."

He dragged both hands through his hair before resting them

on her slender hips. "Honestly? The thought of going home makes me want to throw up."

There was a beat.

And then, "What if I went with you?"

His jaw hit the floor. "Are you serious?"

She nodded, though he didn't miss the brief flicker of anxiety in her gaze. "I've got Thanksgiving weekend off, so I can be your moral support if you want."

"What about Danny?"

"We don't usually do anything special. Last year I went with him to Angie's parents' house, and I felt totally out of place. He was invited there again this year, so he'll be all right if I leave town with you. I'm sure Angie's parents will let him spend the weekend with them."

Jackson was still floored—but also touched. Very, very touched. Mia's offer to accompany him to Abbott Creek for the holiday, while unexpected, was absolutely welcome. He saw it as yet another sign that he was chipping away at her resistance toward a long-term relationship with him. As each day passed, she was acting more and more like a girlfriend than a temporary sexual partner. And as reluctant as he was to go home, he knew he couldn't pass up this opportunity.

Her gesture was a step in the right direction. A promising omen that she cared about more than having sex with him. That she cared about him as a man, and not just a lover. So much that she was willing to be there for him during what was bound to be an extremely painful visit to Texas.

But if he was finally going to face his demons, he refused to be the only one.

"I'll make you a deal," he said quietly. "I'll go home and talk to Shane—and yes, I would love it if you came along, sugar—but only if you keep an open mind about your mother."

She frowned.

"She's already back in your life," he pointed out. "And Danny clearly wants her here, which means you can't get rid of her so easily this time. So as long as she's stickin' around, would it hurt to hear her out? I'm not saying to completely drop your guard and open your heart to her again. Just give her the benefit of the doubt."

Several seconds ticked by, and still Mia didn't utter a word.

"C'mon, darlin', just promise to keep an open mind," he coaxed. "Can you do that for me?"

Her shoulders sagged in resignation. "Fine," she muttered. "I guess it wouldn't kill me to try."

CHAPTER
NINETEEN

Two weeks later

"Isn't this so exciting, Mia?" Brenda bubbled happily as the three of them walked into the apartment.

Mia smiled in spite of herself, then blamed the reaction on the high she was still riding after watching the Warriors clinch a playoff spot. She and Brenda had sat together in the stands, and as her mom cheered for Danny and his teammates with unbridled enthusiasm, Mia had been reminded of the fact that her mother wasn't *all* bad.

When she wasn't chasing after her next husband or drowning her sorrows in a black hole of Häagen-Dazs, Brenda could be a lot of fun. She was like an endearing child, possessing a knack for spontaneity and an unmatched lust for life. Except there was a flipside to that, because children weren't equipped to handle adult problems, so when faced with the not-so-fun grown-up parts of life, Brenda reacted...poorly, for lack of a better word.

Mia refused to let herself forget that, even as she tried to keep her promise to Jackson and remain open-minded about Brenda's motives for being here.

And shockingly enough, her mother *was* here. This was the second weekend in a row that she'd made the long drive from Reno to San Diego, which showed some serious dedication on her part. That alone was enough to make Mia wonder if maybe her mom was sincere about making amends.

"It'll be even more exciting when they win the state championship," Mia said.

"Which we will." Danny's eyes glittered with confidence as he followed them inside.

Just like last weekend, he'd decided to skip the Friday-night post-game festivities so he could spend time with their mother. He was already scrolling through titles on Netflix to pick something for them to watch tonight.

Mia drifted into the kitchen to brew some coffee. Brenda trailed after her and leaned against the counter while she clicked on the coffeemaker.

"Are you sure you don't want to come to Reno with us on Thursday?"

She searched her mom's eyes and detected nothing false in her earnest expression. Brenda had asked both her kids to spend the holiday with her, but while Danny had jumped at the chance, choosing to be with his mom over his girlfriend, Mia was secretly glad she'd already made other plans. Her mother's invitation might seem genuine, but she still didn't entirely trust the woman.

"I promised Jackson I'd spend Thanksgiving with him and his family," she answered as she grabbed two ceramic mugs from the cupboard.

"The two of you are getting serious, huh?"

Her shoulders instantly stiffened. "Not really," she said vaguely.

The last thing she wanted to do was talk to her mother about her relationship with Jackson. Brenda asked about it each time they saw each other, but Mia didn't feel comfortable confiding in her.

Especially when she couldn't put a label on her own feelings about the subject. She'd been seeing Jackson for three months, which was about, oh, two and a half months longer than she'd anticipated their fling lasting. But it wasn't a fling anymore —she'd finally forced herself to accept it. But it wasn't a serious relationship, either.

Bullshit.

As usual, her stupid brain voiced its disagreement. And as usual, she tried to ignore it. But it was getting a lot harder to do that lately.

Over the past few weeks, Jackson stayed over more often than not. He cooked her breakfast and kissed her goodbye before she left for work. Sometimes he dropped Danny off at school if he didn't have to report early to the base. Other times he fixed them dinner. He was sweet and attentive. He was patient. He had the uncanny ability to make her laugh even when she was in the foulest of moods.

And the sex... It only seemed to get better. Whether he was kissing her with infinite tenderness or tying her up to his bed with bungee cords, he treated her as if she were the most beautiful, most desirable woman in the world.

Bottom line: Jackson Ramsey was an incredible man.

Yet despite all the wonderful things, she couldn't stop imagining the worst-case scenarios. Like maybe they'd get bored of each other and break up. Or he'd cheat on her and they'd break up. Or they'd get into a colossal fight—and break up.

Breaking up was always the end result in her pessimistic mind. Either that, or losing Jackson when his chopper crashed in some godforsaken jungle, or when he got shot on a mission in the "desert."

Hard as she tried, she couldn't picture a future with him. With anyone, for that matter. She couldn't see herself growing old with someone, couldn't imagine finding a love that lasted forever. In her experience, happiness was fleeting. The bad always crept in to destroy the good. It was inevitable.

"Mia?"

She lifted her head to find her mother's concerned gaze fixed on her. "Yeah?"

"The coffee's ready."

"Oh. Right." Banishing her disturbing thoughts, she hurriedly prepared two cups, then handed one to her mom.

Before she could take a step to the door, Brenda spoke up uncertainly. "I wanted to talk to you about something."

Cue an instant rush of suspicion.

"What is it?"

"Danny and I were talking before the game..." Her mother hesitated for a beat. "We were discussing his chances of getting a college scholarship. He thinks he's got a good shot."

"He does," Mia said with unfailing conviction.

The faint wrinkles around Brenda's mouth creased as she smiled. "I believe it. But I wanted to ask you about your backup plan, in case the scholarship doesn't pan out. Do you...are you...?" Embarrassment flashed in her eyes. "Do you need any money?"

Her jaw fell open.

"I mean, I don't have a lot saved up," her mom hurried on, "but if you need help paying for Danny's expenses, I'd be happy to contribute."

It was impossible to mask her shock. Her mother was offering them *money*?

God, maybe Jackson was right. Maybe the woman *was* trying to turn over a new leaf.

"That's really nice of you to offer," she managed to say through the lump of emotion clogging her throat, "but we're fine for now. I've got some savings, and so does Danny."

Brenda blinked in surprise. "He does?"

Mia nodded. "He's saved every penny he's made working for that landscaping company. He even has his own bank account. And he's ridiculously responsible with his money—he doesn't spend a dime unless it's for something important."

Her mom's expression reflected back the same pride Mia was feeling. "He's a very smart boy." Brenda's voice cracked. "You've done a wonderful job with him, baby."

"I didn't exactly have a choice, seeing as his mother couldn't be bothered to raise him."

The muttered response triggered a wave of tension that crashed over them and efficiently wiped out the emotional moment they'd been sharing. Mia immediately regretted the verbal jab when she saw the hurt look on her mother's face.

"Sorry," she mumbled. "I know you're trying. I shouldn't have said that."

"I deserved it," Brenda said sadly.

They both went quiet for a moment, and then Brenda offered a smile, albeit a forced one.

"Come on, let's go see what kung-fu movie Danny has decided to torture us with."

Mia responded with a weak laugh. "I'll be right there. I'm just going to make a sandwich first. Do you want one?"

"No thank you, baby. I'm still full from the hot dogs we had at the game."

After her mother left the kitchen, Mia drew in a deep breath. *Keep an open mind*, she thought, repeating the same mantra she'd been relying on for two weeks now. Brenda did seem to be making a genuine effort, and throwing her past mistakes in her face every two minutes wasn't at all beneficial to the situation.

As she prepared a ham-and-turkey sandwich, the sound of footsteps came from behind her and she turned to see Danny enter the kitchen. His hair was damp from the shower he'd taken in the locker room, and his black T-shirt and dark-blue jeans emphasized his tall, broad frame and muscular arms. At times like these, she had to blink to make sure this was actually her little brother and not a grown man who'd somehow moved into her apartment.

She had to face the facts, though—Danny wasn't a kid anymore. He nearly *was* a man, and maybe it was time for her to stop being so overprotective of him.

"Almost done," she told him, slapping a piece of lettuce on the bread.

He walked over and stood directly beside her. "Listen, I wanted to...um...I wanted to apologize to you. I said some really shitty things to you the day Mom came back, and I feel really bad about it."

A soft smile tugged on her lips. Danny hadn't brought up the argument during these past two weeks, but she'd known he'd been trying to find a way to apologize. She hadn't wanted to push him, though, so she'd decided to wait until he raised the subject himself.

"I'm sorry I was so rude," he finished.

"It's all right. I'm sorry I didn't tell you that Mom stopped by."

"It's okay. I know you were just trying to protect me." He sighed. "But you don't have to hide things from me. I know you think I'm a stupid kid and that I'm being gullible about the whole thing, but you only have one mom, you know? I don't want to be one of those messed-up losers you see on some reality show twenty years from now, complaining about his crappy relationship with his mother."

Mia grinned at him. "Mommy issues *are* out of style," she agreed.

"I also wanted to thank you. You know, for making an effort. I know you still don't trust her, but at least you're giving her another chance, and I think that's pretty cool of you."

"You wanna hug it out?"

"You're such a loser." He shifted in embarrassment and grumbled, "Okay, fine."

He gave her a quick hug that made her laugh again, and then the two of them left the kitchen together to join their mother.

CHAPTER
TWENTY

Thanksgiving

"For Pete's sake, can you quit grinning like that? You look like a total goofball." Mia glared at Jackson as they walked through the automatic doors of Dallas-Forth Worth International Airport and stepped into the early afternoon sunshine.

He lugged their carry-on bags toward the taxi stand, the grin never leaving his face. "I can't help it. That was the best plane ride of my life."

Hers too, but Mia refused to give him the satisfaction of admitting it, not after she'd just reprimanded him.

"Uh-huh, Mr. Sex Maniac, I'm sure you've *never* done that before," she said sarcastically.

"Gotten a handjob under a blanket while on an airplane? Nope, hasn't happened before."

She eyed him dubiously.

"I'm serious," he insisted. "My air travel always involves a bunch of sweaty men on a cramped chopper. You popped my airplane cherry, baby."

She snorted, then turned her attention to the cab that had appeared in front of them.

A few minutes later, they were in the backseat of the taxi and heading away from Dallas. Her gaze stayed glued to the window so she could admire the scenery whizzing past them. Gently rolling land, golden dirt, and red clay earth made up the landscape, and when the freeway gradually turned into a winding country road, forested areas started cropping up. Tall oaks, majestic hickories, and sweeping elms inhabited the land, still surprisingly green for November.

The temperature was in the high seventies, and Mia had to roll up the sleeves of her fuzzy blue sweater because the car didn't have air conditioning. She and Jackson didn't say much during the drive, but she didn't mind. She occupied herself by peering out the window and enjoying the sights.

It took less than an hour to reach Abbott Creek, a dusty western town with a main street that featured dozens of little stores and an honest-to-God saloon. Mia felt Jackson stiffen the second they drove into his hometown. His handsome profile revealed an extremely tense jaw, which only hardened further when the driver turned onto the long dirt road that led to the Ramsey Ranch.

A large wooden gate stood at the end of the road, welcoming them to the Double R. Above the gate was an enormous sign with the ranch's brand carved into it.

Despite Jackson's obvious agitation, Mia couldn't help but smile in delight as she examined her surroundings. Beyond the gate was a gorgeous, two-story house with white walls and a dark-red roof. Red was also the color of choice for the front door and the pretty shutters covering the endless amount of windows.

To the left of the house was a large paddock, where three graceful brown mares were grazing beneath a shady elm tree. To the right were a series of outbuildings, all painted white and red like the main house. And all around them was land. Lots and lots of land. Hills, valleys, and trees, farther than the eye could see.

"It's beautiful," she said softly.

Jackson's voice came out hoarse. "Yeah, it is."

He met her eyes for a second, then hopped out of the car so he could open the gate for the driver. Rather than get back in the taxi, Jackson jogged the length of the dirt driveway, reaching it at the same time as the car.

They unloaded their bags and paid the driver. As the car sped away, the front door of the ranch house swung open and a tall, willowy brunette in her late teens or early twenties flew onto the wooden porch.

"Jackie!" She bounded down the steps two at a time and threw her arms around his broad shoulders. "I'm so glad you're home!"

Mia watched as the two of them exchanged a long, affectionate hug.

"Mia, this is my sister Evie."

She barely got out a hello before the door opened again and another brunette raced toward them with an older version of Jackson trailing after her. Mia suddenly found herself surrounded by two incredibly tall men and two incredibly tall women, making her feel miniature in comparison.

After Jackson embraced his parents, he made another round of introductions, while Mia gaped at the Ramseys the entire time.

"Oh, man, you're a family of giants," she blurted out.

Evie's brown eyes twinkled mischievously. "Or maybe you just come from a family of dwarves."

Mia couldn't stop gawking at them. "Seriously. How tall are all of you?"

Jackson's sister laughed. "I'm six feet. Mom's five-ten. And Dad 'n Jackie are six-five."

"Giants, every last one of you," Mia grumbled.

Arlene Ramsey stepped forward with a warm smile. "It's a pleasure to meet you, Mia. I'm so glad you could join us for Thanksgiving."

"Thanks for having me."

"Let's go inside," Arlene said. "Kurt, help Jackson with the bags."

"Yes, ma'am." Jackson's father tipped an imaginary hat at his wife.

The next thing Mia knew, she was sandwiched between Jackson's Amazonian mother and sister, who linked their arms through hers on the way to the porch.

"You're the first girl Jackie has brought home since he moved to California," Evie informed her in a frank tone.

She fought a pang of discomfort. "Oh. Really?"

"Yup. So you must be special." The younger woman looked Mia up and down with unabashed interest. "I demand to know everythin' about you, Mia Weldrick."

"Leave our guest alone, Evangeline," Arlene chided. "We'll get to know Mia in due time."

Both women spoke in the same drawl as Jackson, which Mia found utterly endearing. She followed them into the house and was instantly greeted by the most delicious aromas on the planet.

"Something smells amazing," she commented.

"Thank you, darlin'." Arlene flushed prettily. She had Jackson's dark hair and light-brown eyes, but her face was more rounded and her cheeks seemed to have a perpetual rosy glow. "Dinner will be ready in an hour or two. We usually eat early, around four, so we can catch the game at four thirty. The boys would have my head if we missed kickoff."

"The football game," Evie clarified, her eyes narrowing as if she were waiting for Mia to object.

But Mia just grinned and said, "Awesome. I didn't want to miss seeing the Cowboys kick some butt."

Approval lit Evie's gaze. "You're a Cowboys fan?"

"Not entirely. We moved around a lot when I was a kid so I was never able to form an attachment to one specific home team. So I'm rooting for Jackson's hometown these days."

The two women nodded in approval, and then Arlene addressed her daughter. "Why don't you give Mia a quick tour of the house while I check on the turkey?"

Evie voiced an easy assent. And for the next ten minutes, she showed Mia every inch of the Ramsey homestead, which was as cozy inside as it was out. Wood-paneled walls and weathered parquet floors spanned the large house, and every bedroom featured deep bay windows that overlooked a part of the sprawling ranch. Mia laughed when she got a peek at Jackson's childhood bedroom, a big, airy space with shelves littered with trophies and white walls covered in posters of bikini models draped over sports cars.

"Classy," she said dryly.

Evie laughed again, a high, melodic sound that was downright contagious. "He was obsessed with those posters. Mom decided to keep 'em up even after he moved out. She says they add charm to the room."

Mia snickered and followed Evie down the wide hallway lined with framed family photographs and pretty oil paintings of western landscapes. She paused in front of one photo in particular, a shot featuring two smiling dark-haired boys with their arms slung around each other. The boys were about eight and ten years old. She recognized one as a very young, very adorable Jackson. The other boy was older, but looked so much like Jackson that she knew it must be his brother.

"That's Jackie 'n Shane," Evie told her. "They were joined at the hip when they were kids."

Mia just nodded, not wanting to bring up the brotherly estrangement that was currently wreaking havoc on the Ramsey family. But Evie surprised her by raising the topic.

"I suppose Jackie told you about the beef between him and Shane?"

"He did," she said guardedly.

Evie heaved out a dramatic sigh. "Well, I think you should ride my stubborn brother's ass and tell him to straighten this nonsense up already. It's getting dang old."

She stifled a laugh. "I'll see what I can do." As they headed to the second-floor staircase, she gave Jackson's sister a sidelong look. "How old are you, anyway?"

Evie beamed. "Turning twenty-one next week. Finally! You don't know how long I've been waiting to be legal. I'm tired of bribing Jed at the hardware store to buy me beer."

Mia had to grin. She really liked Jackson's sister. The girl was vibrant and outspoken, exuding the same charm as her older brother, but also a devilish energy that Mia suspected made Evie Ramsey a lot of fun to hang out with.

They went back downstairs, Evie yet again linking their arms on the way to the enormous country-style kitchen. Arlene was chopping onions on the huge cedar work island when they walked in.

She looked up with a smile. "So what do you think of our humble abode?" the older woman asked.

"I love it," Mia confessed. "You have a beautiful home, Mrs. Ramsey."

"Oh, pshaw—call me Arlene," Jackson's mother said firmly.

"Okay. Arlene."

"Thatta girl. Now come pull up a stool and keep me

company while I dice. Kurt's stolen my son away, so we have plenty of time for some good ol' fashioned girl talk."

Jackson had known he'd get a lecture from his father at some point, but he hadn't expected it to happen within five minutes of his arrival. As he set his and Mia's bags down on the porch, Kurt crossed his arms over the front of his blue-and-white Western shirt and gave a stern look.

"Why don't we go down to the barn, son?" It was voiced as a question, but was clearly a demand.

Jackson nodded. "All right."

They walked side by side toward the main barn that stabled the dozen or so mares living on the ranch. The stallion barn stood a hundred yards away, but Jackson forced himself not to look at the big red structure. He hadn't stepped foot inside it since that fateful morning, when his big brother had pummeled him with his fists and probably would've beat him to death if their father hadn't intervened.

"It's good to see you," Kurt said gruffly. "Your mother and I miss you."

His throat tightened. "I miss you too."

"Yeah?" His dad cocked his head. "Sometimes I wonder."

"Shit, Dad, you know I do."

"Funny, 'cause you don't seem inclined to come visit us."

"You know why I can't," he said in a low voice.

"Can't? Now that's bull crap, son. You choose not to come home to see your family. No *can't* about it."

He gritted his teeth. "You say that as if I'm missing out on a welcome parade or somethin', but we both know there's at least one person on this ranch who doesn't want to see me."

His father sighed. "Your brother is a mule-headed fool.

Always has been. I told you this once and I'm gonna say it again —you need to be the better man in this situation. Forgive him, Jack. It's the only way our family will ever be whole again."

"Forgive him?" he echoed incredulously. "For that to happen, Shane needs to actually apologize first. You know, for beating me within an inch of my life? He never told me he was sorry, Dad. Not even once."

"He is sorry," Kurt said quietly. "You can see it on his face whenever y'all are in the same room."

"That's not good enough. I need to hear him say it."

"Lord, how'd I end up with such a stubborn lot?"

Jackson rolled his eyes. "We got it from you, old man."

They reached the barn's big double doors, but rather than go inside, Jackson's father turned on his heel. "C'mon, let's head back. Your mama is clamoring to see you."

Their walk could probably have been considered pointless, but Jackson knew his father had needed to say his piece away from prying eyes.

On the way back to the house, they didn't talk about anything of importance. Jackson simply chatted about his life in San Diego, while Kurt filled him in on what he'd missed on the ranch. The subject of Shane and Tiffany's wedding didn't come up at all, but the couple's wedding photo was the first thing Jackson encountered when he strode into his childhood home. It hung proudly in the front hall, and he had to forcibly tear his gaze off the picture, refusing to let any emotions surface.

He hoped his mom and sister hadn't been grilling Mia in his absence, but when he entered the kitchen, he discovered that Mia was holding her own. She and Arlene were chatting a mile a minute about gardening, but the animated conversation halted abruptly, because the second he walked in, his mother put down the knife in her hand and rushed over to hug him again.

"Sit," she ordered, her soft brown eyes glimmering with joy

and affection. "I want to know everythin' you've been up to these last few years."

He smiled. "You already know. We talk on the phone once a week."

"Oh, is that right?" Her meaningful gaze shifted to Mia. "Because clearly you've been keeping a few secrets from your mama, young man."

"I told you I was seeing someone," he protested.

"Mmm-hmm, but you didn't tell me how delightful she was."

From her perch by the counter, Mia blushed, but she didn't look put off by the compliment.

Chuckling, he slid onto the stool next to Mia while his mom resumed her dicing. Neither Arlene nor Evie allowed the couple to help out with the cooking, so for the next hour they sat there while the two women puttered around the kitchen, the conversation flowing without a single pause or awkward silence. Jackson's father didn't say much—he was more of a listener than a talker—and eventually he excused himself so he could go feed the horses.

A feeling of pure contentedness filled Jackson's heart as his little sister told him about her college classes and his mom talked about her volunteer work at his old elementary school. Lord, he'd missed this. The warmth, the laughter, the love.

And he knew Mia was enjoying it too. She and Evie got along so well it was as if they'd known each other forever. And she'd already won over the gardening-obsessed Arlene thanks to her choice of profession. He was bursting with joy as he watched her interact with his family. Mia hadn't been lucky enough to grow up in a cozy, loving home, and he wanted her to experience it firsthand, to see how wonderful it could be.

But of course, just when he'd allowed himself to relax and was basking in the radiant feeling of being home again, the mood changed from happy to tense as if someone had flicked a switch.

Or rather, opened the front door.

The female voice that wafted from the front hall turned Jackson's spine into a stiff rod.

Tiffany.

And then a male mumble reached his ears, another familiar drawl that produced a more violent reaction—Jackson's hands curled into fists, so tight his knuckles turned white.

"Jackie," Evie murmured in warning.

He swallowed and met his sister's worried eyes. "Don't worry, darlin'. It's all good."

Which was a big fat lie. There was nothing *good* about it, and Jackson was wracked with tension as he waited for the newlyweds to make their appearance.

Shane and Tiffany entered the kitchen a moment later with timid expressions and half-hearted smiles.

"Happy Thanksgiving," Tiffany said in an overly cautious voice. Her eyes darted in Jackson and Mia's direction before focusing on Arlene.

"Happy Thanksgiving, sweetie." Jackson's mother stepped over to give her daughter-in-law a brief hug.

Jackson didn't miss the reluctance in his mom's eyes. He knew that she'd never been able to warm up to Tiff again, not after what the girl had done to her youngest son. And he suspected Tiff knew full well that she'd lost some of Arlene's love and respect, because his ex-girlfriend's body language didn't relax even as she returned her mother-in-law's embrace.

The hug Arlene exchanged with her eldest son was warmer, as was the tender look in her eyes as she kissed Shane's cheek.

Jackson remained on guard as he studied the new arrivals. Tiff hadn't aged at all—her face was as smooth as cream, her long hair fuller and shinier than ever. Shane hadn't changed much, either. He was still tall, still muscular, still wearing his brown hair in a buzz cut. Except he sported a full beard now, which was ironic considering Jackson looked like a lumberjack himself. It only made him all the more eager to shave his stupid precautionary beard.

After Evie went over to hug the newcomers, Shane and Tiffany finally turned to Jackson and Mia, their expressions more suited for an impending visit to the dentist than for greeting a long-lost relative.

"Jackson." Shane cleared his throat awkwardly. "Welcome home."

"Thanks."

No handshake. No hug. Neither man so much as blinked as they eyed each other.

"Hey, Jackson," Tiffany said softly.

"Tiff," he replied with a strained nod.

"I'm glad you were able to make it," she murmured. "Arlene said you might not come."

Silence settled over the kitchen. From the corner of his eye, he noticed Mia shifting on the stool, which alerted him to the fact that he hadn't introduced her yet.

"This is my girlfriend Mia," he said roughly.

Shane and Tiffany extended Mia the courtesy they'd denied Jackson by reaching over to shake her hand.

"Nice to meet you," Mia said, her discomfort written all over her pretty face.

Another silence fell, this one laced with more uneasiness and a shitload of unspoken words.

Finally, Arlene spoke up in resignation. "Evie, why don't you and Mia go and set the table? Tiffany, you can help me fill these water glasses while Shane carves the turkey. Jackson, find your father and tell him dinner's ready."

Arlene Ramsey, efficient as always, and a master at defusing potentially hazardous situations.

With that, everyone split up to complete their assigned tasks, and Jackson hurried out of the kitchen without looking back.

———

"WELL," MIA ANNOUNCED SEVERAL HOURS LATER, HER expression conveying deep weariness. "That was...brutal?"

Jackson followed her into his old bedroom, closed the door behind them, and let out the colossal sigh that had been jammed in his throat all evening.

"I don't know, though," she went on thoughtfully. "Brutal might be too tame a word to describe that dinner. Maybe torturous?"

A tired laugh flew out of his throat. "Yeah, torture's a good way to describe it."

She chimed in with another "helpful" suggestion. "Or how about, 'so uncomfortable I wanted to run out of the house, steal your father's truck, and drive straight to the airport'?"

"Also works."

As they flopped down on the edge of his bed, all traces of humor died. Mia instantly took his hand and squeezed it gently, her head falling against his shoulder as she stroked his knuckles in a soothing gesture.

Lord, that dinner had been one of the most excruciating experiences of his life—and this was coming from a man who'd been bitten in the ass by a pit viper during an op in the jungle last year. Shane and Tiffany had been seated right across the table from him and Mia, and neither one had said a single word to Jackson the entire time. His parents had tried to coax the two brothers into conversing with each other but failed every time.

And Evie, God bless her soul, had filled the numerous awkward silences by babbling on about absolutely nothing, until Arlene eventually had to silence her with a sharp shake of the head.

Mia hadn't said much either, except to exchange some gardening tips with Jackson's mother or to answer a few of his father's rare questions. By the time dinner had been cleared away, Jackson was dying to take Mia and flee the house, but that was a big no-no on Thanksgiving Day. Instead, they'd watched the Cowboys game in its entirety, sitting on the massive sectional sofa as far away as they could from Shane and Tiff. Then, at his mother's firm insistence, they stayed in the living room to eat dessert and watch the first half of the next game. But Arlene's blatant attempt at prolonging the evening in order to spark some sort of conversation between her two sons yet again failed.

Jackson still couldn't believe how cold Shane had acted toward him. Even colder than usual, which was completely baffling. Usually his brother was more aloof than rude, but tonight he'd been sending a helluva lot of scowls in Jackson's direction.

Needless to say, he'd been relieved as heck when Shane and Tiff finally left. Now it was ten o'clock, his parents and sister had already turned in, and he and Mia were finally alone.

"It's the guilt, you know."

He turned to Mia with a frown. "What?"

"That's why your brother and Tiffany were acting like that. They're guilty as hell and neither of them know how to deal with it."

"An apology would be a start."

"Obviously. But I think they don't know how to open that dialogue. I get the feeling they're scared of you."

He wrinkled his forehead. "Why would they be scared of me?"

"Because you're the wronged party in this situation. They're scared of how you'll react if they try to drag up all those old issues—they were probably scared of how you'd react back then, too. And I think they're also a bit resentful. I mean, it's clear that your parents are squarely on your side in this matter. Your mom wasn't very friendly to Tiffany, and even though it's obvious they love Shane, they don't look at him with the same adoration they give you." Mia shrugged. "I think Shane and Tiffany pick up on that."

"Maybe." An unsteady breath left his mouth. "Whatever. I don't wanna talk about this anymore."

She gave his hand another squeeze. "Okay," she said simply.

He shifted around so he could meet her gaze. "I really appreciate you being here. I don't know if I could've gotten through that dinner without you."

"Sure you could. You're a big, macho Navy SEAL. You can tackle any obstacle in your path."

He smiled weakly. "And yet tonight I was tempted to bolt out the front door."

His mind continued to run over the day's events, dwelling on the icy stares Shane kept hurling his way. *He* was the one who ought to have been glaring. Because of Shane and Tiffany, he couldn't go into town without being the object of vicious gossip. Because of them, he'd once lain in a bloody mess on the barn floor. And because of them, he didn't feel comfortable staying in the house he'd grown up in with the parents who'd loved and supported him all his life.

"All right, I can't believe I'm about to do this."

Mia's cryptic words jolted him back to the present. The determination lining her eyes sparked his curiosity.

"Do what?"

She ignored the inquiry and said, "I'll have you know I'd

way rather be singing an '80s pop song, but here goes..." She took a breath.

And started to sing.

Jackson burst out laughing as she softly belted out the lyrics to "My Girl," his all-time favorite oldies tune.

And as he listened, his heart grew so full it felt like it was going to burst. This woman truly was somethin' else. She'd known exactly what to do to raise his spirits, and he loved her for it.

He'd known it for a while, but right here, right now, he could say without a single shred of doubt that he was wildly, passionately and unequivocally in love with Mia.

When she opened her mouth to start the next verse, he cut her off by capturing her lips in a deep kiss.

"You—" he pulled back to meet her eyes, "—are absolutely fuckin' wonderful."

Pleasure washed over her face, and then she grabbed him by the collar of his button-down and kissed him again.

They fell back on the mattress, their mouths locked together. His pulse raced when their tongues met. His brain went fuzzy when Mia sucked on his bottom lip. And his cock dang near exploded when she shoved her hand between their bodies and squeezed it.

Somehow their clothes disappeared and they wound up naked beneath the thick duvet, exploring each other's bodies with their hands, mouths, and tongues.

"You're so beautiful," he mumbled, propping himself up over her warm, slender body.

"So are you." When her hand came up to stroke his cheek, he sagged into her touch, loving it, welcoming it.

Neither of them was interested in foreplay anymore—their hands collided down south as they both tugged on his cock to guide him inside her. They laughed at their own eagerness, then released simultaneous moans when he slid into her wetness in one smooth glide.

She wrapped her arms around him and ran her fingers over his back. He shuddered, not just from the feel of her tight pussy clutching his dick, but from the overwhelming love flowing inside him.

"Mine," he choked out. "You're mine, Mia."

"I'm yours," she whispered, and the sweet confirmation sent his heart, mind, and body soaring to a new plane of joy.

He wasn't rough tonight. Didn't fuck her hard. Didn't go fast. Rather, he made love to her. Slow and gentle, rocking into her with infinite tenderness while his mouth sought out hers in a never-ending kiss.

When he climaxed, it wasn't so much an explosion as a drawn-out rush of bliss that washed over him. Mia's orgasm was equally low-key, eliciting a quiet cry and a shiver that seemed to ripple through her body.

After their breathing had steadied, Jackson rolled them over so they were lying face-to-face, his cock still buried inside her. Their skin was sticky from his come and her wetness, but Jackson didn't mind and Mia didn't seem to either. She just moved closer and rested her head on his biceps.

"I'm so sleepy," she murmured.

"Go to sleep," he murmured back.

"You sure? You don't want to stay up late and talk?"

He smiled. "Not really. I'm feeling sleepy myself. It's probably from all the turkey we ate."

She snuggled against his chest, making no attempt to separate their joined bodies. "What's the plan for tomorrow? Are we going to that Thanksgiving parade Evie mentioned?"

"Yeah, it's a family tradition." He didn't want to spoil the mood by warning her that they'd probably be subjected to stares and whispers when they went into town tomorrow, so he kept the grim thought to himself. "It's not until late afternoon, though. Oh, and tomorrow my dad and I are goin' for an early-morning ride. He wants to show off the new stallion he picked up at auction last month."

"What's early?"

"Seven a.m. probably. Maybe eight."

"Okay." Her voice was growing drowsier by the second, and when he peered down, he saw that her eyes were firmly closed. "Told your mom I'd help her in the garden around eight. Don't wanna accidentally sleep in, so wake me up before you go, 'kay?"

He smiled in the darkness. "Don't worry, I'm really good at wake-up calls." He paused meaningfully. "Of the sexy variety, of course."

Her sleepy laughter was muffled against his chest. "God, I love you."

Jackson froze, his heart coming to a grinding halt.

He waited a couple of beats, but Mia didn't say another word. She was fast asleep, he realized. Probably wasn't even conscious of what she'd just said.

I love you.

Goddamn.

He suspected she wouldn't remember this moment when she woke up tomorrow, but he was never gonna forget it.

She loved him.

She fuckin' loved him.

He carried that spirit-lifting thought with him as he drifted off and fell asleep with a smile on his face.

CHAPTER
TWENTY-ONE

The next day, Mia learned what it felt like to be the subject of unwanted attention. She'd spent a wonderful morning on the ranch working in the garden with Arlene and then taking a long walk on the Ramsey property with Evie, but the second she and Jackson had driven into Abbott Creek's downtown core, the fun atmosphere evaporated into a cloud of friction.

Everywhere they went, people stared at Jackson. He was gawked at, glared at, whispered about. The short walk down the cobblestone street toward the town square was utterly unbearable and succeeded in making Mia understand precisely why Jackson didn't like coming back here. If she was treated like a specimen under a microscope each time she came home, she'd probably stay away too.

And yet with the understanding came the fierce need to defend the man by her side. What had he ever done to these people? And what the hell gave them the right to judge him? Jackson had been a nineteen-year-old kid who'd indulged in some kinky bondage sex with his willing girlfriend. So fucking what? He didn't deserve to be ostracized for it, not one goddamn bit.

Mia wasn't normally into PDA, but today she went out of her way to shower Jackson with affection. She held his hand while they stood on the sidewalk to watch the parade, kissed him at every available opportunity, and gave him more than one bear hug over the course of the afternoon. She wanted him to know that he was worthy, that he deserved none of the scorn being directed his way.

And he seemed to appreciate her efforts, smiling at her whenever she touched him and always making sure she remained close to his side.

His family had come into town with them, including Shane and Tiffany, who'd driven over separately and were keeping their distance by standing several feet away. Throughout the day, Mia had been shooting surreptitious glances in Tiffany's direction, trying to locate any outward flaws in the woman, and it really grated that she couldn't.

As irritating as it was, it didn't surprise Mia that Jackson had loved the girl. The blue-eyed blonde was undeniably beautiful, and the air of fragility that surrounded her made it easy to see why Casper Griffen had believed his daughter had been victimized. Tiffany emitted an innocent vibe that only annoyed Mia all the more, especially knowing that the woman liked it *real* dirty behind closed doors.

Jackson's brother was even harder to read. Shane didn't say much, not even to his wife, and Mia would've given anything to get a glimpse into his mind. Did he still believe Jackson had forced himself on Tiffany? Did he long for reconciliation? Or did he still harbor deep hatred and resentment toward his younger brother?

"The last float is coming up."

Mia glanced over at Evie, who practically had to bend her

entire head to get her mouth close to Mia's ear. The cheers and applause of the crowd on each side of the street made it difficult to be heard, so Evie raised her voice even higher.

"Trust me, you're gonna love this one."

A moment later, Mia understood Evie's mischievous prediction. The float that appeared on the street featured half a dozen shirtless men, ranging from twenty to forty years old and wearing bright red fireman helmets.

"Abbott Creek's volunteer fire brigade," Evie declared with a grin. "See the one over on the far left?"

Mia followed the young woman's gaze and grinned when she spotted the muscular firefighter. "A friend of yours?" she teased.

"Not yet, but I intend to change that once I'm legal." Evie sighed loudly. "His name's Kellan and he has a strict rule about not dating anyone under twenty-one. We've been flirtin' for the last year, but the pigheaded fool refuses to make a move."

Jackson cleared his throat. "Can you please not subject me to this, Evangeline?" he griped to his sister. "I don't wanna know who you're making eyes at."

His sister stuck out her tongue. "Tough. 'Cause Mia wants to know all about it. Right, Mia?"

She laughed. "I don't know... I say we put your brother out of his misery and talk about it later in private."

"Deal," Evie said immediately.

After the final float disappeared around the corner, Jackson's parents drifted over to the trio. While the Ramseys tried to figure out where to go for dinner, Mia discreetly snuck a peek at Arlene's and Kurt's interlaced fingers. She'd noticed that the older couple never stood more than an inch or two apart. And they always stole kisses when they thought no one was looking.

The love they felt for each other was so evident it might as well have been advertised on a billboard. Mia had never met a couple who was still so in love even after decades together. Arlene and Kurt acted like newlyweds, and seeing them brought a strange pang of longing that Mia didn't understand.

She'd been trying to make sense of the troubling emotion since they'd arrived in Jackson's hometown, but she hadn't figured it out yet. And she had no time to dwell on it now. The Ramseys had reached a decision about dinner, and the group was moving away from the crowded sidewalk.

As she and Jackson fell into step with each other, he looked over and said, "Did you still want to go to the saloon after dinner?"

She answered without hesitation. "Hell yeah. Every time I see those swinging doors I'm just dying to go in."

"Then we'll go." The smile he gave her seemed incredibly strained.

"Or we don't have to," she said hastily.

"Nah, it's cool." He lowered his voice. "Just be prepared to get stared at some more."

Her heart ached for him, and the unfairness of the situation really hit home when she noticed a passing trio of women smile at Shane and his wife, who were walking ahead of them. Those same ladies frowned the moment they saw Jackson, which irked the hell out of Mia.

She suddenly had to wonder if maybe Shane and Tiffany were contributing to the icy reception Jackson received each time he came home. Maybe if the two of them made an actual show of solidarity with Jackson, the townsfolk would realize there was nothing for them to gossip about, that it was all water under the bridge.

"Why don't we invite your brother and Tiffany to come with us?" Mia spoke in a barely audible voice, but she knew Jackson had heard her, because his wide shoulders went rigid.

"You really think that's a good idea?" His lack of enthusiasm showed on his face.

"You're going to have to talk to them eventually, right? Wasn't that the plan?"

"Yeah...but in public?"

"Might as well." Anger colored her tone. "At least if it's in public, he won't be able to lay a hand on you."

"Now, sugar..."

"Sorry. Uncalled for."

He sighed. "I guess it wouldn't kill me to make the first move. Y'know, extend the olive branch or whatnot."

She had learned that when Jackson made up his mind about something, he didn't dilly-dally. He was the kind of man who followed through immediately, and that was exactly what he did now.

"Shane," he called out gruffly.

His brother's back tensed for a moment. "Yeah?"

"Mia and I were gonna head to the saloon after dinner. Do you and Tiff wanna join us?"

Shock flared in the other man's eyes. "Uh..." He exchanged a quick look with his wife, then nodded awkwardly. "Sure. We'll join you."

Jackson nodded back. "'Kay."

Just like that, the "date" had been set, and Mia didn't miss the wave of surprise that traveled over the rest of their little group. Jackson's parents looked like they'd just seen an elephant lumbering down Main Street, while Evie was completely agape.

"This has the potential to end very, very badly," Jackson told Mia in the softest of voices.

She attempted to be optimistic. "Or it could go great."

He didn't look convinced.

And frankly, neither was she.

Two hours later, Jackson knew with absolute certainty that he'd made a mistake.

The Creek Saloon was filled to the gills, and every head swiveled to the door when the foursome strode inside. He suddenly wished he and Mia had just gone home with Evie and his parents. He could've ridden Glory over to Shane's cabin and they would've had this unpleasant reunion in private, rather than in front of the whole dang town.

But it was too late now. He'd made his uncomfortable bed and now he had to lie in it. So he swallowed his reluctance, gripped Mia's hand even tighter, and followed his brother and ex-girlfriend toward a semi-private booth against the far wall. The bar's dim lighting made it easier for him to ignore the cutting stares of the other patrons, and the country tune blaring out of the jukebox drowned out the whispers that were no doubt being exchanged as the two couples settled on opposite sides of the booth.

"Uh...so..." Jackson pasted on a cordial expression. "I never had a chance to congratulate y'all. Y'know, the wedding and all."

Shane responded with a brisk nod. "Thanks."

"Thank you," Tiffany echoed. She looked distinctly uncomfortable as she played with a strand of her hair.

"Did you get married here in town?" Mia's casual tone sounded as forced as everyone else's.

"We did," Tiffany confirmed. "We were married in the same church where Shane's folks got hitched."

"Oh, that's nice."

There was a beat of silence.

"So you work for a landscaping company," Tiffany said clumsily. "Do you like it?"

"I love it," Mia answered.

Another silence.

"How are you enjoying military life, Jack?" Shane finally spoke up.

He shrugged. "It's a lot different than ranching, but just as back-breaking."

"I imagine so."

More silence. Then all four of them spoke at once.

"So—"

"Well—"

"How do—"

"Are you—"

A wave of uneasy laughter washed over the booth, but none of them got to finish their sentences because a very familiar woman in an apron had appeared out of nowhere.

"Well, as I live 'n breathe," the waitress drawled. "Jackson Ramsey, back in Abbott Creek."

He studied the dark-haired woman, scanning his memory as he tried to figure out how he knew her.

"Crissy," she prompted. "I was on the cheerleading squad with Tiff."

"Right. How've you been, Crissy?" he asked politely.

"Can't complain. Bobby and I tied the knot—you remember Bobby, don't cha? He played for the Steers, same as you. Anyway, we tied the knot, happily married for four years now."

"I'm glad to hear it, darlin'."

"You look good, Jackson. Real good. I'm feeling a little tongue-*tied* lookin' at you."

Crissy's smirk annoyed the shit out of him. So did the way she'd used the word "tied" three times in less than a minute.

Not as subtle as you think, Miss Crissy.

He smothered his irritation as he responded with, "You're lookin' good too. Bobby's a lucky man."

"Damn right." The brunette glanced around the booth. "What can I get y'all? A cold Bud for Shane, Long Island iced tea for Tiffy—I already know that. What else?"

After Jackson and Mia both ordered, Crissy flounced off, leaving the foursome to their nervous small talk.

He ought to put an end to this nonsense, Jackson knew that. He needed to look Shane in the eye and demand an apology, but before he could, another unwanted visitor dropped by their booth.

"Jackson Ramsey!" The bulky man was a former classmate of Jackson's, who'd gone by the nickname Rocky back in the day.

"Rocky, good to see you," he said guardedly.

"Don't go by Rocky anymore, man—it's just Stuart now. But then you'd know that if you came home more often." Stuart's dark eyes gleamed. "But I suppose you're too busy having a ton of kinky sex over in Cali."

Jackson set his jaw and refused to take the bait. "Nah, I'm busy saving the world."

"Yeah, I heard you were some kind of SEAL," Stuart retorted, sounding unimpressed. "Bet that really gets the chickies goin'. Prolly makes it easier to get 'em to agree to all that bondage shit you're into."

"Stuart," Shane said with a note of warning.

"What? I'm just messin' around. He knows that, right, Jackson?"

He grunted in response, his hands tingling with the urge to clock the son of a bitch.

Fortunately, Rocky AKA Stuart didn't stick around. The beefy man stumbled away when somebody called his name, much to Jackson's relief.

When Crissy returned with their drinks a moment later,

Jackson immediately reached for his beer and chugged half of it straight away.

"Shit, I'm sorry about that."

Shane's gruff words surprised the heck out of him. "No biggie," Jackson mumbled.

"Maybe we should just go," Tiffany said timidly, running one finger along the rim of her glass. "Everyone keeps staring at us."

Mia, who hadn't said a thing during the last five minutes, suddenly snorted. "And why do you think that is, *Tiff?*"

The blonde shifted on the hard wooden bench, ill at ease. "I don't like being the center of attention, is all."

Jackson felt Mia's body stiffen with disbelief. He quickly rested his hand on her thigh and gave it a reassuring stroke.

Unfortunately, his attempt at calming her down didn't work.

"And you think Jackson likes it?" Mia shot back. "Do you realize how humiliating this is for him? Everywhere he goes people look at him like he's either a sexual deviant or a rapist—you think that's fun for him?"

"Mia," he said quietly.

"No," she snapped. "I can't stand the way they're just sitting here, acting like all this shit isn't their fault." She glared at the other couple. "Well, guess what, dum-dums, it's *directly* your fault."

Shane and Tiffany recoiled.

"Mia," Jackson started again.

Her hands trembled as she wrapped them around her beer bottle. "Don't worry, I'm done," she muttered.

"Listen, I get what you're saying," Tiffany told Mia in a wobbly voice. "I messed up, okay? I shouldn't have lied eight years ago, and Shane shouldn't have done what he did. But we've moved past it. We—"

"Okay, I'm *not* done," Mia interrupted in another explosion of incredulity. "You've *moved past it*? Well, gee, how wonderful for you, Tiffany. You accused your boyfriend of rape, a lie that led to him getting beaten senseless by his own brother, but life goes on, huh? You just married the other brother and now you're living happily ever after. Doesn't matter that Jackson is treated like a pariah by everyone in town, or that he and your *husband* haven't spoken in years—as long as *you've* moved past it...well, congratu-fucking-lations, Tiffany."

Deafening silence crashed over them. Jackson noticed in dismay that half the bar patrons were looking their way, and even though the jukebox belted out an up-tempo Garth Brooks song, a flurry of whispers could be heard over the music.

"I want to go home now."

Tiffany's meek voice brought a sigh to Jackson's lips.

His brother, whose expression had remained shuttered throughout Mia's entire tirade, wasted no time ushering out his shaken wife from the booth.

Mia gave Jackson's leg a little push. "I want to leave too," she said tersely. "I can't spend another second with these people."

He'd never felt so helpless in his life as he followed Mia out of the bar. Her body radiated anger, and he didn't know whether to be touched or upset. He shared in her frustration. He'd always resented the fact that Tiff and his brother had come out of that awful situation unscathed while he'd been hung out to dry. But he'd held his tongue for his parents' sake, to spare them from another potentially violent altercation between the two sons they desperately loved.

Fuck. Bringing Mia and Tiff along tonight had been a bad idea. He should've spoken to Shane alone.

He hadn't expected Mia to jump to his defense, but he couldn't fault her for it. He'd been too agitated to regain control of the situation.

But he would find a way to get his brother alone. He had to, for everyone's sake. His and Mia's flight didn't leave until noon tomorrow, so he was confident he'd be able to speak to Shane before they left.

Not tonight, though. Tonight he needed to get Mia home, pronto. She was too volatile at the moment.

Far more volatile than he'd thought, in fact. Because the second they stepped outside, they encountered a sobbing Tiffany in Shane's arms. And the second Mia overheard Tiffany's muffled words, she exploded like a cannon again.

"It's not like what they're saying isn't true," Jackson's ex mumbled. "He *is* a deviant! I know that now. I was young and stupid back then and I didn't realize how wrong what we were doin' was—"

"You're a goddamn liar," Mia spat out, advancing on Tiffany like a lioness protecting her cub.

The couple broke apart, but while Shane's expression flickered with wariness, Tiffany's eyes took on an incensed glint.

"You don't even know me!" she snapped. "Who the heck are you to come here and call me a liar? You know nothin' about me or Shane or even Jackson, for that matter! You're a nosy city girl who thinks she's better than a country hick like me, is that it? Well, you're *not* better! You're just a judgmental bitch who—"

Before Jackson could blink, Mia punched his ex-girlfriend right in the face.

CHAPTER
TWENTY-TWO

Mia had never hit another living soul in her entire life. She didn't use violence to solve problems. She wasn't that kind of girl. Or at least she hadn't *thought* she was.

But clearly she was the person who slugged someone for calling her a bitch.

Sheer mortification flooded her body when she saw Tiffany's head snap back from the force of the blow. Mia's breaths were shallow pants, and the guilt that streaked through her veins caused her hands to shake ferociously.

"Oh my God," she burst out. "I'm sorry. I didn't mean to…"

"I can't believe you did that," the blonde whimpered, pressing her palm to her red cheek.

Mia was relieved to see she hadn't drawn blood, but she knew Tiffany would have a hell of a bruise on her cheekbone tomorrow morning. Which only set off another rush of shame that almost knocked her off her feet. Jackson immediately came up beside her and she sagged against his solid frame, still stunned by what she'd done.

"I'm so sorry," she murmured.

Tiffany didn't answer. She just gazed imploringly at Shane. "Can we please go?"

Without another word, husband and wife stalked off toward the red pickup parked several yards away.

As an engine roared to life, Mia peered up at Jackson in pure misery. "I'm sorry," she whispered. "I can't believe I hit her."

"She provoked you," he said gruffly.

"That's no excuse." An anguished moan slid out. "Oh fuck, I'm a terrible person. I *hit* her, Jackson."

Tears filled her eyes, then spilled over and streamed down her cheeks in hot, salty rivulets. She felt so ashamed she couldn't even breathe.

And she was scared. Honest-to-God scared.

Because deep down, Mia knew the provocation that led to her punching Tiffany wasn't the woman's use of the B-word. It was Tiffany's character-bashing of Jackson.

She'd called him a deviant! And then she'd lied through her teeth by saying she believed their past relationship had been wrong.

The woman's nerve had made Mia see red. Acting like there was something wrong with Jackson? Un-fucking-acceptable. In that moment, her sole goal had been to silence that sniveling liar, to punish her for having the nerve to imply that Jackson was anything other than the amazing and honorable man he truly was.

And in that moment, Mia had realized just how much she cared about him. So deeply that she'd *assaulted* someone for him.

Somehow, over these last three months, she'd fallen for the guy without even realizing it.

That was the most terrifying thing of all.

"C'mon, let's go home." His warm hands cupped her chin, his thumbs sweeping away the tears staining her face.

She nodded weakly, allowing him to take her hand and lead her to his father's truck.

The drive back to the Double R was a quiet one. Mia battled tears the whole time, unable to get a grip on her emotions.

She'd punched another person.

She loved Jackson.

The two thoughts tangled together and ravaged her tired brain, but she refused to give them the attention they demanded. She didn't want to think about how guilty she felt about the former, or how confused and scared the latter made her.

When Jackson finally pulled into the ranch driveway, relief crashed into her and had her diving out of the pickup. All she wanted to do right now was lock herself in Jackson's bedroom and bury her head under the covers. She didn't want to think. Didn't want to *feel*. She would simply sleep, and then tomorrow she'd be back in San Diego, where she'd sift through her thoughts and emotions and hopefully be able to make sense of them.

"Mia, wait."

His gruff voice stopped her when she was halfway to the porch.

"Do you mind being alone for a little while?" he asked, his worried gaze probing her face. "I'm gonna drive out to Shane and Tiff's place."

She blinked in surprise. "What for?"

"I think it's time my brother and I had that talk we've been trying to avoid."

"That's probably a good idea." She bit her lip. "Can you...

will you apologize to Tiffany again? I feel so awful about what happened. I really do, Jackson."

"I know you do, sugar."

His long strides ate up the distance between them, and then he was kissing her, his lips warm and reassuring.

"Go upstairs and get ready for bed, darlin'. I'll be back soon, okay?"

She swallowed. "Okay."

With a sweet smile, he left her on the porch and headed back to the truck. Mia watched until his taillights disappeared in the darkness, then took a breath and walked into the house.

She knew Evie had gone out after dinner with some friends, but Jackson's parents had come straight home. As Mia entered the front hall, she prayed that Kurt and Arlene had already retired for the night. She didn't have the energy or the brain capacity to maintain a pleasant conversation, and she suspected that if either of Jackson's parents saw her face, they'd immediately know that something terrible had happened tonight.

She quietly slipped out of her sneakers and took a hesitant step toward the hallway. Luckily, the kitchen was dark, which told her Arlene wasn't doing any late-night baking or anything. But up ahead, light spilled out from the living-room doorway.

She tiptoed toward it and hoped that if Jackson's parents were inside, they wouldn't spot her. When she neared the doorway, however, she realized there'd been no reason to worry. Kurt and Arlene were in the living room, but they were sound asleep on the couch.

Her heart jumped to her throat as she stared at the sleeping couple. Kurt was on his back with one arm propped behind his head, the other wrapped tightly around Arlene, who was nestled at his side. The older couple looked so peaceful lying there that Mia almost started crying again.

Something happened to her as she stood there staring.

She suddenly wanted...

She wanted *forever*, damn it.

But forever didn't exist.

Yes, it does. You're looking at it right now.

But maybe this was a fluke. Maybe Kurt and Arlene's long-lasting relationship was a gift for them, and them alone.

You can have it too. With Jackson.

But...could she? Her own mother had tried to find true love ten times—and she'd gotten ten divorces out of it.

Fear and turmoil clogged her throat. She'd avoided serious relationships her entire life. Shied away from forming any attachments in order to avoid getting her heart broken. But was she right to be scared? Or were her fears simply a knee-jerk reaction to watching her mother's life shatter every other year?

God, she couldn't think about any of this right now.

Her gaze darted back to Jackson's parents, and a rush of panic swarmed her belly. She had to leave. Had to go home. Now.

The anxiety attack came so fast and so unexpectedly that Mia couldn't think straight. All she knew was that she couldn't stay in this house. She couldn't face Jackson's family after what she'd done to Tiffany. She couldn't face *Jackson*. Not tonight. Not when her heart was trying to pound its way out of her chest and her lungs refused to accept the oxygen she was gulping in. Not when her mind was a jumbled mess and her emotions were so out of control she feared she might actually pass out.

Everything after that initial siege of panic was a blur.

Somehow she ended up upstairs.

Somehow she wound up on the porch with her carry-on hastily packed.

Somehow she was sliding into the backseat of an Uber she didn't remember ordering.

And somehow she found herself at the airport, buying a ticket for the next available flight to San Diego.

It was only when she entered the gate that Mia became aware of what she was doing. And once she did, a flash flood of guilt whipped through her.

She fumbled for her phone, horrified that she'd left the ranch without saying goodbye to Jackson. Without thanking his family for their hospitality. Without apologizing to Tiffany again.

But despite the deep remorse seizing her insides, she couldn't bring herself to go back. She wanted to go home and sleep in her own bed, to take advantage of Danny's absence and really think about what all this meant.

What loving Jackson meant.

Fighting back tears, she sent Jackson a brief text letting him know she was at the airport and flying home early. Then she shut off her phone and sat in the gate until it was time to board. Luck had been on her side—the flight was scheduled to leave in twenty-five minutes, and somehow she'd managed to check-in before the kiosk closed and zip through security without a hitch. It had all gone so smoothly she felt like one of those unrealistically fortunate characters in a movie.

Like *The Runaway Bride*.

Or maybe *The Worst Girlfriend on the Fucking Planet*.

She took a breath, trying not to let the guilt consume her, but it was impossible. For the next two hours, guilt seemed to be the only emotion she was capable of registering. It plagued her during the two-and-a-half-hour flight. It constricted her heart when she arrived in San Diego, and followed her all the way home.

Exhaustion crushed down on her chest as she climbed up to the third floor of her building. It was nearly two in the morning. She was desperate to slide under the covers and pretend tonight had never happened. She hadn't even turned her phone back on, for fear that Jackson would call and she might be tempted to answer. She couldn't hear his husky voice right now. She'd be liable to burst into tears if that happened.

The apartment was engulfed in shadows when she walked inside. She welcomed the dark, the silence, the familiar sturdy hardwood beneath her feet.

But the overpowering relief she experienced from being home was suddenly replaced by a burst of sheer terror as a blurry figure lurched into her line of sight.

The indistinct monster wielded an aluminum baseball bat that gleamed in the darkness, swinging it around in a menacing whirl that promptly took ten years off Mia's life.

"Don't move!"

The command sent her pulse careening—until she blinked, recognition dawning in her eyes.

"*Danny?*" she screeched.

"*Mia?*" he exclaimed at the same time.

Her heart rate steadied, but the alarm rushing through her only increased, drawing an incredulous question from her mouth.

"What the *hell* are you doing here?"

CHAPTER
TWENTY-THREE

"I figured you'd show up." Shane was standing on the porch of his small, A-frame cabin when Jackson's boots connected with the dirt.

He slammed the door of his dad's pickup and strode toward the cabin, no hesitation, nothing but steely determination.

"I figured you'd be expecting me," he replied with a shrug.

When he reached the porch, he noticed the two unopened beer bottles on the ledge.

Shane followed his gaze and smiled wryly. "I thought we'd need the liquid courage."

Jackson had to chuckle. "Probably a good idea." His eyes strayed toward the door. "Is Tiff all right?"

"She's fine. Just suffering from a case of embarrassment and some bruised pride." Remorse flickered in Shane's eyes. "She doesn't blame Mia for what happened back there. Tiff knows she provoked it, and she feels crappy about it. She's already planning on drivin' up to the big house tomorrow to apologize to your girl."

"Mia feels bad too," he said roughly. "You don't know her

well, but trust me when I tell you that she's not the kind of woman who goes around assaulting folks."

Shane let out a low laugh. "A wee lil' thing like her? I doubt she's ever thrown a punch in her life. C'mon, why don't we go round back?"

Beers in hand, they rounded the side of the cabin and settled in a pair of Adirondack chairs on the patio. Jackson noticed that Shane and Tiff had made a lot of changes to the sprawling land behind the cabin. A large wooden gazebo stood on what had once been an empty stretch of grass, and natural flagstone paths now wound through newly planted flowerbeds and stone planters overflowing with greenery.

"Mom's been helping Tiff in the garden," Shane said quietly.

"That's nice of her."

"Yeah, it is. Tiff really appreciates it." Shane paused, regret flashing on his face. "Mom's never forgiven her for what she did to you, but they're slowly rebuilding their relationship. I'm hoping one day they can be close again."

Jackson twisted open his bottle and took a long sip, hoping the cold beer would ease his rising agitation.

"I never forced myself on her, Shane."

His brother jerked as if he'd been struck.

"Never," Jackson repeated, his throat so tight it hurt.

"I..." Shane's expression swam with shame. "I know that."

Surprise jolted through him. "You do?"

"'Course I do. You're not that kinda man, Jackie. Never have been, never will be."

"Then why..." He took another hasty sip. "Why did you follow me into the barn that day? Why did you..."

"Beat my little brother senseless?" Shane's voice cracked. "Because I didn't take a moment to think. I reacted, pure and simple. I loved Tiff, loved her so fuckin' much, and the thought of anyone hurting her made me crazy. I snapped. Think I might've even blacked out, Jackie. One minute I was walking toward the barn, the next I was being pulled off your bloody, broken body."

The horror on Shane's face was impossible to miss, and when he went on, his voice shook so hard he was nearly stuttering. "I couldn't believe what I'd done to you. I was so fuckin' ashamed of myself, and still am. When I saw Dad carrying you to the house, reality suddenly came rushing back. I knew you couldn't have done what Tiff accused you of. And I knew I'd never be able to look you in the eye again."

Jackson's hand trembled as he set his beer on the ground next to his chair. "You never apologized," he said hoarsely.

"I didn't know how to. And not just that. I didn't wanna tell you I was sorry—so fuckin' sorry—only to have you deny me the forgiveness I was desperately craving. So I didn't say anything, and eventually shit got so bad between us I didn't know how to bring it up. I thought maybe if I ignored it, pretended it never happened, it would just blow over. But it didn't blow over. It got worse, and then you were gone. You left, and I had no fuckin' clue how to make you come back. But...fuck, Jackie, I missed you. I missed my brother, and I didn't know how to deal with that or how to make things better."

Jackson raked his hand through his hair. "I thought you still believed Tiff's lie. Even after she came forward and told the truth, I thought you still believed it."

"Never," Shane said fiercely.

"Then why...I mean..." Frustration surged in his blood. "Why all the nasty looks? You've been eyeing me these past couple days like you want to throttle me."

His brother let out a ragged breath. "I know. I...dang it...I was jealous, okay? Every time you come home, Mom and Dad act like the messiah just showed up. And to top it off, this time you brought this amazing girl who instantly earned Mom's approval, somethin' my own wife has had to beg for every day for the last eight years."

As they both went quiet, Jackson listened to the crickets chirping in the distance and the rustling of the trees all around them. He'd never realized how tormented his older brother had been all these years. He'd assumed that Shane hated him, but now he knew that wasn't the case. His brother had been overwrought with guilt and shame, with envy thrown into the mix, and that made Jackson damn sad.

"I'm sorry."

Shane's gruff words hung between them, bringing a lump to Jackson's throat.

"I'm so sorry, Jackson. For beating you that day, for being too much of a coward to apologize for it, for marrying Tiff even though I knew it would cause more friction for the family. I'm sorry for all of it."

He slowly met his brother's gaze. "Thank you. I appreciate that." He stopped, breathing through the pain and sorrow. "I forgive you."

"You do?"

"Yeah, I do."

Ever so slowly, the tension that had plagued them for so many years seeped away like groundwater soaking into dirt. In that quiet moment of forgiveness, Jackson felt a sense of peace and liberation that lightened his chest and soothed his heart. He'd needed this. Goddamn, he'd needed it.

And clearly Shane did too, because his face relaxed and a smile lifted his lips.

"Do you wanna come in and catch the highlights from yesterday's games?"

Jackson's regret was genuine as he shook his head. "I would, but I've gotta check on Mia. Poor thing's more upset than I've ever seen her."

Shane nodded in understanding. "You're right—go take care of your woman. And make sure she knows there's no hard feelings on Tiff's part. She didn't mean what she said back there. This whole mess has been tough on her too, Jackie."

"I know. I'll talk to her tomorrow before we leave, try to make things right," he said gruffly.

"I know she'd appreciate that."

They rose from their chairs, eyeing each other for a moment. Then Shane stepped forward and hugged him.

Jackson's heart ached as he returned the embrace. It was the first physical contact he and Shane had had since the incident in the barn eight years ago, and when they finally broke apart, they both had tears in their eyes.

"I love you, Jackie. I need you to know that."

"I love you too."

The emotion tightening his chest didn't let up, not even when he slid back into the truck and made the short drive back to the main house. He was suddenly itching to see Mia, to throw his arms around her and thank her for persuading him to come home. Because of her, he'd finally mended the rift with his brother and found the solace he'd been seeking all these years.

He parked the truck and jumped out eagerly, but when he glimpsed his parents sitting in a pair of wicker chairs on the porch, his happiness dissolved like a cloud of smoke. It was past eleven, way past their bedtime. His folks woke up at the crack of dawn every day. They didn't normally shoot the shit on the porch this close to midnight.

Their identical grave expressions brought a frown to his lips. "What's goin' on?" he demanded.

Kurt and Arlene exchanged a look.

The frown deepened. "Tell me."

Jackson's father cleared his throat, distinctly uncomfortable. "Your woman's gone."

His pulse sped up. "What?"

"Mia's gone," Arlene said softly. "She left."

Shock and confusion spiraled through him. "What do you mean, she *left*? Why didn't you stop her?"

"We were asleep," his mom admitted.

"Woke up when we heard the taxi pull into the drive," Kurt said. "By the time we got outside, she was gone."

"We tried calling you, sweetie, but your phone went to voicemail."

As his heart thundered in his chest, Jackson dug his phone out of his pocket and frantically searched the screen. He'd put it on silent before heading over to his brother's. Sure enough, he had several missed calls from the ranch number.

Along with a text message.

From Mia.

He quickly read the text, unable to believe his eyes.

"She's catching a flight home." He checked his watch and cursed. "Son of a bitch. The flight was at ten thirty. It's already taken off."

His mother's eyes filled with sympathy. "Oh, sweetie."

"It's too late to stop her," he mumbled. "She's already gone."

"Why?" his father asked, looking bewildered. "Why would she go?"

Jackson set his jaw and took a step to the door. "Shane'll fill you in. I've gotta pack."

He flew into the house without another word. As he sprinted up the stairs, he heard footsteps pounding behind him. A glance over his shoulder revealed Arlene, whose cheeks were red as she struggled to reach her son.

"You're leaving?" she said in dismay.

"I have to." Misery clogged his throat. "I have to go to her."

His mom didn't voice another objection. She simply followed him into his bedroom and stood in the doorway while he rapidly shoved items of clothing into his bag.

"She's the one."

He froze.

"You know that, right?" Arlene said gently.

He met his mother's eyes, his heart squeezing painfully. "I know."

She gave a brisk nod. "Good. Now go get her, son."

CHAPTER
TWENTY-FOUR

Standing in her dark apartment, Mia stared at her brother and waited for him to explain himself.

But rather than shed light on his startling presence, Danny turned the tables on her. "What are you doing home? I thought you were coming back tomorrow!"

"I caught an earlier flight," she sputtered. "And don't you dare make this about me, pal! Why aren't you in Reno with Mom?"

Very slowly, Danny lowered the baseball bat. "I didn't feel like going," he mumbled.

Mia narrowed her eyes. "Daniel."

"I..." He sucked in a breath. "She..."

After a beat, the bat slid out of his hand and clattered to the floor with a sharp, metallic ding.

"What happened?" she demanded.

Danny's entire face collapsed. "Mom never showed up."

Those four desperation-laced words hovered in the air.

And broke Mia's heart.

As nausea churned in her stomach, the six-foot-tall young man standing in front of her transformed into a lost little boy right in front of her eyes. Danny's bottom lip trembled, his broad shoulders drooping as if he couldn't support his own weight.

Mia didn't waste time—she threw her arms around him and hugged him with everything she had.

"Oh Danny, I'm so sorry."

Moisture soaked her skin as he buried his face in her neck. His tears triggered a jolt of anger that blasted into her chest. She suddenly wished their mother were here so she could strangle the living shit out of that bitch. How could Brenda have done this? How *could* she?

Mia stepped back. "You've been here all alone for the past two days?"

He nodded wordlessly.

Drawing a steady breath, she led her devastated brother over to the couch and forced him to sit while she went to switch on the floor lamp. A moment later, light flooded the room and revealed Danny's red-rimmed eyes and wet cheeks.

She sat beside him and wrapped one arm around his shoulder, speaking in a firm voice. "It's all right, baby. We've dealt with this before, remember? She shows up and then she leaves. That's just what she does. I know you were hoping it would be different this time, and I'm so sorry it didn't turn out the way you wanted. But we'll get through it, the way we always do. It's okay to be sad and hurt and upset, but it's not the end of the world."

"Yes it is!"

The certainty in his voice and vehemence in his eyes startled her. "It's not, sweetie, I promise you that. I know she hurt you again, but—"

"She hurt my future."

Mia was caught off guard. "What are you talking about?"

Danny looked up with a crestfallen expression. "She took

my savings."

A wave of horror rammed into her. "What?"

"She emptied out my bank account," he mumbled, then let out an agonized moan that sent a knife of fear straight to Mia's heart.

She had no idea what he was saying. How was that even possible? She and Danny had opened his account together. They were the only ones who could withdraw or deposit funds into it.

"Danny," she said softly. "What did you do?"

Tears welled up in his eyes again. "She told me she wanted to help out," he whispered. "She said that college would be really expensive even if I ended up getting a scholarship, and she offered to throw money my way whenever she had some to spare. She told me it would be easier if she could just deposit money into my account through her online banking."

Ice crept through Mia's veins, making her entire body run cold.

"So we went to the bank together and we spoke to the manager..."

She could hardly breathe now.

"He made us fill out this form that would link our accounts. That way Mom could transfer money directly into my account from hers." Danny's lower lip started to quiver. "I signed the form, Mia. I didn't think it was a big deal. I mean, it wasn't like it was just Mom who could access my account—I could access hers too." He shrugged helplessly. "I thought it was really cool that she trusted me and didn't think I would try to take her money or anything."

Mia's pulse roared, nearly drowning out his voice. "The bank manager shouldn't have let that happen," she growled. "She's not your guardian, damn it. She shouldn't have been given access to your account."

In fact, Mia was already planning on marching into the bank the second it opened and demanding that motherfucker be fired.

"So on Thursday morning, I was waiting for her to pick me up," Danny went on, "but she never showed. I hung out here, and then the next morning I got an email from the bank. It was a confirmation of a transaction, and I clicked on it and saw that she transferred all my money into her account. I had almost ten thousand dollars saved up and she took it all! I tried to transfer the money back, but I kept getting an error message saying her account number was no longer valid."

His face scrunched up as if he was fighting back tears, and Mia quickly pulled him into her arms again. Silent sobs wracked his shoulders, and each time he sniffled, another chunk splintered off her heart.

"Why didn't you call me?" she asked. "And why didn't you tell me about the bank thing?"

"Because I knew you'd get mad. I knew you'd tell me I was being a gullible idiot. But I thought she wanted to help me, Mia. I really thought that."

She sighed. "I know you did, kiddo."

"And then when I got that email from the bank, I was so embarrassed." Another round of tears shook his body. "I didn't want you to be disappointed in me. I didn't want you to hate me."

"I could *never* be disappointed in you and I could *never* hate you," she said fiercely. "I love you, Danny. And one of the things I love most about you is the way you always try to see the good in people."

Her brother looked up, his expression absolutely ravaged. "I love you too."

"I know you do."

He rested his head on her shoulder, and she gently stroked

his hair, wishing she could take away his pain. Brenda deserved to burn in hell for what she'd done to him. If the woman ever showed her face again, Mia was going to throttle her, no mistake about it.

"Do you think there's any way to get the money back?" he asked in a small voice.

She hesitated. "I don't know. We'll go to the bank tomorrow and talk to the idiot who signed off on it. Your account is set up so that both of our signatures are required in order to make any major changes. Anything you do on your own is restricted to withdrawals and deposits. I don't give a shit if Brenda told him she was your mother—the manager shouldn't have approved your request. Believe me, I'm going to have his job for this."

Danny smiled weakly. "Maybe we should bring Jackson. You know, so he can scare the manager with all his muscles."

Her heart clenched. God, she'd completely forgotten about Jackson. About the way she'd deserted him in Texas and scurried back to San Diego like a petrified animal.

"He came back with you, right?"

She avoided her brother's eyes. "No, he's still in Texas."

"How come?"

Mia shrugged.

"Seriously, why?" Danny pushed.

She let out a sheepish breath. "Let's just say you're not the only one who screwed up."

"Oh, crap. What did you do, dum-dum?"

She and Danny didn't usually discuss each other's love lives, but Mia found herself blurting out everything that had happened in Abbott Creek. Confiding in Danny probably wasn't the best idea, but it was past two in the morning, she felt battered and exhausted, and words just kept popping out of her mouth before she could stop them.

When she finished, Danny was staring at her as if she'd just told him she'd joined the circus and was leaving tomorrow.

"What is the matter with you?"

Her brow puckered. "What do you mean?"

"Why don't you want to be with him? Jackson is, like, the coolest guy on the planet," Danny announced. "And for some reason, he actually loves you."

"Ha ha," she muttered.

"I'm serious, Mia, you're being so dumb right now. He loves you, you love him. So what's the problem? And PS, that was a dick move, leaving without saying goodbye to him."

She swallowed. "I know."

"Oh, and PPS—I don't think you should be scared. You're not like Mom." Danny's tone turned ferocious. "You're *nothing* like her. You're strong and awesome and you put everyone's needs ahead of yours. She's selfish and spoiled and doesn't care about anyone but herself. So are you really surprised that all her stupid marriages failed? She can't stay in love with anyone because the only person she loves is herself."

He finished in a thundering rush, daring her with his eyes to disagree.

But she couldn't. She couldn't argue a single thing he'd said because he was absolutely right. Brenda hadn't gotten her happy ending not because forever didn't exist, but because she was a flawed, self-absorbed woman doomed to destroy every relationship in her life.

But happily ever after *did* exist. All of Jackson's friends had found it. Kurt and Arlene were living it.

So why couldn't Mia?

"You're too smart for your own good," she told her brother.

"Um? Mia?" Danny pointed at his own chest. "Guy that just had ten grand stolen from him?"

Laughter was probably not the most appropriate of reactions, but Mia couldn't help it.

"Good point," she said between giggles. "Obviously you're as dumb as I am."

Danny started laughing too, and suddenly they were both crying again, but this time because of the ridiculous hilarity of the situation. Eventually they hauled their asses off the couch and drifted side-by-side toward the hallway, pausing in front of Danny's bedroom door to exchange another long hug.

"We'll try and straighten everything out in the morning," she assured him as she ruffled his hair.

"Thanks, Mia." He paused. "And you're going to straighten things out with Jackson, too. Right?"

"Don't worry, I have every intention of fixing what I broke." A ripple of worry tugged on her stomach. "I just hope Jackson is able to forgive me."

IT WAS NINE IN THE MORNING WHEN JACKSON LET HIMSELF into Mia's apartment with the key she'd given him weeks ago. He knew he was probably abusing his key privileges by sneaking into her place without warning, but he didn't give a shit. He was tired, hungry, mad, and worried, a four-way punch that made it impossible to care about etiquette at the moment.

In fact, there wasn't a single trace of Southern gentleman in him as he threw open the door to Mia's bedroom and stormed inside.

"Wake up, sugar."

Her dark head popped up, those beautiful green eyes more alert than he'd expected them to be.

He realized then that she hadn't been sleeping. Wasn't even lying under the covers. She was fully dressed and sitting on the bed, almost as if she'd been waiting for him.

Her next words confirmed his thoughts. "Took you long

enough." She sighed. "I checked the airline website and it said the next flight out of Dallas was at five o'clock this morning."

"It got delayed 'til seven." He approached the bed with wary strides. "You knew I'd come, huh?"

"Of course."

He narrowed his eyes. "Was that why you left? To see if I'd chase after you? Because that's fuckin' crazy, sugar."

"I left because I got scared," she replied quietly. "Once I was gone, yes, I figured you'd come after me, but that wasn't why I ran away." She hopped off the bed and walked over to him, keeping a foot of distance between them. "I'm so sorry I took off without telling you. That was a really shitty thing to do."

He scowled. "Damn right."

"The only excuse I have is what I just told you. I was scared." Her expression conveyed a whole lot of regret. "I was really, really scared."

"Why?" His forehead creased. "Because you thought you'd get in trouble for sluggin' Tiff?"

"No, because of the reason I slugged her in the first place. I didn't hit her because she called me a bitch," Mia confessed. "I did it because I couldn't stand knowing how much she'd hurt you. I hated the way everyone treated you in town, Jackson. You didn't deserve it, not one fucking bit."

He was confused. "And that scared you enough to send you packing?"

"I realized..." She trailed off, taking a deep breath. "I realized I cared about you much more than I thought I did. And then when you dropped me off at the ranch, I saw your parents lying together on the couch, and I wanted that, Jackson. I wanted what they had so badly, but with *you*. Because I love you."

His heart did a somersault.

"I mean it. I love you so much it hurts, and when I realized it yesterday, it scared the crap out of me."

"Because you don't want a relationship," he said in a low voice.

"Because I never thought relationships were capable of lasting." Her eyes softened, shining with certainty. "But ours can, and it will."

"Oh, really?" he couldn't help but taunt.

Her tone grew fierce. "It *will*. You said so yourself—I'm yours. And you're goddamn mine. We belong together and we're going to get our happily ever after, got it? You and me? We're forever, Jackson, and we're—why are you smiling like that?"

He could barely contain his glee. "Because you're making my job too dang easy, sugar."

"What do you mean?"

"I came here to win you back, but you didn't even give me a chance to make the big speech I was practicing on the plane. You stole the words right outta my mouth."

A smile lifted the corners of her mouth. "Sorry?"

"Don't you dare apologize." He reached for her hand and tugged her toward him. "I'm glad you finally came to your senses and realized that we're meant for each other." He brought his lips close to her ear and added, "I love you too, by the way."

The way her entire face lit up made him grin. "You do? Even after I abandoned you in Abbott Creek?"

"I love you," he repeated, his tone clear and unwavering. "I fell in love with you on our very first date and I'm gonna love you 'til the day I die. I hope you know that, and I hope you're cool with it, because you're never gettin' rid of me. "

Mia stood on her tiptoes and smacked a kiss directly on his mouth. "Good, because I'm never letting you go."

Their lips met in another kiss that sent a rush of pure joy to his heart. He'd truly expected to show up and have to use some serious persuasion to woo her back, but as usual, Mia surprised him. She was the most incredible woman he'd ever known. Quick to apologize, willing to own up to her mistakes, unafraid to tell him exactly how she was feeling when she was feeling it.

He should've known that once she became aware that she loved him, she wouldn't hesitate to let him know, and a thrill traveled up his spine as he anticipated their future together. *This* was the relationship he'd longed for, one chock full of honesty and patience, laughter and challenge. And no-holds-barred sex.

When the kiss ended, Jackson beamed at the woman he adored. "Should we get naked now, sugar? Because no declaration of love is official until the two parties involved get naked."

Her laughter echoed in the bedroom. "You're going to have to take a rain check, *sugar*. Right now you're accompanying me and Danny to the bank. We might need your muscles."

His eyebrows shot up. "What for?"

"I'll tell you all about it in the car." She laced their fingers together. "Oh, and before I forget—how did it go with your brother?"

"I'll tell you all about it in the car," he mimicked.

They stepped into the hall, rapping a wake-up call on Danny's door on their way to the living room. As they waited for her brother, Jackson cocked his head and said, "So what do you wanna do later? After we're finished being naked, that is."

She mulled it over. "Well, I guess we can grab some dinner from Tonio's." She thought about it some more. "And then I'm sure we'll get naked again at some point."

He smiled. "And then?"

Mia smiled back. "And then we can get started on the forever part."

EPILOGUE

Six months later

"Ladies and gentlemen—and Seth—will you please do me the honor of welcoming the miracle before you." Lieutenant Carson Scott stepped through the waiting-room doorway and held up a tiny infant swaddled in a blue blanket. "Feast your eyes on Jacob Thomas Sullivan Scott."

"Two middle names?" Seth cracked. "Isn't that overkill?"

"And did you really just *Lion King* that baby?" Dylan piped up.

"Seriously, dude, put the kid down," John Garrett advised. "Holly'll kill you if you drop her precious bundle."

Carson rolled his eyes, but he did lower his infant son and cradle him protectively against his chest. "Who wants to hold him?"

Every girl in the room jumped out of her chair and hurried over to Carson with outstretched arms.

Jackson rubbed his clean-shaven chin and hid a grin as he watched the women battle over which one of them got to hold baby Jacob first. Shelby Garrett ended up getting the honors, and as Carson carefully transferred the valuable cargo into her arms, the others gathered around her to take a peek.

"Oh gosh, he's so beautiful!" Claire gushed.

"He's perfect," Annabelle agreed.

"Absolutely perfect," Savannah echoed.

Jackson's gaze focused on Mia, who wore an awed expression as she admired the baby. He couldn't help but imagine the day that his and Carson's roles would be reversed. *He* would be the proud father showing off his kid to his friends and teammates. And Mia would be the proud mother catching a much-needed nap in her hospital bed, as Holly Scott was currently doing.

Don't put the cart before the horse, a little voice chided.

Yeah, he should probably take things one step at a time. Babies would come eventually. But first he had to make an honest woman out of Mia—which he planned on doing.

Tonight.

The ring his mother had given him during his last visit home had been burning a hole in his pocket for weeks now, but tonight was finally the night. Danny had left for football camp yesterday, and the Imperial Beach house the three of them had moved into last month was finally starting to look and feel like home. Danny had insisted on paying a small percentage of the down payment using a portion of his savings, which the bank had returned to him after an outraged Mia stormed the branch manager's office and demanded he fix his employee's irresponsible mistake. There'd been no word from Brenda since she'd stolen her son's money, and none of them expected to hear from the woman anytime soon.

Mia and Danny weren't heartbroken about it. They had each other, and that was enough for them. And now they had Jackson, too.

Only thing left to do was for him to get down on one knee and slide that diamond ring on Mia's finger.

He couldn't wait.

But that was later. That was *their* moment.

Right now, it was Carson's moment, and Jackson quickly walked over to give his lieutenant a hug.

"Congratulations." He snuck a peek at the gorgeous, healthy baby who was now being cooed over by his Auntie Jen. "You've got yourself a beautiful boy there, LT."

"Damn right," Carson said proudly.

One by one, Carson's teammates came up to embrace him, thump his back, and offer their congratulations. Jacob Two-Middle-Names Scott was passed around from one set of arms to another, his big blue eyes flickering with interest as he peered up at each person. The baby didn't cry once, but by the time he'd been held by everyone in the waiting room, a big yawn overtook his tiny face and he was promptly spirited away by his father, who, with an overprotective glare, told them all to quit tiring out his son.

After Carson was gone, everyone drifted toward the elevator bank, raving about how cute little Jacob was. Cash and Jen stayed behind with Carson and Jen's parents to spend more time with Carson, Holly, and the newborn, but the rest of the group rode the elevator to the lobby and left the hospital.

They walked out to the visitor lot, and then everyone went their separate ways.

Garrett and Shelby headed home to their daughter Penny.

Seth and Miranda went home to their twins.

Former SEAL Will Charleston and his wife Mackenzie made the long drive back to the small town they resided in, where their son Lucas awaited them.

Jane and Thomas Becker dashed off to get back to their daughter Sadie.

Ryan and Annabelle carpooled with Matt and Savannah to the building where they all lived.

Dylan, Claire and Aidan left hand in hand in hand to the trio's downtown condo.

And Jackson and Mia drove back to Imperial Beach, smiling the entire time.

The End

Read about the couples that came before Cash, Seth, Dylan, and Jackson in these two *Out of Uniform* anthologies.

Six sizzling-hot stories from *New York Times* and international bestselling author Elle Kennedy!

HOT & BOTHERED

Give a SEAL an inch, and he'll take your heart.

Heat of the Moment

For almost a year Shelby has lusted over swoon-worthy Garrett, but she can't figure out why he's not interested...until she overhears him saying she's too vanilla for his taste. When a heat wave sends the sexy Navy SEAL into her bakery, she finally has the opportunity to show him exactly what he's missing...

Heat of Passion

Holly has too much on her plate to think about a serious relationship. A hot fling with a SEAL, though, is the perfect way to take the edge off. The last thing she expects is to run into her gorgeous one-night stand weeks later, and to discover that Carson wants the one thing she doesn't: more. In the face of his methodical seduction, her resistance is crumbling...

Heat of the Storm

Will has waited fifteen years for the storm that sends Mackenzie into his arms. He's the one man not scared of her psychic gift, and their one night of passion is enough to convince this tenacious SEAL that they are much, much more than friends. Now he just has to convince her of that...

HOT & HEAVY

When a SEAL goes after your heart, don't put up a fight. They don't like to lose.

Heat It Up

One minute broody SEAL Becker is responding *hell no* to a pesky reporter's interview request. The next, he's trapped in an elevator and calming Jane's confined-space panic attack—with a kiss. Once he caves in to the fierce, unexpected need, there's no turning back. Beck's not looking for long-term, but a fling with a redhead with a brutally honest mouth and a body made for sin? Abso-effing-lutely...

Heat of the Night

When her long-time fiancé breaks off their engagement, Annabelle sets out to prove she's not a prude. Only problem is, her list of sexual fantasies winds up in the wrong hands, and now she's got a sinfully sexy SEAL offering to help check off every last wild and wicked item. Resisting Ryan is futile, but protecting her heart? It's necessary...

The Heat is On

Matt thinks he's a bad boy...until he finds himself face down on the floor during a bank robbery, arguing with a sexy blonde who wields her sharp tongue with surgical precision. Savannah eagerly follows the adrenaline rush she feels with Matt to the nearest bed, but when tangled sheets begin to feel like tangled heartstrings, commitment-shy Savannah's first instinct is to cut him loose. Problem is, Matt's not going anywhere...

ABOUT THE AUTHOR

A *New York Times*, *USA Today* and *Wall Street Journal* bestselling author, Elle Kennedy grew up in the suburbs of Toronto, Ontario, and holds a BA in English from York University. From an early age, she knew she wanted to be a writer and actively began pursuing that dream when she was a teenager. She loves strong heroines and sexy alpha heroes, and just enough heat and danger to keep things interesting!

Elle loves to hear from her readers. Visit her website www.ellekennedy.com or sign up for her newsletter to receive updates about upcoming books and exclusive excerpts. You can also find her on:

Facebook (ElleKennedyAuthor)
Twitter (@ElleKennedy)
Instagram (@ElleKennedy33)
TikTok (@ElleKennedyAuthor).

Made in the USA
Coppell, TX
10 December 2022

88422449R00174